Across Borders

Lee Ducote

Raccoon Bend Publishing

Across Borders

ISBN-13: 9780996643269

In Publication Data
DuCote, Lee

FICTION / Thrillers / Crime

FICTION / Action / Adventure

Editor – Merrell Knighten
Cover Designer – Marianne Nowicki

Visit Lee Ducote's website and sign-up for his newsletter at:.
www.leeducote.com

Printed in the United States

To the men and women who help keep this country safe by protecting us at the borders. I thank you for giving the ultimate gift, life!

Acknoledgments

My deep and profound thanks to those who have helped put this novel together: my editor, Merrell Knighten; my coach and editor Alice Sullivan; and my proofreading team Janet Nolan, Randy Allums, Leo DuCote, Michaele Edwards, and Katie Holmes.

Chapter 1

A strong warm breeze blew dust past a patrol truck as it stopped shy of the white wooden frame house. With the heat of the summer, the grass in the yard had burned leaving only a dry vegetation that was more vulnerable to fire than kindling. Lawson sat behind the wheel of the truck stopped in the dirt and gravel drive that led to the house. The picket railing that lined the porch was half painted, a project he had let go only a few days ago.

Lawson's hands gripped the steering wheel, turning his knuckles white before he let go, allowing them to drop to his lap. A border patrol badge hanging from his rearview mirror threw a spark of sunlight in his eyes, causing him to take a deep breath as he glanced down at a picture of him and his best friend that was shoved in the dash, hiding part of his gauges.

Another strong wind blew against his truck, causing a cloud of dust to form from his driveway. It was a tell-tale sign that fall was soon approaching, not that the temperatures dropped in Presidio, Texas, but a sure sign of high school football and the Friday night lights that came with the favorite sport—something Lawson enjoyed doing on the weekends, watching West Texas Football at its finest, and this year the Blue Devils were predicted to go deep into the playoffs.

Lawson Caine was a fifth-generation lawman who had moved to the small town of Presidio after joining the United States Border Patrol, a dream he had since his high school days. A border patrol agent had visited and made a presentation on the agency and the training that came with the job. Lawson was hooked.

The Caine family had lived in Paris, Texas, since the early 1800s, and Lawson was the great-great-grandson of the famous Bill Caine, a U.S. Deputy Marshal. Bill was commissioned in the Southern District of Indian territory in Paris, Texas. He was shot and killed in 1893 while attempting to arrest Bud English, a prominent stockman. Caine was riding with a posse tracking a gang of horse thieves when a gunfight broke out, leaving him lying dead beside his trusted horse. Years later, one of the posse members recognized Bud English in the streets of Ardmore, Oklahoma, and had him arrested, nine years after the death of Bill.

Since then, the Caine family had gained the respect from the townspeople of Paris and become the trusted lawmen that followed their reputation. Lawson's dad and two uncles all worked for the sheriff department and headed up the mounted patrol. Dave, Lawson's father, was a talented calf roper and had the buckles and trophy saddles to show for it. Lawson, however, had football fever and lived every waking moment with a football in hand. He knew that his football career would end with his high school days, and after walking off the field his senior year, he placed his attention on the US Border Patrol.

Lawson found himself in Artesia, New Mexico, at the Federal Law Enforcement Training Center 14 months after graduation, getting the life kicked out of him at Border Patrol training. He thought two-a-days football practice in the summer was tough, but it was not even close to this. Still, with a strong background in Spanish and being in the best shape of his life, he managed the 19 weeks of hell and was assigned to the Marfa Sector, now the Big Bend Sector, with the United States Border Patrol.

After meeting with the Chief Patrol Agent, Lawson was placed on a team located in the station at Presidio, Texas, a team headed up by Deputy Patrol Agent James D. Garrett, a former Captain with the Texas Rangers who preferred to be called "Captain," but all the men under him adopted him as "Cap."

Cap and Lawson hit it off immediately, both having ties to Paris, Texas. Cap was a distant relative of the famous lawman Buck Garrett, the nephew of the infamous Pat Garrett who killed Billy the Kid. Buck Garrett was born in Tennessee and had moved his family to Paris in the late 1800s with his two brothers.

Cap was often given young rookies fresh out of the academy to train them up and send them to other stations and sectors, but Lawson and a few other young men had decided to stay with Cap. They loved his non-managing attitude and slow pace to life. His theory was there was no rush to get to the grave.

Now, eight years after moving to West Texas to join the agency, Lawson was sitting in his driveway in Presidio, Texas, wondering how he got to the stage of life he was now sitting in. He took another deep breath and reflected back to the last two years.

Chapter 2

Sitting on a boulder, Cap carefully rolled his cigarette from the tobacco that was balancing on his leg in the leather porch handed down from his father. He pulled out a Zippo lighter and lit the freshly rolled cigarette, drawing in a deep breath of smoke. Exhaling toward the sky, he looked back down at his team, who were taking a mid-day break in their favorite swimming hole just south of Presidio. He smirked and made his usual sound, "huh," with all the young men in their boxer briefs, all with the exception of one.

Alex Sweeny, the craziest one of the team, was baring all as he stood on a taller boulder antagonizing the men below by slapping his butt. "Here's a full moon cannon ball!" he yelled, taking a running jump into the water.

"You're such an idiot! Nobody wants to see you naked," Dale yelled, splashing water toward Sweeny as he emerged. Dale was the youngest of the five team members and only a few months out of the academy, and his expressive, outspoken, chatty nature fit him in perfectly with the rest of the team.

"You're just jealous because I'm ALL MAN!" Sweeny said, trying to wrap his arms around Dale. Dale did his best to fight him off while the others were laughing.

"Cap, you going to join us?" Lawson yelled up at the grey-haired, thick-leather-skinned man propped up against a boulder.

"Nah, I don't swim with naked boys," he yelled back down. Everyone laughed. Cap was set in his ways, but enjoyed the energy of the team that was placed under him. He took another drag and looked up at the sky, the sun beaming down on the red clay rocks as white clouds raced by. With sweat dripping off his forehead, Cap looked down at his watch. "Whatcha say? Give 'em another hour?" he asked a black Rottweiler that was lying in the shade under an overhanging rock. The dog looked up at Cap, panting and showing her teeth as if she understood.

Valentine was not your typical law enforcement dog; not many Rottweilers were made into patrol dogs, but she was special and never missed a command. Sandra, Cap's wife, had rescued her as a pup and had full intentions of making her a house dog, but Valentine quickly fell in love with Cap and became his partner. It was February 14th when Sandra found her, and the name "Valentine" stuck.

"Come on, girl!" Sweeny yelled from the middle of the creek. Valentine lit out from under the rock and bolted toward the men with her tongue hanging out. Without missing a step, she soared into the water and swam toward Sweeny.

"Damn," Cap whispered to himself. "She's riding with you now," he yelled down at Sweeny.

"Well, Probie, looks like you're riding with a wet dog," Sweeny said to Dale.

"I'll dry her off," Dale replied.

"Lawson!" Terry, the other agent, yelled from the edge of the creek with a football in hand. Lawson threw up his arms anticipating the pass, and Sweeny quickly swam over to intercept the incoming pass.

"It's all you," Lawson said, moving out of Sweeny's way.

"Y'all are a bunch of little girls. I don't have cooties," Sweeny
replied.

"Are you sure?" Dale asked.

"Shut-up, Probie," Sweeny said, catching the ball.

"Cap! Heads up!" Sweeny yelled, then threw the ball in his direction. The pass came up short and hit the rocks below Cap and fell back into the creek. Everyone started laughing at his failed pass. "Oh, all you shut-up. The ball is wet."

"Give it to me," Lawson demanded. "Cap!" he yelled. Cap put his cigarette in his lips, knowing that Lawson wouldn't miss his mark. The ball left Lawson's hands with a tight spiral, shedding water and missiling toward Cap. Cap's firm hands clinched the ball as it nailed him without moving.

"Show off," Sweeny said.

"It's all in the arm." Lawson curled his arm, making his bicep muscle flex.

Cap threw the ball back, and Lawson and Terry threw it back and forth half a dozen times. Terry was the quiet one of the bunch; he had been with the Border Patrol four years and lived with his wife, who was from Atlanta, Georgia. She had followed him to West Texas for his dream job, but lately had complained that she was melting in the heat and wanted to move back home.

"It's a warm spot," Sweeny exclaimed to the guys looking down at the water.

"It could be because Valentine is upstream from you," Dale replied.

"Is my little girl peeing in the water?" Sweeny said in a baby voice, swimming toward the Rottweiler, who seemed to be relaxed in the water.

"Are we still grilling at your house tonight?" Dale asked Lawson while swimming toward the shore.

"Yep, you know what to bring?" he asked.

"The beer," Dale replied in a lower tone.

"Aw, don't worry, Probie, there'll be another probie coming soon," Sweeny said.

"They need to hurry; you guys are breaking me," Dale answered.

"If you need me to buy, I will," Terry said as Dale reached for his towel.

"No, I got it."

A call came over the radio for the local BORSTAR team to help with the possibility of a stranded Mexican family found north of Presidio in a remote area. BORSTAR, the Border Patrol Search Trauma and Rescue team, was created in the mid-1990s to help with the growing number of migrant deaths along the border of Mexico and the US. Within the last few years, a large number of families were being led across the border, robbed, and left to die by their own countrymen. These evil individuals were given the nickname *coyotes* by the Border Patrol, and neither side had any mercy on each other.

Cap and his team were often called to aid the BORSTAR team and saw firsthand the cruelty and deceitfulness these coyotes had on innocent families. They had found men with their throats cut as their children witnessed and women raped and left to die with their children. The horror and evil left a hardened heart in the team members toward the coyotes and the smuggling lord who controlled them.

In the last few years, there had been an individual in Mexico that hired these low life's to do his dirty work for him while he sat back and got rich. All the branches of law enforcement and military had been working hard to capture this smuggling lord, but had come up short in all extremes; only his name was known as Jose Emmanuel.

Dale and Terry made their way over to Sweeny's truck with the door open and listened to the action unfold on the radio as BORSTAR made their way to the location.

"I hope when we catch Jose, they hang him like in the old days," Dale commented.

"He'll probably never make it to jail," Terry said.

Chapter 3

Pulling onto the pavement of Hwy 170, Amalia Gonzales held on to the sack of prescription medicine she was delivering. Amalia had just opened a local pharmacy in Presidio a few months earlier and had already made many customers, but with many of her customers in their elder years, she made frequent deliveries. Amalia was nicknamed "Lia" during elementary school when the students and teachers had a hard time pronouncing her name.

"I'll hold them," a young female said from the passenger seat.

"Thanks Erika," Lia answered. Erika Santeljo was not only Lia's best friend, but helped run the pharmacy. Today Lia had asked Erika to ride with her because their first stop was to a schizophrenia patient who made her nervous.

"I told you he'd be OK. As long as you get his meds to him in time, he'll act normal," Erika said, tucking the sack under her feet.

"He still creeps me out."

Driving back north toward Presidio, Erika turned the radio station to the only country channel they could receive. With Hank Williams blaring from the 6X9 Sony speakers, the girls sang along. Lia turned down the radio. "While we out here, I can drop off Mrs. Jones' meds," she said, slamming on the brake.

"Not if you kill us both."

Lia looked over her shoulder and slammed the Jeep Grand Cherokee in reverse. Spinning the tires, she backed to the street she had just passed. Then turning onto the dirt road, the Jeep fishtailed as she floored the gas, nothing Erika wasn't used to.

Flying over a hill, they noticed the three Border Patrol trucks off in the distance with one of the trucks' cabs disappearing just over the ridge. Lia pointed to the trucks. "I have a prescription for one of the Border Patrol guys. Check in the bag and see if Alex Sweeny's bag is in there," Lia asked.

Erika dug through the sack. "Yep. What is he taking?" She examined the bottle. "Victoria?" she asked Lia.

"It's his daughters."

The Jeep jetted by the road that led to the trucks, "If they're still there on the way back, we'll stop."

"Why take the chance? I could see me some Border Patrol officers," Erika replied with a devious tone. Lia looked over at her with a smile and slammed on the brakes. "Lia! You're killing me!"

The Jeep fishtailed the opposite direction as Lia turned down the road and straightened up just in time to cross a cattle gap. As they approached the three trucks, they noticed the farthest truck doors were open. The Jeep crawled to a stop.

"Drugs, please." Lia held her hand out.

"You're not going without me." Erika opened her door and climbed out.

"You don't think we are going to interrupt them on a bust or whatever they call what they do?" Lia asked.

"Not with their radio blaring country music across the open country." Erika pointed at the truck.

The two girls walked side by side past the trucks and appeared over the hill on the creek that was nestled below between two small ridges. At first they thought the four agents were looking for something in the water until one of them climbed up a boulder and shouted something. It wasn't what he shouted—it was the fact that he wasn't wearing anything.

"Get down!" Erika whispered to Lia and pulled her down out of sight from the men.

"What are you doing?"

"Getting a better look at this," she smiled. Lia rolled her eyes, but didn't argue. The two girls bear crawled up to a spot where they could peer down onto the swimming hole. Sweeny had already jumped in, and Lawson was climbing out to accept his challenge for a bigger splash.

"Dang! That one has on his boxer briefs. Take em off, take em off." Erika chanted.

"Shhh. They're gonna hear you. I swear, Erika, you are just as childish as they are."

The girls studied the creek in hopes another would immerge from the muddy water. "Stupid muddy water," Erika said unbeknownst to Cap, who was still leaning against the boulder just above them. He leaned over and laughed at the two who were stealing a glimpse of the young men, but it was Valentine that sold them out.

"Girl, what are you barking at?" Sweeny said, looking in the direction of Valentine's stare.

Erika looked over at Lia. "We've been spotted."

"Let's get out of here," Lia said.

"OK," Erika answered with no intentions of leaving. She stood up from their view area. "Which one of you is Alex?" she shouted.

Lia thought she was going to either pee herself or pass out. "Oh, dear God," she replied.

One of the men waved his arm. "That would be me. Who wants to know?" Sweeny asked.

"Your local friend pharmacy store," Erika shouted back.

"You girls are delivering out here?" Cap asked, still perched above them and scaring them both.

"How long have you been up there?" Lia was embarrassed to ask him.

"Long enough."

"You saw us drive up?"

"And fishtailed the corner before ramping the cattle gap."

Lia had a hard time swallowing. The girls looked back in time to see Sweeny exiting the water with a straw hat covering his privates and walk toward them.

"Damn, Sweeny, put some clothes on," Lawson said.

Looking back at Lawson. "They're kinda like doctors— they've seen it all. Right?" Sweeny asked.

"Not exactly," Lia said.

"It's fine with me," Erika replied with a smile that a good coroner couldn't remove.

Sweeny stood motionless for a brief second with a wide-eyed expression. "Hum, well... I guess I should find some clothes," he said in a coy tone.

"Don't trouble yourself on my account," Erika said. Lia threw an elbow in her side. Sweeny laughed and walked past them to gather his uniform from his truck. Lia was just through turning every shade of red in the rainbow when Lawson walked up with a towel wrapped around him.

"Sorry, we normally don't have visitors out here," he said, pulling his pants out of his truck. Lia stood paralyzed and speechless. She couldn't help but notice his toned chest and ripped abs. "I'm Lawson." He said, standing on the other side of his truck.

Lia let out a whimper sound; she couldn't talk. *What the hell is wrong with me?*

Erika stared at her with a funny look on her face, "What was that?"

"I'm Amalia," she stuttered and gasped for a breath of air.

Lawson laughed, "It's nice to meet you. OK boys, swim time is over," he yelled back at Dale and Terry. Cap was climbing down from his perch and Sweeny was getting dressed.

Lia looked at Erika as they walked back to their Jeep. "I'm going to kill you!"

Chapter 4

The following day Lawson and Dale pulled up to the store for coffee and Dale's favorite breakfast, cupcakes and zingers. Lawson barely had the truck in park before Dale bailed out in a sprint toward the bathroom from all the coffee he had already drunk. A half-ton pickup truck pulled up beside Lawson as he shut his door. Turning, Lawson noticed it was the local football coach, Coach Willis. Coach Willis had been coaching the Presidio Blue Devils for 20 years and had had his success. With four state titles and an overall winning record, he had become the local celebrity.

"Coach," Lawson nodded his head toward the overweight man.

"Lawson, how's the border?" Coach asked, striking up a conversation.

"Still there," Lawson smiled, holding the door open. "Looking forward to this year," he added.

"Me too. Got lots of talent on the team. If they'll leave the girls and booze alone," he smiled back.

"Good luck with that."

Coach headed toward the coffee that was tucked in the corner as Lawson walked up to the counter. He heard the front door open again and turned to see two Mexicans walk in eyeing him down. Lawson nodded his head toward them as they walked down an aisle toward the coolers. He turned back to the cashier and bought two cans of smokeless tobacco, said goodbye to Coach, and walked back out to his truck. He sat in the driver's seat opening his can of tobacco and watching the two Mexicans glancing back at him as he waited for Dale. Dale exited the bathroom, grabbed his breakfast plus a 32-ounce soda, and walked out to the truck.

"Ready," Dale announced to Lawson, who was still watching the two men. Dale took notice. "Something wrong?"

"No, I don't guess so." He began backing out when Cap called them over the radio.

Dale picked up the mic. "Go ahead," he answered Cap's call.

"Meet us at the station," Cap responded.

"10-4," Dale replied.

Five minutes later, Lawson and Dale pulled up to the station and parked in front of a cyclone fence that led to the administration and training facilities. Cap was sitting on a 2-foot stone wall that lined the yard of the first building. The building that was open to the public was a small white brick building with two small trees and a flag pole in the front. Cap rose to his feet and stomped out his cigarette. "Good morning, compadres." he said in his typical raspy voice.

"Morning," Lawson said, rolling down his window.

Cap walked up to a key pad and entered a five-digit number. The gate opened, making a grinding noise as the chain dragged across the pavement. "Age before beauty." Lawson gestured to Cap, pointing to the opening. Cap made his usual "huh" sound and walked in the gate.

"Where's Sweeny?" Lawson asked, opening his truck door.

"He's on his way. He had to do something at school for Vicky," Cap replied, pulling out another cigarette.

Victoria Emily Sweeny was Sweeny's eight-year-old daughter and had earned the name Vicky from her mother after the little girl became one of the toughest kids on her neighborhood street. It had been five years since Sweeny lost his wife in an automobile accident. He had contemplated moving back to Houston, Texas, where his parents lived to help raise Vicky, but decided to come to the Big Bend Sector. After moving to Presidio, Cap and Sandra agreed to help with Vicky so Sweeny would have time to adjust. With Cap's team, Vicky had four more dads and one mom. Sandra picked her up from school every day and hauled her around everywhere she went. Sandra, whose two daughters were grown and living in Dallas and New Orleans, claimed Vicky and Sweeny as her kids.

Sweeny's truck slid to a stop as the dust was swept up by a north wind. "Good morning, ladies," he said, shutting his door. Terry waved the leftover dust out of his face with his hand.

"Head in," Cap ordered, flicking his cigarette.

"What were you doing at the school for Vicky?" Lawson asked Sweeny.

"I had to pay for her field trip and check on her outfit for the dance recital," Sweeny replied, walking ahead of Lawson.

"When is she coming back from your parents'?" Lawson asked.

"This Sunday evening," Sweeny answered.

The team made their way through the white hallway lined with pictures of past border patrol members and into a patrol room. Each member took a seat behind tables that formed a classroom-type environment. Cap stopped at the lecture pulpit and opened a file folder, putting his glasses on he looked up and motioned for Dale to turn off the lights. "Last night, agents received word through an informant that a large shipment of drug are coming through today. The word is these smugglers are using false floors in the back of pickup trucks." A picture formed on the screen of a white pickup truck with half of the bed removed, showing several kilos of cocaine. "Our boys at the crossing have been informed and are going to let the first suspicious truck through, and we are going to follow them to their state side distributers."

"We're going to let them enter?" Lawson questioned.

"Yes sir. Our informant claims they deliver right here in Presidio," Cap answered.

"Chancy, don't you think?"

Cap raised one of his eyebrows. "You planning on losing them?"

"Haven't lost one yet," Sweeny answered in a cocky tone. Cap motioned for the lights back on. "Questions?"

Before anyone could ask, Cap's cell phone rang, and looking down at the number, he quickly answered and then shot a strong stare at his team. Everyone stood motionless as he spoke to the person on the other end of the line. Putting his phone in his shirt pocket, he added, "Looks like they're making an early trip—our boys at the gate are going to contain them until we get there. Sweeny you have the tail vehicle. Terry, you're with me. Lawson, you and Dale back up Sweeny. Let's head out." Cap was through the door before he had finished his sentence.

The border was only minutes from the station, and the team was in place in no time. Lawson and Dale parked between a convenient store and a beer truck just two blocks from the border and waited for directions from Sweeny. Dale rocked back and forth in his seat, feeling his heart pounding in his chest.

"Relax," Lawson said, looking at him. Dale wanted to, but this was his first time to trail smugglers, and with the stories from other agents, he knew they would see some action.

"All right boys, they're letting them go," Cap said over a private station on their radios.

Within a few minutes, Sweeny reported, "I have two men, one in a blue cap and white t-shirt and the other in a blue short-sleeved button shirt. We are moving north on 67, they are driving a white single cab truck, maybe a mid-1990s model."

Lawson and Dale watched from their back window as the white truck came into sight. "We got 'em in sight," Lawson added over the radio. Lawson waited for the truck and Sweeny to disappear before they pulled out. Just as they pulled onto Hwy 67, Sweeny came back over the radio.

"We are turning left on Leaton Street. I'm going to the next street and turn in," Sweeny informed everyone.

"I'm on Porto Rico Street," Cap said.

"Hold back, Cap, they may turn your direction," Sweeny said.

"10-4."

The radio was silent for a minute. "Sweeny?" Lawson asked.

"The truck has turned into a drive on Rosedale and they're just sitting there. Hold on—they are exiting the truck. This is it," Sweeny replied.

"10-4, I just let the state police know and they are on their way. Everyone get to a staging area," Cap ordered.

"Cap! I've been made!" Sweeny's voice sounded through the radio.

"Move in!" Cap shouted on the radio. Lawson and Dale could hear the acceleration of his truck as he instructed them to move in. Lawson's truck peeled out on the gravel as they raced down Hwy 67, and coming to the intersection of Rosedale and 67, the tires boiled on the pavement as they cut the corner. Sweeny was out of his car with his M4RIFLE in hand and crouched beside a wooden fence waiting on Lawson and Dale.

Stopping short and out of sight of the house, Lawson slammed the truck into park and both he and Dale grabbed their M4RIFLE's and headed toward Sweeny. "You stay behind me! Understand?" he barked at Dale.

"Got it," Dale answered.

"Sorry boys, I got too close," Sweeny apologized as they kneeled beside him. Cap and Terry's truck appeared from down the street and parked shy of the driveway. Cap gave them a thumbs up.

"Let's get these boys before they have time to set up for the long haul," Sweeny said, making his way toward the house. Stopping, he signaled to Cap and Terry to go around back.

Sweeny, Lawson, and Dale ran to the rear of the white truck that was parked in the drive. "Ok, let Cap and Terry get in place before we take a peek," Lawson said, but before they had confirmation from Cap, gunfire rang out from the front of the house. The white truck was pelted with a hail of bullets with the occasional bullet ricocheting off the concrete. Sparks flickered from the lead hitting the driveway.

Sweeny looked at Dale with a smile, "Probie, go tell them to stop shooting."

"Me?" Dale's face was already white from the excitement.

"Wait for them to reload and I'll make it to the side," Lawson replied.

"Nah, you better stay here with Probie. I'll go."

The gun fire died down. "Go now!" Lawson said, raising his rifle on the house and opening fire on the front door. Sweeny quickly disappeared around the truck and toward the side of the house. The gun fire returned from the front window.

"When it dies back down," Lawson ordered, "open fire on the window and only the window." He looked directly at Dale's face, seeing his fear. After a short time the gun fire stopped again, and Lawson and Dale raised their rifles and aimed at the window. Just before Dale squeezed the trigger, Lawson raised his barrel. "Hold fire! Where in the hell is Sweeny?"

While the men inside the house were blasting shots in the direction of Lawson and Dale, Sweeny kicked open the side glass door and rushed in. Cap, seeing Sweeny entering the house, rushed through the back door. With Sweeny from the side of the room and Cap and Terry from the rear, they laid their sights on the three men crouched down in front of the window.

"Hold fire!" Cap yelled over the radio so loudly that Lawson and Dale could hear him from inside.

Lawson stormed the front door, kicking it open to find the three men with their hands behind their heads and fingers inner locked. Terry was already cuffing one of the men. "Probie, cuff the other two!" Cap said as Dale entered.

After Dale had both of them cuffed and all three men laid on the floor, Cap turned to Sweeny. "Outside." Lawson followed them. "Pull another stunt like that and you'll be sidelined. Understand?" Cap said, pointing his finger at Sweeny.

"Cap, I could see all three through the glass door."

"But you had Lawson and a fricking rookie filling the house with lead."

Without any argument, "Yes sir," Sweeny answered. One thing the team members knew was never to argue with Cap.

"You two boneheads are filling out the paperwork," Cap said, lighting a cigarette.

Chapter 5

Sitting at a restaurant table, Sweeny leaned over to Lawson and watched him type out the report from yesterday's bust. Cap blew on the steam that was rising out of his cup as Dale and Terry scrolled through their phones. Cap shook his head and rolled his eyes watching the two so fixated on their phones that they didn't hear or see the waitress ask if they wanted their cups topped off. The table shook with Cap kicking his foot into the shin bone of Dale.

"Ouch!" Dale looked at Cap, confused.

"Answer the lady," Cap said, now combing his mustache with his free hand.

"I'm sorry. A little more would be fine." He slid his cup to the edge. Terry followed suit, not interested in the same attention from Cap.

"You boys are going to go blind always looking at those damn phones," Cap commented.

Sweeny and Lawson smiled and then returned to the computer screen, arguing how to describe Sweeny kicking in the glass door from yesterday. Cap took another sip from his cup and followed with a wipe of his mustache. "If you trimmed your mustache, you wouldn't have to wipe it all the time," Dale commented. Everyone at the table stopped moving, talking, and cut their eyes at Dale. He felt the tension rise and all eyes on him but Cap's.

"Sandra says that, but I like it the way it is," Cap answered. Lawson looked up at Sweeny as he shrugged his shoulders, and then they went back to work on their report. Dale looked around the table, still confused on the attention he got for his comment.

"You boys about finished?" Cap asked in his raspy voice.

"Just about," Sweeny replied.

"Take a break; breakfast is here," Cap said, smiling and nodding at the waitress, his cowboy hat hanging off the back of the chair he was sitting in. The last plate was placed in front of Terry, and the waitress asked if they needed anything else. "No ma'am, thank you." Cap paused then looked at Terry. "You want to bless it?" Without an answer, Terry gave thanks, and the team dug into their breakfast.

With Lawson and Sweeny's back to the door, they never saw Lia and Erika walk in. "Hey, it's the two girls from the swimming hole," Dale said. The girls felt five pairs of eyes lock on them as the door shut.

"Well, howdy, boys," Erika said in a bubbly tone. All five of the men nodded simultaneously. Lia turned a light shade of red with the attention from not only the table of border patrol agents, but a few other tables. "Hello, Mr. Sweeny, I see you found more to wear than just a straw hat," Erika added.

"Yea, they make us wear these clothes in public. Suppose to be good PR or something like that," Sweeny answered, pulling at his shirt from the front pockets.

"How's the pharmacy business?" Lawson asked Lia.

"Good," she answered softly.

Erika rolled her eyes and tilted her head toward Lia on her one word answer. "Better than good—she's putting in one of those old-time soda fountain bars."

"Oh, yea," Cap perked up. "I grew up around one of those bars at the local dime store."

"Yep, and back then 10 cents was like a hundred dollars now," Sweeny shot at Cap with a smile on his face.

"Damn right. A dime would get you a movie, drink, and a popcorn," Cap returned the remark.

"When do you open it?" Lawson asked, trying to get the conversation away from inflation.

"They are finishing up the final touches, and I hope to have it open next week," Lia answered with a smile that revealed two small dimples that appeared on her flawless dark complexion. Lawson paused with an answer after receiving the soft smile and a hypnotic glance from Lia's brown eyes. For a moment there was an awkward silence before Lawson was able to muster up something to say. "Cool," he replied. She smiled again.

"We better get a seat," Erika pushed Lia past their table, pausing for a brief second to whisper to Lawson. "She's available," she said in a sarcastic tone.

"Erika!" Lia said under her breath, trying not to let the table of agents hear. She pulled Erika toward a vacant table in the corner.

"Looks like someone needs to get sick so they can have a prescription called in," Sweeny said, looking at Lawson.

"Shut up and eat your breakfast," he replied.

Dale turned in his seat toward the girls, adding "She is pretty."

"Turn around, Probie, dang!" Lawson quickly reacted to his obvious demeanor.

"Ahhh, there *is* something there," Sweeny replied. Lawson shook his head and tried to ignore the men. Glancing in the direction of the girls, Lia and Lawson locked eyes, and with no-one else noticing, he gave her a gentle, warm smile. She returned the smile. *I wonder what his story is?* she thought before the waitress blocked her view.

The door burst back open with the sheriff making his entrance into the busy dinner. A few of the tables closer to the door exchanged greetings with the overweight sheriff before he made his way to the table with Cap and his men. Pulling back the empty chair at the end of the table, the sheriff ordered his normal cup of coffee, then sat. "Morning, boys!"

"Sheriff," Cap said, holding his coffee with both hands.

"Hell of a shootout yesterday," the sheriff started. The men shrugged their shoulders as if it were a normal day for them. "We ran a check on the guns those Mexicans had. Turns out two of the guns was from the Fast and Furious Sting." Lawson and Cap looked up from their breakfast.

"Fast and Furious?" Dale asked.

"It was a sting operation that our government did on the Cartel, only for it to go bad, and our government lost tens of thousands of automatic weapons," the sheriff cheerfully answered, thinking he was teaching something. But it was nothing new, since the team knew the story. It had been only a few years since they lost a neighboring agent to one of the guns that was lost in the sting operation. It was definitely a sore subject with all border patrol agents.

"I remember learning about it at the academy," Dale answered.

"Well, something else." The sheriff moved to another subject he hoped would be new to the agents. "Those Mexicans had strong ties to Jose Emmanuel."

"How strong?" Cap asked, giving the sheriff his full attention.

"One of them confessed he worked for him."

"Really? Any other information?" Lawson asked.

"Not yet," the sheriff replied, leaning over the table for the creamer, "but my boys are at your disposal until we catch this low life."

"You mind if we talk to this guy?" Cap asked.

Sheriff shook his head. "Nope, not at all."

"Are they coyotes?" Terry asked the sheriff

"Don't think so," he replied, shoving bacon in his mouth.

"Finish up breakfast and that report; our day has started," Cap replied, throwing a five-dollar bill on the table and reaching for his hat.

Chapter 6

A few passing clouds broke down the heat for the morning as three border patrol trucks came to a simultaneous stop outside a Catholic church north of the patrol office. Cap looked in the rearview mirror and combed his grey hair, taking the hat marks out of the side of his head. A white Ford Taurus pulled up alongside his truck with Sandra in the driver's side. Cap quickly climbed out of the truck and opened her door as she checked her lipstick one last time in her mirror. He tapped on the passenger window of his truck, getting the attention of Lawson. "You want to come in with us?" he asked just as he did every Sunday they had to work.

"Thanks, but I'm good," Lawson replied.

"Devil is gonna get you one of these days," Cap joked back.

"He's too scared of Sweeny," Lawson answered.

Before he could roll up his window, Sandra handed him a note. "You boys pick this up from the store before church is out and bring it with you for lunch."

"Yes ma'am," Lawson respectfully answered.

Sandra had asked the boys to go with them to church many times and had received the same answer time and time again. She had always prepared Sunday lunch for the team and figured since they wouldn't go to church, they could always pick up things from the grocery store. It was a compromise the boys didn't mind.

The Catholic Church was one of the older buildings in Presidio and matched the backdrop of a desert landscape with its light brown stucco siding. A set of weather-beaten wooden doors centered the front with a steeple growing from the top reaching high into the Texas heat. The priest stood in the doorway greeting everyone who came to service, and as the last people entered, he too would always offer church to the four team members that waited in the parking lot. Conveniently located next to the old building, though, was a basketball court for the young men, who had always turned down church. It was their Sunday tradition, 2 on 2.

"Terry! Grab the ball," Sweeny yelled across the parking lot as he tied his shoes. A few short moments later, a basketball came bouncing toward Sweeny. Lawson reached behind his truck seat and found the shoes that he always stored for their Sunday ball game. He sat down on the floor board with   the door open and pulled off his boots. A red Jeep Grand Cherokee caught his attention as he pulled the laces on his Nikes. Lia stepped out into the bright sunlight in a light blue dress and checked herself in the mirror on the driver's side door. Lawson, still holding his shoe laces, stared as she flipped back her dark hair and checked her teeth. He was so fixated on her that he didn't notice Erika standing in front of the jeep tapping her foot.

"Lia, you look fine. You drug me here, and now we're going to be late."

Lia stood up and glanced in Lawson's direction. "Good morning," she smiled.

"Yea….hi." He found himself lost for words. She giggled, thinking it was him this time to lose his words.

"Are you guys going to church?" she asked Lawson.

"If you girls want to join us we could make it three on three!" Sweeny yelled, holding the ball.

"Maybe next time. I've got to go to church to be forgiven of all the bad thoughts I had this week," Erika answered.

"Oh yea, what thoughts?" Sweeny smiled.

She laughed back and turned back to Lia. "Come on!"

Lia made a head motion toward the old church, "Want to join us?"

Lawson paused for a second, looking back at Terry, Dale, and Sweeny, who were already standing on the court. "Sure," he replied and shut his truck door.

"Are you kidding me? How are we going to play with just three of us?" Sweeny asked.

"You'll figure it out," Lawson said, walking toward the double doors. Sweeny stood in place with his hands on his hips staring a hole through the back of Lawson's head.

Just as Lawson reached to open the door for Erika and Lia, he heard Dale say, "I'll take you two on."

And the reply from Sweeny: "Shut up, Probie."

The door screeched as he pushed it open to reveal a small church with freshly waxed tile floors and rows of dark old mahogany pews that lined both sides of the building. The stained glass windows threw different colors of light from the east side of the building with the bright Texas sun beaming through. Everyone was quiet with their heads bowed as the priest led them through the first prayer of the morning. Cap and Sandra turned to see who was entering, and she wasted no time scooting her purse down the pew, making room for the three latecomers. The priest looked up at the tip toes of two pair of high heels and two Nike sneakers; he smiled, not missing a word of his prayer.

Sandra reached over Cap and patted Lawson on the knee with a big welcoming smile and then sat up proud that she had her two favorite men in church. Lawson's phone buzzed with a text from Sweeny, and after he opened it he found a picture of Sweeny's hairy butt with the basketball balancing on his back. Both Erika and Lia burst into laughter, trying to muffle their mouths with their hands, and the priest looked back at the trio. Cap rolled his eyes at the picture, and Sandra firmly kept her eyes closed as the priest ended the prayer.

After the service was over, Sandra quickly stood and introduced herself to Lia and Erika as Cap talked with a few elderly men. Sandra led the girls and Lawson toward the doors and happily introduced them to the priest. "Glad to have you girls in service this morning," he said, shaking their hands.

"Thank you, it was nice," Lia replied.

"You are the young lady that has opened the pharmacy store?" he asked her.

"Yes, sir."

"Well, it's good to have you here," he added, turning his attention to Lawson. "And it was good to have you as well. Even though it took two girls to get you here." He smiled, and Lawson just smiled back, not knowing how to answer.

"Girls, what are your plans for lunch?" Sandra asked.

"We'll probably go to the diner," Lia answered.

"Nonsense. You two come to our house for lunch."

"Oh, we couldn't at the last minute," Lia answered, being polite.

"Nonsense, I won't take no for an answer. Follow the boys." She turned back toward Cap, who was lighting a cigarette, "Not on the steps of the church!" She hit him with the church bulletin, and he rolled his eyes and put it out.

Lawson texted Sweeny, who was at the store picking up Sandra's list, "The girls are joining us for lunch. Pick up more rolls. Per Sandra's orders."

A few minutes later, Sweeny texted back a picture of a box of mashed potatoes with the focus on the word printed on the box: *whipped*.

Chapter 7

"Dale, will you set the table for two more," Sandra ordered as she hustled inside the house. There were many things that she looked forward to, but having the boys over for Sunday lunch was her favorite. She tied her apron around her waist and barked out a few more orders in the manner of a loving mother.

Standing outside, Lawson pointed to a spot behind his truck on the street for the girls to park. "I can get used to this," Erika said.

"What's that?" Lia asked as they both stared in their mirrors fixing their hair.

"Lunch with a bunch of single young men."

Lia smirked. "I'm going to splash some cold water on you if you get out of hand."

"Whatever it takes," she smiled and smacked her lips.

Lawson moved to the yard, patiently waiting for the girls to get out of the red jeep. He knew if he walked in too early, he would be caught up in the orders of setting lunch. He spotted

Sweeny's truck flying down the street kicking up dust, and he had an impulse to rush the girls inside to miss whatever comment Sweeny was going to say. His curiosity held him in the yard for Sweeny to park behind the jeep.

"You two owe me a ball game," Sweeny said to the girls, pulling out a sack of last-minute items for lunch.

"Anytime!" Erika answered.

Sweeny stopped and lifted one of his eyebrows. "You're too short to be a baller."

Putting her hands on her hips and bowing up to him, Erika replied, "This little Latino can kick your butt. I should know—I've seen that hairy thing recently." Sweeny laughed and followed them to the front door that Lawson was holding open.

Walking past Lawson, Sweeny whispered, "You're using religion to get to a girl? You're going to hell." Lawson pushed him in the door.

Sandra stood at the head of the table and lightly clapped her hands together. "I'm so happy you two came."

"She didn't really give us a choice," Erika said under her breath.

Lia elbowed her in the side. "Thank you for inviting us."

"You girls can sit on this side." She pointed to two chairs. "James, please bless the meal."

Cap looked at everyone and then bowed his head, "God, thanks for a good day. Thanks for these young men and their sacrifices for freedom. Thank you for our new friends today and bless this food and the hands that prepared it." He reached back, grabbing Sandra's hand, and started to end the prayer when Sandra spoke up and finished it.

"And thank you, Father, for Lawson joining us this morning and be with Vicky as she travels home," she added.

"Even if it took girls to get him in there," Sweeny said, thinking no one would hear him, but with Dale chuckling, he knew it was louder than intended.

Sandra looked up at him and added, "And may Lawson's example reflect to others. Amen."

"Amen." Cap shook his head and sat in his chair, throwing in a "Good grief!"

"I hope you like fried chicken. Sandra cooks the best," Dale said, passing a large platter of chicken.

"I do like fried chicken. Thank you," Lia answered taking a piece.

The radio centered in the middle of the table blared out a call to a group of agents that were stationed just north of the town. Cap leaned over, snatched up the talkie, and turned down the volume, holding it close to his ear to listen to the call.

"That's the one thing I just don't care for on the table," Sandra commented, scooping a small portion of green beans on her plate.

"How long have you been married?" Erika asked.

"44 years," she smiled.

"How long have you been in law enforcement?" she asked Cap.

"Too long," he replied in his raspy voice.

"Hopefully he'll retire soon and leave this outfit to Mr. Cain." She smiled at Lawson. Cap ignored the comment about retirement. He had worn a badge for 43 years and didn't plan on taking it off any time soon.

"How long have you been with the Border Patrol?" Lia asked Lawson in a soft voice.

He wiped his mouth with the napkin draped over his leg. "Seven years."

"Are you from here?"

"No. Paris, Texas," he answered.

"Most of the young men that serve here are from other parts of the country," Sandra volunteered her input.

"What about you?" Lawson asked.

"I grew up across the border in Ojinaga and moved to Laredo to go to college. Erika and I recently became citizens."

"Congratulations," Sandra replied.

"We'll need to see your papers after lunch," Sweeny said with a mouth full of chicken.

"Behave!" Sandra scolded him. Everyone laughed.

The radio blared out again. Cap listened intently to the call, "We might be called out on this one," he said aloud.

"So your family is back in Paris?" Lia questioned him.

"Yep, but this my family too," he said, hoping to score points with Sandra. He did. "Are you two kin?" he added.

"No, just friends." She looked at Erika, giggling. "I have a big family with four brothers and six sisters."

"What does your dad do?" Lawson asked.

"He and my brothers have a plumbing business."

"Maybe I should have him over here. The back bathroom faucet has been leaking for a while, and I can't seem to get anyone to fix it." Sandra looked at Cap, who was still listening to the radio.

"Maybe so." Lia didn't know how to answer the statement. Dale looked at Erika. "Where are you from?"

"Oh, around," she answered, avoiding the question.

Cap wiped his mouth with his napkin and threw it on the plate, "Ah right, boys, we have to roll." He stood up and grabbed his hat from the back of his chair. The men followed suit, with Dale and Sweeny quickly washing down their food with the sweet tea. "Sorry, sweetheart." Cap kissed Sandra on the lips and then looked in the kitchen at Valentine, who had been quietly lying against the refrigerator. "Let's go, girl." She scrambled to her feet and beat everyone outside.

"It's OK," Sandra said in a disappointed tone. The boys all filed out, each hugging Sandra and grabbing a few pieces of chicken. "This is something I'll never get used to," she said, looking at the girls, who didn't know how to act.

"Sorry, duty calls. Thanks for having lunch with us," Lawson said.

"Leave your number and he'll call you!" Sweeny yelled from the other room as Lawson pushed him out the door.

Three Border Patrol trucks peeled out in front of Cap's house as they rushed to the aid of a neighboring team.

Chapter 8

A few days later, Lawson was sitting at his desk catching up on some much-needed paperwork. The office was tight with five desks situated so each team member had his space. The aroma of coffee lingered in the air, with a fresh cup always sitting on Cap's desk while he was working. Terry's desk was covered with pictures of his wife and vacations they had taken in the last few years. Sweeny walked in and set a half-eaten bag of chips on his desk across from Lawson. "You're not done yet?"

"Just about," Lawson answered with a pencil in his mouth. Sweeny sat in his chair and propped his feet on his desk with the bag in his lap.

"Where's Probie?" Sweeny asked.

"I don't know," Lawson answered, fixated on the computer screen. Sweeny looked around the room as if bored and looking for something to do. "Don't you have a report to fill out?" Lawson asked him.

"Yea." He spit a few crumbs of chips on his shirt. His phone buzzed with a text. Reading the text, he added, "It'll have to wait. Sandra can't get Vicky today. You want to ride with me to get her?"

"Ok, five minutes." Lawson's foot shook back and worth at a rapid rate as he tried to hurry his work. Dale walked in with a clear container of corn sticks and a bottle of Fiji water.

"What are you eating?" Sweeny asked.

"Cajun Corn Sticks."

"What?"

"It's healthy snack food."

"Sounds like yuppie food with girly water." Sweeny picked up his bottle of water.

"I like the taste of Fiji water." Dale snatched the bottle out of his hand.

"Probie, water is water. I bet I can give you a taste test and you fail."

"What's the bet?" Dale asked.

"We'll take this up later—I have to go get Vicky. You coming?" He turned his attention back to Lawson.

"Just finished." He closed his laptop and followed Sweeny out the door. The two of them walked out into the office yard that was surrounded with a cyclone fence and a roll of razor wire that capped it off. A few small buildings and a set of gas pumps were all that was in the lot. Lawson climbed in the passenger seat and barely had his door shut before Sweeny started backing out.

"You haven't said much about this pharmacy chick the last few days," Sweeny commented, putting on his sunglasses.

"Not much to say."

"You interested in her?"

"Maybe," he answered in a nonchalant tone.

"Don't play that with me—if you're interested, call her."

"If I were to ask her out, would you ask out Erika?"

"She doesn't seem the type to go out with a single father," Sweeny answered.

Sweeny had been single for a couple of years, something he didn't talk a whole lot about. Rachael Sweeny, his wife for five years, was a beautiful, inspiring country singer who had caught the attention of a few music labels before tragedy struck.

Alex and Rachael had met at college in Oklahoma during a fraternity party. Alex, as usual, was drawing attention to himself with the hair-brained idea of swinging from the second story balcony into the bed of a pickup truck filled with water. Earlier that day, the fraternity brothers had placed a tarp in the back of a truck, filled it with water, and driven around campus advertising their spring bash party.

Rachael and two of her sorority sisters had met the guys earlier, and after losing a small bet to her friends, Rachael had to ask Sweeny for a date. The girls came to the party to film the proposal when they found him holding onto a roped tied off in a tree and preparing to swing into the water-filled truck.

"I think we need to change the bet," Rachael said, trying to back out.

"Oh no, a bet is a bet," they taunted her.

She turned her attention to the crazy Alex Sweeny as he announced to the world his death-defying act, one mostly driven by the beer they had drunk all day. He took a deep breath, questioned himself, then swung from the second story. He was right on target as he twisted over the bed of the truck, and estimating his landing, Sweeny let go of the rope. Unfortunately, he overshot his target and landed flat on his back on the hood of the truck, crushing it into the engine.

"Damn, that's gonna hurt tomorrow!" he said, looking up into the night air.

"You think?" Rachael said, standing over him.

"Hi," Sweeny replied, half dazed and half drunk.

She didn't hesitate. "You want to go out tomorrow night?" "Sure."

"Sweeny! You fricking ass! You caved in my hood!" an overexcited frat brother screamed, holding a beer and his forehead.

"Yeah, but I got a date out of it." Sweeny rolled off the hood and landed face down in the drive. It was the beginning of a true and beautiful relationship between the two junior college students, and before graduating they tied their love in marriage. A short year later she gave birth to Alex's pride and joy, Victoria Sweeny.

They had decided to move to Del Rio, Texas, as Alex started his Border Patrol Career and Rachael began her music career. She had been in San Antonio recording a couple of new songs and was driving back in a west Texas downpour. As she rounded a corner, a moving truck lost control and changed lanes, hitting Rachael's vehicle head on. The coroner's report claimed she died instantly, but Sweeny found a scribbled note on the console that read, "I love you both!"

Shortly after he moved to Presidio and with the help from Cap and Sandra and the deep friendship that he made with Lawson, Sweeny found a second home. Still, not a day went by that he didn't think about Rachael and the beautiful time they had together. He often worried about Vicky going up without a mom, but he wasn't ready to find that person.

"There she is," Lawson said, pointing to the little eight-year-old girl with her backpack on standing patiently with her teacher. The truck rolled to a stop before she ran out with a smile from ear to ear. Sweeny opened the driver's door, and Vicky climbed in.

"You got a kiss for daddy?" he asked with her climbing in his lap.

She gave him a big smack and smile, "And this." She handed him a picture she had painted. "Hi, Uncle Lawson, did you ask out that girl yet?"

Lawson shot a look at Sweeny. "What? I don't know where she hears stuff like that," Sweeny defended himself and looked down at the painting. "Hey, it's Valentine."

"Yep!" She pulled the center buckle over her lap and snapped it shut.

Chapter 9

Cap walked into the office with his coffee mug close to his face, the steam from the cup making its way through his mustache. He stopped shy of the desks and examined his team, half working, half awake, and not acknowledging his presence in the room. He took another sip and pushed back his cowboy hat from pressing on his forehand. "A rancher called and said he has been seeing illegals crossing his place just west of Redford. Lawson, you and Sweeny bring one truck, and Dale and Terry, ride with me," he said, setting his cup on his desk and picking up his radio. The other men scrambled to close their computers and gather their gear.

Once outside, a set of keys thrown by Sweeny missed Lawson's head without him noticing. "You awake?" Sweeny asked.

"Yea?" Lawson answered, clueless of the keys resting in the dirt behind him.

Walking past him and retrieving the keys, Sweeny replied, "I was going to ask you to drive, but never mind."

"I'll drive," Lawson turned and held out his hand for the keys.

"You sure? You need to go ahead and ask out that pharmacist."

"I don't know." Lawson opened the truck door.

Both trucks threw gravel against the concrete culvert as they peeled out of the drive and jetted down Hwy 170 South. Lawson could see the heads of Dale and Valentine sharing the back seat of Cap's four-door truck as they led the way. Lawson slowed down in front of the elementary school with children outside being led from the football field across the street. The field was the second greenest field in Presidio, next to the baseball field that was closer to the high school. With the lack of rain and the West Texas heat, both coaches struggled to keep their fields in playing condition.

"Football season is starting this week," Sweeny said, looking at the field that was bordered by a red track.

"Yea, I believe the Blue Devils will have a good shot at going deep in the playoffs."

"You need to ask Pharma to a game," Sweeny suggested. "Pharma? She has a name, Lia!"

"Already protective?"

Lawson shook his head, knowing there was no winning with Sweeny. The two border patrol trucks blasted southward for close to a half hour before turning off the pavement onto a rock road that lead to a set of houses, a few barns, and a couple of equipment sheds. The old rancher standing near one of the equipment sheds was wiping his hands with a red tool rag. Lawson parked and stepped out to be greeted by a border collie. Valentine barked twice and quickly stopped as Cap shot her a look.

"James," the rancher said, greeting Cap.

"Morning," he replied. "Gets any drier, you gonna have to import water," he added.

The old rancher just laughed and dusted his pants off with the back of his leathery, calloused hands. He then turned and walked toward a vegetable field located behind the equipment shed, expecting the agents to follow. "We've always had folks crossing the borders to pick some of the vegetables, and honestly, I don't care. I normally calculate extra just for hungry people. But I found a spot that some of them made camp last night, and well...." He pointed to a spot beside a dike with trash, empty bottles, and bloody rags.

Lawson climbed down and examined the area with Dale leaning over his shoulder. Lawson pointed to the massive amount of paw prints in the dirt around the area. Sweeny walked down the embankment. "Pack of coyotes?"

"Looks like it," Lawson replied.

"What do you think?" Sweeny asked Lawson.

"I don't know."

"This is the scene of someone delivering a baby," Dale replied. Sweeny and Lawson turned simultaneously and gave him a funny look. Dale pointed at a few items lying nearby. "The coyotes came later," he added.

"You sure, Probie?" Cap asked.

"Yes sir, I'm sure," he answered, confident.

"Aw right, boys, get your radios and water. We're going on foot. The odds of a new mother surviving out here is slim to none," Cap ordered. The boys hustled back to their trucks and gathered their gear and looked at a map. After planning their search, they left their trucks and started walking east.

"Let's go, girl," Cap yelled at Valentine. She bailed out of the window and ran to catch up with Cap as he called in for the local BORSTAR team and air support.

Dale jogged up with Lawson. "Why are we heading east? There isn't anything for miles but the Big Bend Ranch State Park. Don't you think they would hitch a ride somewhere?"

"Not if they are being led by a coyote. You'll learn the thought pattern of these smugglers," he answered.

"But how do you know?"

"You just learn to know after a while. Let's just hope we find them before someone dies."

The team hadn't walked an hour before Valentine picked up on a scent that she alerted. Cap held everyone up and pointed to the sky; they could hear a helicopter in the distance. Within a few more steps, Terry pointed to a set of footprints, and walking around a bend, the team found a pack of prints leading into the hills. Cap called to the helicopter, reported their location, and asked the pilot to keep their distance. He knew that this group of individuals was being led by a coyote and didn't want to spook them.

Lawson stopped and held up his fist, motioning for everyone to stop and get quiet. Looking at Sweeny, he motioned with his hand for everyone to get down. "I bet they are right around this bend." Everyone remained quiet and listened. Before long, they heard someone yell something in Spanish, but couldn't make out what they were saying.

Pointing at Sweeny, Cap whispered, "You and Probie flank to the north and wait on my signal."

"Yes sir."

"Wait on my signal!" he made sure Sweeny heard him. They waited a few minutes, then approached the group. "Terry, stay back with Val," Cap added as he and Lawson stood up.

"Border Patrol! *Quedarse donde esta*!" Lawson yelled, coming in view. Everyone froze. Lawson and Cap couldn't believe the number of people, close to twenty. Cap radioed for the helicopter to move in.

"Cap!" Lawson yelled as one of the Mexicans raised an AK- 47.

Chapter 10

There was one thing about Cap—he had a sense of things before they happened. Once the coyote pulled up an AK-47 on Lawson, Cap already had a bead on him with his issued H&K 40 cal. Two other men pulled out AK's, and Lawson looked over his shoulder at Cap. "*Bajar su arma… compadre,*" Cap said in a loud and raspy voice. There were a few secret words the team shared, and *compadre* used in a confrontation meant one thing: Back up!

Sweeny and Dale appeared from their left side with their M4A1 carbines aimed at two of the three. Terry appeared from their right with his H&K pulled and aiming in the direction of the men. But it was when Valentine appeared behind Lawson with teeth showing and a demon-sounding growl that three Ak-47's hit the dirt.

"Sweeny!" Lawson yelled for him to gather their weapons.

"*Las manos detras de la cabeza y en el terreno!*" Lawson ordered the three men to the ground with their hands behind their heads. Cap ordered the helicopter to touch down with medical supplies and called their location to the BORSTAR team that was already heading their direction. As soon as the helicopter touched the earth, one of the Mexicans leaped to his feet and bolted over the hill. Lawson and Sweeny, who were standing the closest, looked at each other for a brief moment. "Damn!" Lawson shouted as they sprinted after him.

Sweeny was fast and agile, but no-one could hold a candle to the speed Lawson demonstrated. Many new young rookies fresh out of the academy would often challenge Lawson to a foot race, mostly because the training officers would always talk about the speed he had and heckle them to race him. It was fun for Lawson to stay side by side with his opponent until halfway through the race, then kick it in high gear and smoke them. A coyote that had been in the heat for three days didn't have a chance.

"Get your cuffs," Lawson said as he blew by Sweeny. The coyote made it to the next ridge before Lawson tackled him from behind. As the man splattered face forward, Lawson landed on his back, but accidently slid his knee over a rock, tearing his pants. Sweeny was on top of the coyote within seconds, pulling his arms to the small of his back and slapping the cuffs around his dirty wrist.

Sweeny glanced to his left as Valentine jogged up with her tongue hanging out and teeth showing as if smiling. "Where the hell were you, girl?" Sweeny said, out of breath. She sat and licked the slaver off her mouth.

"You boys good?" Cap yelled over the noise from the helicopter powering down. Lawson gave him a thumbs up, still sitting with his knee pulled to his chest.

"You OK?" Sweeny asked.

"Yea, hit my knee on that stupid rock."

They stood the man up, and Sweeny checked his pockets for any weapons, finding a cell phone. Sweeny marched him back to the group with Lawson limping behind them. By the time they got back, the EMT on the helicopter was examining the young woman and her baby. "She can't be 14," Dale said.

The EMT looked at him, "Thirteen. And neither would live another night out here."

Four border patrol trucks came over the ridge and parked with serval BORSTAR team members climbing out. "Well, Cap, you did all the hard work," their supervisor replied.

"Just in the right place at the right time."

"This one had this on him." Lawson pointed at the man that had run, handing Cap a cell phone.

"Probie." Cap handed the phone to Dale. Dale ran through the contact list that had only two names. Eddie and Jose. Dale showed the name Jose to Cap.

Cap casually walked over to the coyote. "This phone to contact Jose Emmanuel?" he asked.

"You might want to ask him in Spanish," the supervisor said.

"He understands me! Well!" He shoved the phone in the man's face.

"I don't know nothing," the coyote replied. It was a common phase the agents heard when they apprehended one of Jose Emmanuel's men. They knew it was better not to answer to the US agents than answering to Jose—their lives depended on it. "Cap, we're going to take them in. Let me know if you want to question them." The supervisor motioned for his men to gather the three coyotes. "I've called for an ambulance for the young girl and her baby. They should be on the road once we get out there," he added.

"Have 'em look at this one," Cap pointed at Lawson.

"Cap, I'm OK," Lawson said, but that only got the look from Cap not to argue.

"Come on, Lawson, we'll give you a ride out," the supervisor said.

Once they got the young girl loaded in the ambulance and Lawson's knee taped up, the team walked slowly back to their trucks that were still across the highway. What started out as an hour investigation had turned out to be an all-day event. The five of them stopped at their trucks and downed a bottle of water, with Valentine drinking out of her bowl that Cap took everywhere they went. He set his leather pouch on the hood of his truck and rolled a fresh cigarette as the sun started its descent into the Mexican landscape.

"I guess I'll stop by the pharmacy and get some bandages," Lawson said, wondering why he was volunteering the information. Everyone started laughing, and the comments came out randomly, with everyone getting a word in about Lawson going to see Lia.

"Get in! I'll drop you off by the station," Lawson said to Sweeny, who wasn't going to let his comment go. Once on the road, Lawson change the conversation to the one subject that Sweeny loved to talk about, Vicky.

After dropping Sweeny off at the station, Lawson's truck slid to a stop in front of Lia's pharmacy, and he crept into the door hoping she would notice him limping. The smell of fresh-cut wood lingered in the air from the construction on her soda bar. On one side of the store were shelves with over-the-counter meds, bandages, and other anointments and first aid; the other side was snacks and the bar. Lawson slowly walked toward the back counter looking for someone, and Erika appeared from the back room.

"Well, well, if it isn't our favorite Border Patrol Agent," she said.

"I figured you would put Sweeny as your favorite" he joked.

"Well, not wearing clothes is a bonus for him," she smiled. Lia walked out, hearing their conversation. "I got to go. See you kids later," Erika added, holding a bag and walking out.

"Don't let me run you off," Lawson said. She smiled and waved over her head as she walked out the door.

"What brings you in?" Lia asked.

"Well, I kinda fell today and cut my knee. The EMT said I should keep it wrapped up for a few days. I didn't have any bandages."

"Come around here and let me look." She pointed to a chair behind the counter.

"It's nothing—"

"Let me look," she interrupted him. He pushed on the counter with his hand to relieve pressure on his knee walking to the chair.

"You can barely walk," Lia said, kneeling in front of him to roll up his pants leg.

Erika burst in the door. "Forgot my keys," she said, stopping shy of the counter. "Well, that didn't take long," she laughed.

"Shut-up—I'm looking at his knee." Lia began rolling up his pant leg.

"Might get a better look if you take your pants down instead of rolling the pants leg up," Erika said, leaning over Lia to look at Lawson's knee.

"Don't you have your keys?" Lia said, getting upset.

"Yea, yea. Bye again," Erika hollered, walking out.

"Sorry, she's always like that," Lia said, embarrassed.

"It's OK, I work with one," Lawson said, referring to Sweeny. She carefully unwrapped the bandage the EMT had placed around his knee. The touch of her hands on his knee sent chills up his spine, and it wasn't from any pain. *She has the softest hands, man, she's a beauty.*

"Let me clean it out a little better and put something on it. Is that OK?" She looked up at him with her spellbinding brown eyes. Lawson didn't say anything. "Is that OK?" She softly asked again.

"Yea," he squeaked out.

She looked up at him and cocked her head sideways with a smile from his unique answer, then walked to an aisle and gathered bandages and ointment. He studied her while she took the items from the shelf. *Man, she is courteous.*

She knelt back down and set the items beside her, opening the box with the ointment. She gently placed the medicine cream on the cut, and with her fingers carefully massaged the area around the injury. After placing a 4x4 bandage, she wrapped his knee with an Ace bandage. He began to feel guilty with his staring and couldn't hold in his question any longer.

"Would you like to get some coffee later?" he asked.

"Maybe some other time. I have to see my family tonight," she answered in a lie.

"OK, maybe tomorrow?" He shrugged his shoulders.

She took a long look at him. "I have to work."

"OK, maybe some other time, then." He started regretting that he had asked.

She walked to the cash register and rang up the items. "It'll be $14.97."

He dug in his wallet and gave her a $20, and after she gave him his change, added "Let me know if that doesn't get any better."

"OK, thank you." He limped to the door. Opening it, he turned and waved and then walked to his truck. *Well, that went about as bad as it gets! I guess I read her wrong, crash and burn!*

She watched him back out of the parking lot, "Dang, he's good looking," she said to herself. "Who am I fooling? Dad would never allow me to date him. Stupid, stupid, stupid. Maybe I don't tell Dad? Urgg, probably too late now. I've screwed that up!"

Chapter 11

"How did it go yesterday?" Sweeny asked as Lawson hoisted himself into Sweeny's truck. He had been debating whether to be truthful with Sweeny or not. He pulled his seat belt across his lap and started to answer, but Sweeny beat him to the question. "That bad, huh?"

"Let's just say we can probably still be friends." "Ouch! She said that?"

"For the most part. She said she was busy."

"Maybe she's busy?" Sweeny replied, looking out his window to make sure his lane was clear. Lawson cut his eyes at him. "I'll talk to her," Sweeny added.

"No, thanks, I don't need help getting shot down twice. Let's drop it."

"OK," Sweeny answered, but Lawson knew that he wouldn't be able to let it go.

Their truck barreled north through the rugged terrain on Hwy 67 toward Marfa, Texas, to the Big Bend Sector Headquarters. It wasn't often that the team was called into headquarters, but with the increasing activity of Jose Emmanuel, there was a growing concern to catch him. Lawson watched as the West Texas desert passed by through the window of their patrol truck; the endless view of dried vegetation and brush trees brought a sobering thought of his relationship status.

"Did you ever think you'd be out here?" he asked Sweeny. "Nope. I ask myself that question every day."

The view disappeared as their truck passed through a cutout hill of clay and dirt and reappeared with an unending barbwire fence. Streaks of white clouds crisscrossed in the deep blue sky from jets streaming their way to their destinations. Lawson thought about the people on board and wondered if they were looking down and thinking the same thing he was: *Where am I going?*

"You're not thinking about leaving?" Sweeny asked. "No, just wondering what's in store for me here." "Man, this girl did a number on you."

Maybe so, he thought. He drifted in thought to his family and his parents in Paris, Texas. He remembered the day he left like it was yesterday—and his father's words: "You will always have home." He studied an old school house and an old wooden church with a steeple that looked like it was struggling to hold the bell as they sped through a small community. Shafter, Texas was a blink as they drove north.

Thirty minutes later, they pulled into the headquarters and stopped in front of a cyclone fence. Sweeny leaned out his window and punched in a code. Within a second the gate jerked open, and as it slid across the tracks, they pulled in, parking beside Cap's truck.

Sweeny put the truck in park and with both hands resting on the steering wheel, asked, "What's up? It's not like you to let getting shot down by a girl bother you."

"Are you saying I've been shot down so many times I'm good at it?"

"I don't know—I mean, I've never experienced being shot down," Sweeny smiled and opened the door. It was times like this that Lawson wasn't sure if Sweeny understood him and dropped the subject or just his nature. Cap was sitting on a bench that was a few feet from the entry door for agents smoking a cigarette.

He looked down at his watch then back at the duo. "Five minutes early? Either it's a miracle or you thought the meeting started 25 minutes ago." Cap blew a puff of smoke in the air.

"We're turning over a new leaf. Always early, always turning in our reports on time, and always quiet during these meetings," Sweeny replied.

"Always full of BS." Cap thumbed his cigarette in the dirt and followed the two of them inside. After stopping by the coffee pot, he joined the rest of the team and other agents in a large meeting room. Within moments the Border Patrol Chief walked into the room with a vanilla file overflowing with papers and set them at the podium facing rows of tables. He glanced over to the corner of the room to see Valentine sprawled out on the cold tile floor, and he rolled his eyes and put on his reading glasses.

"Gentlemen, thank you for coming in. I have some information for you." He passed out stapled papers to each member and returned to the podium. "The two men you arrested last week after your shoot out." He paused and looked at Sweeny, expecting his input.

Sweeny looked at Cap and mouthed the word "always." Cap smiled and shook his head.

"These gentlemen are key players with the Juarez Cartel. We learned that Jose is helping with an extreme amount of drugs to be smuggled into the US within a week. We have also learned there is a house in Presidio that we believe the Cartel is using for a meeting place," the Chief lectured.

"And we get to watch the house." Sweeny couldn't hold it in any longer.

"Yes. We don't want to alarm them in any way. Hopefully this is a place that Jose will come to." The Chief continued, "You will find the briefing in your notes. I want surveillance on this house." He looked at Cap. "Gentlemen, this is the closest shot we have had to catch Jose. Let's put this scum bag down."

"What about the coyotes we took down yesterday?" Lawson asked.

"We know for sure they worked for Jose. You probably saved the lives of the aliens you intercepted in that group. I am calling in the BORTAC team to assist in with this operation. I don't want to lose this guy. Any questions?" He glanced at Sweeny, who just shook his head and remained silent. "All right, gentlemen, good luck. Cap, can I see you for a moment?"

The guys walked out into the office and ran into a couple members of the BORTAC team. BORTAC—Border Patrol Tactical Unit—is a special response unit of the Border Patrol. It was formed in 1984 to respond to terrorist threats of all types anywhere in the word in order to protect our nation's homeland. Most agents had a great respect for the members, not only for their special assistance, but for the harsh training they went through for five weeks. Lawson had been heavily recruited to join the team, but he didn't think he was ready for the training and hell they go through.

"Looks like we'll be partnering on this operation for a while," Lawson said.

"Looks that way," one of them replied.

"Johnson, when are you going to start working out? Your arms are getting a little flabby," Sweeny said to the other officer.

"You wish! Nothing wrong with this cannon," he replied, bowing up his bicep and slapping it. Lawson and his group walked on past the BORTAC agents and headed outside.

"How do you become a BORTAC member?" Dale asked.

"Steroids," Sweeny answered.

"Three years of service, first," Lawson answered. Dale shook his head with acknowledgement. "Those guys have saved our butts a few times," he added, taking up for the members. Before Sweeny could come back with anything, the doors burst open, and Cap and Valentine walked out.

"Head back to the Ponderosa. Sweeny, Lawson, you got first shift on this house tonight," Cap said as the team loaded up in their trucks.

Chapter 12

Sweeny reached in the backseat of the Honda Accord they were using for the stakeout and nabbed another piece of pepperoni pizza. Between his Mountain Dew, the pizza, and the bag of M&M's on the dash he was set for a long night. Lawson sat quietly in the passenger seat playing a game on his phone. "Why are we watching this house and not the sheriff's office? He said he wanted to help," Sweeny asked with a mouth full of pizza.

"You're gonna choke on that," Lawson replied. Sweeny opened his mouth and showed the chewed-up piece. "You know they're under staffed." Lawson answered, turning away from Sweeny.

"Well, I'd be better off setting up cameras on the house and watching from my couch. Cap and his old school ways." He turned up the Mountain Dew and took a huge swig.

"I'd rather be here tonight than during the day," Lawson said, taking a drink from his Fiji bottled water.

"Has Dale got you drinking that hotty totty water?"

"No, he left a bottle in my truck."

"You still bummed out?"

Lawson thought for a moment; he wasn't interested in getting in a conversation about feelings, but when things were serious, Sweeny was a good friend to talk to. "I don't know," he started. "It's just got me thinking. I'm 28, got a good job, and still single."

"That's not a bad thing; you get to play the field," Sweeny said.

"Here? I don't know—I haven't really dated much since academy, and I don't see a whole lot of opportunities here."

"Maybe you're reading into this too much. She just said she was busy. If you really think there is something there, you should go for it. Don't take 'no' for an answer."

Lawson started to answer him when a dark Ford Fusion with tinted windows pulled up. He sat up. "Someone's here."

Sweeny pulled out a Yukon Centurion night vision scope and focused on the car. "Four guys," he said. "I can't see if anyone else is in the car." The four men walked up to the front porch, where another man met them and walked inside with three of them, leaving one on the porch. "Oh yea, something is happening. Let's take a closer look."

"No, stay in the car," Lawson said, but before he could finish his sentence, Sweeny slipped out of the car and crouched across the street. "Damn it!" Lawson quietly opened his door and ducked behind the car to check to see if he had been spotted. He saw the man light a cigarette and took the opportunity to catch up with Sweeny.

"I bet if we get to that window, we can hear what they're saying." Sweeny pointed to a window on the front of the house with a large hedge in front of it.

"We can't tip anyone off. Now let's get back to the car," Lawson said. Suddenly the neighbor's outside light came on. Both of them dove behind a car on blocks, and the neighbor walked out and set a garbage can by the road. The man on the porch watched as he walked back in and turned the light off. "Come on," Lawson insisted on moving back to the car.

The front door of the house swung open, and the same three men exited the house. It was apparent that the older man was in charge. He ordered the three younger men to get in the car as he followed them. "Could this be our guy?" Sweeny looked at Lawson. Lawson remained silent. As soon as the men pulled out of the drive and drove past, Lawson and Sweeny sprinted to their car and followed from a distance.

"Fall back, not too close," Lawson said, pulling his seat belt around his chest.

"I know—this isn't my first rodeo."

The car drove slowly down Largona Street and took a right on Hwy 67, and Sweeny pulled out and held back. Lawson texted Cap on his phone: "Might be following Jose. We are following, hopefully they will cross and we can get agents to hold them up."

"10-4," Cap texted back.

The Fusion's left blinker turned on and slowed at the intersection of 67 and Louvain. "The same street we had our shoot out on," Sweeny said.

"Not too close," Lawson repeated.

Their car disappeared as it turned onto the street, and Sweeny sped up and took the left to follow. What he wasn't expecting was the Ford Fusion was stopped in the middle of the street only a half block from the intersection. "Get down!" Sweeny pushed on Lawson. He slowed down, then drove past the car. He couldn't tell through the tinted windows if they suspected him. Sweeny drove past the house where the gun fight had broken out and pulled into a driveway.

"What are you doing?" Lawson asked, still ducked in the passenger seat.

"Acting like this is my house. Be right back." Sweeny popped the trunk and stepped out of the Honda Accord, acting as if he was gathering bags in the truck, then shut it and slowly walked toward the front door. The Fusion slowly crawled by the house with the driver window down, stopped at the stop sign, then turned left, heading toward the border crossing. Sweeny sprinted back to the car to find Lawson holding the night vision googles.

"Same guy I saw in the convenience store last week. I knew those guys were eyeing me down for something," Lawson explained. Sweeny backed out as the outside light came on at the house where they were parked and drove the opposite way. Turning right onto Hwy 67, they drove one block before the Ford Fusion appeared at the next intersection.

"Damn! We're made!" Sweeny snapped. The car spun out leaving the stop sign and flew past the Accord. Sweeny cut the wheel in the middle of the street and fishtailed the car as he sped after the Ford.

Lawson picked up the radio and called in for backup. They blasted past the border patrol station, *ironic!* Lawson thought. The Fusion was pulling ahead when it veered off on another highway leading out of town, and the tires from the Accord squealed as Sweeny took the turn without slowing down. Sweeny watched as the taillights from the Ford disappeared around a corner, and leaning into the turn, Lawson yelled, "Watch out!" The Ford slid to a stop in the middle of the road, and three Mexicans bailed out with automatic weapons in hand. Sweeny slammed on the brakes, and as the front of the car was being riddled with gunfire, he cut across the field to their right.

Glass blew over them and through the inside from the gun fire, but with luck Sweeny slid the car behind a nearby building. Both boys fled the car with their M4RIFLE's in hand. Lawson ran to the corner of the building to get a peek. As he slowly looked around the corner, he saw the taillights disappearing over a hill. "They're gone."

"You OK?" Sweeny asked.

"Yea."

"Didn't see that coming." Sweeny walked up to the Accord and examined the bullet holes in the side of the doors, then reached in the broken back window. "They shot the pizza." He pointed at a hole in the box.

Lawson leaned on the car. "Man, I could use one of Cap's cigarettes."

"I'm sure he'll be here any minute," Sweeny answered, taking a piece of pizza out, brushing off the glass, and taking a bite.

Chapter 13

Lia pushed open the door to her pharmacy with her foot and worked her way through the door with an arm full of bags and a backpack. The wind pushed the door shut before Erika could walk through carrying Lia's hiking boots. "Why in the world do you need all this stuff if you're just going to be gone overnight?" Erika asked, pushing the door with her back against it.

"I am going to leave some things for my younger sisters," she said, loading her bags.

"I don't think these are going to fit them," Erika observed, handing her the boots.

"I'm going to see Abuela."

"You're going to see your grandmother? Bring me back something," Erika replied.

Lia threw the boots in the back and hugged Erika. "Don't close the store before time," she said. Erika just smiled with the full intention of leaving early. Lia waved out the window as she pulled out onto the highway and drove toward the border. Within a few blocks of the pharmacy, she pulled in line to cross the border. The thought of running into Lawson at the checkpoint crossed her mind, but she had never seen him there before, so her hopes weren't high.

Lawson had been on her mind since Sunday, but after the awkward encounter at the pharmacy, it was something she couldn't get off her mind. *I'm grown now and have my own business, Papa will just have to accept who I am dating. Or will I be banned from the family? Why does it have to be so complicated?*

Once through the checkpoint, she crossed into the desolate town of Ojinaga. The town was poor, much like the rest of Mexico, and even with a slowly growing population, it resembled a ghost town. She continued through the dusty town and hung a left on Hwy 18 and drove to the edge of town before following a narrow dirt road to her home, a route she had driven many times in the last few years.

Two dogs ran out to the Jeep to greet her, followed by a little boy without a shirt. She could barely open her door with the greeting party of her father's dogs and her little brother. "*Hola*," she said, giving her brother a high five.

Grabbing her hand, the little boy led her to the party in the back of the house. Walking around the corner of the light brown brick home, she found the rest of her family around a long table and a giant BBQ grill. A huge smile formed across the face of her mother, who was wearing a red plaid apron and cutting lettuce and tomatoes for their burgers. "Amalia! I am happy you came."

Her father looked up from the grill. "My sweet Amalia."

"Hello Papa." She wrapped her arms around him, but with spatula and knife in hand, he could only turn and kiss her on the cheek.

"Come help me set the table," her mother smiled.

"Are your arms broke?" she asked another brother, who was watching his father cook.

"It's a woman's job," he laughed and stood to hug her.

"You all act as if I've been gone forever; I was just here last

week."

"A week is too long," her father replied, waving the smoke out of his face.

Soon the long table was filled with her brothers and sisters and her father sitting at the head of the table. They blessed the food and began eating, and halfway through their meal, Lia's two older brothers walked into the yard. "Our American sister is back," the taller one said. Lia leaped up from her seat and jumped into the arms of Roberto, her oldest brother that she hadn't seen in over a year.

"How's the Caribbean life?" she asked.

"Oh you know... awesome!" he said with a smile. Roberto had left his father's business and taken a job with a dive company south of Cancun, Mexico, after he and his father had a falling out. Carlos, the next brother in line, was by far their father's favorite son, and Lia knew it had definitely gone to his head.

"When are you going to get a haircut?" Lia punched Carlos in the arm, observing that his hair was passing his shoulders and shining with grease.

"Someday," he answered and found a seat at the table.

Lia's father stood and raised his red solo cup in the air. "Today, my family is home."

After their meal, the younger siblings helped Lia and her mother clean off the tables and wrap up the leftovers. Her mother handed one of the girls the last tray of food and sent them inside to put it away. Turning to Lia, she said, "You seem different today."

"Just happy to be home."

"You met someone," her mother smiled.

Lia paused to answer the question. Yes, she had met someone, but more than likely had already run him off. "How would you know that?"

"Call it mother's intuition. But I am right?"

"Yes and no. I have had someone ask me out, just for coffee.
But I turned him down."

"Why?"

"He's American." She waited for her mother's reaction and thought this conversation was happening quicker than she expected.

"I figured this much." Lia gave her a funny look; it was not the reaction she was expecting. "Amalia, you've always been the rebel of the family," her mother went on. "You became a US citizen, put yourself through school, and opened your own business."

"Rebel?"

"Maybe I say it wrong... you are...."

"Independent?"

"Yes, independent."

"So you think Papa will be OK with me seeing an American?"

"No. You know how he feels." That was the answer she thought she'd get. "Are you going to stay with Abuela?" Her mother quickly changed the subject.

"Yes ma'am, I should probably start heading that way." She stood up and walked in to visit for a short time before venturing to her grandmother's place.

Lia drove through the deserted countryside of Mexico as the sun dipped into the distant mountains. The sky exploded into a bright, deep red with the rays from the sun breaking through the hypnotic color. The sound of gravel beneath the tires and the dust flying into the air caught the attention of an elderly woman standing outside an old, dilapidated mud house.

The old woman was dressed in a long sarape dress with a string necklace of rattlesnake heads dangling from her neck. A band of hawk feathers wrapped her arm, and the straw hat she wore shaded her eyes. She leaned on a tarnished white oak stick that was two feet taller than she was, and furs from different animals hung off a front porch that was falling in on one side. The Jeep came to a stop feet from the old woman, and Lia opened her door and stepped out. "*Hola,* Abuela."

Chapter 14

Rolling over, Lawson grabbed the phone buzzing on his bedside table. Looking at it, he saw it was a text from Sweeny: "Are we going tonight?" Lawson rubbed his eyes and sat up, trying to focus on the phone.

"Do we have to stake out tonight?" he returned.

"Cap said we are laying off the house for a few days."

"OK, I told Derrick we would come." Lawson set the phone back down. Derrick Owens was on his third year as principal at the high school and had befriended Lawson and Sweeny during his first year. They had participated in a career day at the high school his first year and with their witty attitudes had attracted most of the students to their booth. They had become instant celebrities the following week when the paper posted a story about the duo involved in a gun fight south of town.

Every year they returned to the high school for career day and seminars, Mr. Owens gave them an open invite to lunch. He enjoyed having them as role models and mentors to the teen boys, but Lawson questioned his decision every time he witnessed Sweeny doing something stupid.

Lawson rolled out of bed and placed his feet on the cold hardwood floor of his one-bedroom house. The clock told him it was 11a.m. "Did you not go to sleep last night?" he texted Sweeny back.

"Picked up Vicky from Sandra's this morning and we made pancakes." Lawson smiled at the text and put his phone back. He stumbled into the kitchen and started a pot of coffee, then made his way to the bathroom. Turning on the hot water and cracking open the cold, he closed his shower curtain and walked back to his bedroom.

He carefully unwrapped the ace bandage from his knee and inspected his cut. *Maybe I should have got a stich or two.* He finished undressing and threw his shirt and shorts in front of the closet. Tip toeing across the cold floor, he made his way to the bathroom and faded into the steam cloud coming out of his shower.

After showering and wrapping a towel around him, he walked to the kitchen to pour a cup of coffee and warm up a bagel. He sat at the small table with beads of water running down his chest from his drenched hair. He thought about his parents and retrieved his phone. Dialing the number, he waited for someone to pick up.

"Hello?" A female voice answered. "Hey, Mom."

"Hello, sweetie, how's work going?"

"It's going good. Slow, not much happens around here," he lied, not wanting to alarm her about the work he did. But being a wife and sister-in-law to law enforcement officers, she knew better about an answer that things are slow. "How's Dad?"

"He and your uncle are rebuilding a truck. As if they need an extra project. The garden is just about done, so I'll have him till it under. Do you want any tomatoes?"

"I would, but I don't know how I would get them."

"You would come get them," she quickly answered.

"Mom, it's a ten-hour drive. I'll be home for Thanksgiving."

"Make sure Sweeny and Vicky come this year; he is so entertaining."

"Yes ma'am, he is." Their conversation continued for the next thirty minutes about Church, football, flowers, her friend Janet and her llamas, and other things to catch up. After they said their 'love you's' he hung up feeling a little guilty for not seeing them more than he did. He felt his phone buzz again and looking down, found another text from Sweeny.

"Derrick asked if we could bring the trucks and wear uniforms an hour before the game. I said yes."

"No prob," Lawson returned the text.

He left early to stop by the station and wash his truck and ran into Cap filling up. "You going to the game tonight?"

"San's got me going to the picture show."

"You're missing the first game for a movie?" Lawson asked, dumbfounded.

"Gotta make the bride happy," Cap replied, lighting a cigarette.

"You're gonna blow yourself up." Lawson pointed to the fuel pump.

"I'd miss the picture show then. I'll take my chances," he smiled.

Water dripped from Lawson's truck most of the way to the stadium, and he'd hoped that it would be dry before he got there. Mr. Owens was holding the gate open for him to drive in. Sweeny was parked and drying off his truck with half a dozen teenage boys standing around talking to him. The boys gravitated to Sweeny, and Lawson understood why. Vicky was standing on the tool box waving a red and white pom-pom and waving at Lawson. "Hi, Uncle Lawson."

Stepping out in full uniform, Lawson caught Vicky as she leaped off the tool box and into his arms. "Don't worry, Uncle Lawson, that girl will say yes. Just keep asking." Lawson paused and shot a look at Sweeny.

"I don't have a clue where she hears these things."

Lawson put her down and opened his truck doors so kids could climb in and look at their radios, lights, and blast the sirens. Sweeny encouraged them to make all the noise they could, and they did. Within 15 minutes to kickoff, the majority of the student body were surrounding the trucks, with girls taking selfies and guys talking about the guns they had shot. Mr. Owens walked up and took one large group picture with Lawson and Sweeny in the middle and then shuffled the students to the stands.

"Thanks for coming out, guys," he said.

"Anytime, you know we don't mind," Sweeny replied.

"Funny you say that—I have a young man that has gotten himself into s sticky situation here at school. He doesn't have much of a home life. Would you visit with him?"

"Sure."

"I'll bring him by and introduce you in a little while. Enjoy the game." They shook hands, and the boys and Vicky hurried to the concession before kickoff. They had just gotten seated when the Blue Devils kicked it deep into the end zone, starting the game. Vicky was busy trying to open her peanuts when they heard a voice coming from behind them.

"Wearing your uniforms gets you into the game for free?" Erika asked.

"And the movies," Vicky quickly answered.

Sweeny put his hand over her mouth. "Haha, we were helping the high school."

Lawson turned to find Lia seating beside her. "Hey," he nodded.

"Hi, Lawson, how's your knee?"

"It's just about healed. Thanks." Sweeny shook his head no.

"Uncle Lawson, who's that?" Vicky asked.

"It's just some friends."

"She's the one! She owns the pharmacy store!" she said, excited.

How would you know that? he thought. "Yes, but please don't say anything, OK?"

"OK, I won't, but you should ask her out. We're going to the pizza place after... ask her!"

"Honey, watch the game. Uncle Lawson is scared of her," Sweeny replied. But Vicky couldn't let it go, and during the first half the girls witnessed the commotion between her and Lawson. At half time, Lawson excused himself to the restroom, and as soon as he was out of sight, Vicky turned to Lia.

"Hi!" she started.

"Hello." Lia was surprised at her persistence in saying hi.

"I'm Vicky."

"I'm Lia."

Sweeny was talking to another couple and didn't notice that Vicky had climbed up the bleachers to sit between the girls. "If Uncle Lawson ask you out again," Vicky was asking, "would you say 'yes'?"

Erika starting laughing, and Lia just stuttered, "I don't know."

"Please! He is a super nice guy."

She bent down closer to Vicky. "Well, since I have your word that he's a nice guy, I might consider it."

"Awesome, we're going for pizza after the game. You promise?" Vicky pointed at her.

Lia kissed her pinky, crossed her heart, and held it out for Vicky to do the same. With pinkies locked, she added, "I promise."

Lawson came in sight and saw Vicky sitting in between the girls. *Uh oh,* he thought, *this can't be good.* As soon as she saw him, she scurried back to her seat, Sweeny never seeing a thing. Lawson lifted one eye brow handing her a bag of popcorn. "What were you talking to them about?" he whispered.

"Don't worry—I got it all worked out for you."

"What?" He spilled his popcorn on the people in front of him. "Sweeny!?!" He started to turn red.

"What?" Sweeny was dumbfounded about their conversation.

"Just ask her out," Vicky said with a smile on her face.

"No."

"Ask her!"

"No!"

"You know you're arguing with an eight-year-old?" Sweeny leaned over and asked Lawson.

"And a very hard-headed eight-year-old." Lawson gave her a funny look. With the sound of the horn on the scoreboard, the Blue Devils had won their first game of the season, and as Lawson predicted, they were going to be a tough team to beat this year. The bleachers started to empty, and Erika and Lia stopped to talk with the guys. Vicky threw an elbow into Lawson's thigh.

"Well, it's time for pizza!" Vicky yelled over the crowd.

Lawson felt his blood pressure go up.

"Are you guys going for pizza?" Erika asked with a big smile.

"We are!" Vicky didn't give anyone a chance to answer.

"Yea, we are. Would you guys like to come?" Lawson looked

at Lia.

"That sounds like fun. We'd love to go," she smiled at Vicky.

"Finally!" Vicky said as if she were going to pass out.

Chapter 15

Monday morning rolled around, "Hey, sweet, we need to leave before we're late for school," Sweeny yelled through his house, holding a Transformer backpack. "Mrs. Sandra is picking you up from school today and wants to take you shopping." Vicky walked into the kitchen with a t-shirt, shorts, and sneakers. "Don't you want to put on a prettier shirt?"

She gave him a funny look. "Dad, I'm not interested in dressing up." It was times like this that worried Sweeny about Vicky not growing up with a mom. She was mostly around the guys and loved to roughhouse like a boy. He hoped that she would grow out of it and become a little girl. Sandra often reminded Sweeny it was just a phase.

"How long are you going to be this afternoon?" she asked, staring out the window of his truck.

"Not long."

"OK. Sometimes Mrs. Sandra takes me to girly stores, and I don't want to go," she replied.

"What's got you worried about girly things?" Sweeny smiled.

"I don't know," she answered. Sweeny let the subject drop.

They pulled up to the circular drive that led to the school drop off spot. "Have a great day!"

She leaned over and kissed him. "I will. You too." She slid out of the truck and shut the door, running to join her friends. Sweeny watched her for a moment until an anxious mom honked the horn behind him. He gave a wave and drove to the station. Pulling in, he noticed Cap's truck by the pumps with Dale filling it up. He parked and climbed out.

"You going with us?" he asked Dale.

"No, Cap asked me to fill it up. Terry and I are heading north today."

Walking in the back door to the offices, he could smell a cigarette that wasn't completely stomped out. A cool breeze blew through the patrol yard, and he stopped and looked toward the sky, thinking fall was already here. For the most part, Presidio has decent temperatures with normal lows in the 50s during winter, but summer can become a squelcher at temperatures rising well above 100.

Cap walked out carrying his normal travel coffee mug, greeting Sweeny with "You better get your coffee and gear, we need to roll." Cap had planned to ride with Sweeny down to a small area named Castolon, deep in the Big Bend Park and close to a small Mexican town. Sweeny walked in and grabbed his gear for the three-hour drive they had ahead of them. Lawson was already out and working at the crossing for the day.

"All right, Cap, you ready for our all-day venture?" Sweeny said, walking up to his truck.

"I don't know," Cap mumbled to himself.

The Big Bend Park was one of the hardest places in the country to regulate aliens from crossing into the US. Many of the ranches and land owners in south Texas had developed a volunteer group in 2006 called Texas Border Volunteers. The group was designed not to hinder Border Patrol Agents, but assist them in protecting the borders. This group of mostly older men and some women would patrol their areas and call the agents if they found any aliens. The Chief Patrol Agent, in Marfa, had received a call that a group of volunteers had organized and was in the park area, something that was out of the ordinary for the group.

Cap turned on his newly acquired satellite radio to his favorite country channel and fired up a cigarette. Sweeny rolled down his window to allow the smoke to funnel outside, and they were quiet for the first 30 minutes before Cap broke the silence.

"Heard the boys looked good Friday night," Cap commented.

"Yep, heard you went to the movies. Chick Flick?"

"No, went to the new Captain America movie. Pretty good."

"Vicky has been asking me to take her."

Cap pulled the truck into a parking lot of a local mom and pops diner. "Let's eat before we get down there." There was no arguing coming from Sweeny. The bell on the door sounded as Cap swung it open. A dozen tables filled the small restaurant with only a couple of them with people. Cap pulled back his chair, rested his cowboy hat on the back, and nodded hello to a neighboring table with an elderly couple. Sweeny picked up the menu and was studying it when the waitress walked up and ask what they would be drinking.

"Water is fine with me," Cap replied.

"Water...." Sweeny froze.

The waitress gave him a funny look. "I'll get those while y'all decide on what you want to eat." It had been five years since Rachael was killed in the accident, but Sweeny had never forgotten what she looked like. Her tall slender figure, long brown hair, and dimpled face were permanently edged in his memory. Now he was staring at a very close resemblance of Rachael.

"You OK?" Cap asked.

"Yea."

"Look like you saw a ghost."

"I did," he said under his breath.

He couldn't take his eyes off the waitress and did his best to hide them when she looked his way. Cap talked about the volunteer group and expressed his worry that if radicals were to join, the Border Patrol would have more of a problem with them. They scarfed down lunch, and as Cap paid, Sweeny walked outside.

"What was that all about? You know her?" Cap walked out with a tooth pick hanging from his mouth. Sweeny slid into the truck and pulled out his wallet. Fumbling through some pictures, he pulled out the last picture of Rachael, showing it to Cap. "She gave you a picture of herself?" Cap asked, confused.

"That's Rachael." Sweeny pointed at the picture.

"Oh... yea. I guess you did see a ghost."

Sweeny took a deep breath. "That is the first time since her death that I have been shaken. Is that bad?" he asked.

"Bad? You saw someone that reminded you of your late wife. I wouldn't say it was bad. More like good. Memories are important."

Sweeny felt a lump in his throat and his stomach sink. *Late wife* rang through his head. It wasn't something that he had thought about himself, a widower. He always thought of it as though Rachael went somewhere and he would soon join her—a temporary separation. It was a large part of why he had never given any thought to dating someone else.

"Cap, am I screwing up?" he choked out.

"With Vicky?" Cap knew before he asked.

"Yes."

"Well... I will always say every little girl needs her daddy. It's a role that is most absent in the lives of kids these days. There's a saying that if a dad points his kids in the right direction, when they're old they won't be lost."

"You preaching to me?" Sweeny asked.

"Nope."

"Doesn't the Bible also say *it takes a village to raise a child?*" Sweeny asked, knowing Cap was known to read his Bible.

"Nope, it says it's the parent's job, not the village or the schools. I live a simple life that I learned from my dad and his dad and so on." Cap flicked his tooth pick out the window and lit another cigarette. "I wasn't the perfect father for my two daughters, but I worked my ass off trying to be. I believe God wants us to be over the household and for us to lead our own families. Having a mother is important for a child. She provides things we can't, but ultimately it comes down to the fathers... and if your reason for not having a woman around the house is because you're not ready, well compadre... I'd say that's selfish."

Sweeny didn't like his answer. "I'm not selfish," he defended himself.

Cap rolled his eyes over to him. "I didn't say you were."

"The night of the accident, Rachael had called me." Sweeny took a deep breath. "She told me that she was thinking about staying another day. I got mad. She had been gone two or three days, and I had been home with Vicky. I felt like I was doing all the parenting and she was off running around with her music friends. Well... I told her that if she didn't come home, it was going to be over between us. I only said it because I was mad." He paused again. "You know the rest of the story." Cap remained silent and stared straight ahead. "Selfish, huh? How's that for being selfish? I killed my own wife."

Cap slammed on the brakes and pulled to the side of the road. "You think it was your fault that girl died? Son, we don't control life! When God is ready for us, he's coming. If you've been living the last five years believing a bunch of crap that you killed your wife, then you've bought into a lie!"

Sweeny just stared at Cap. "What is your heart telling you, son? You'll never go wrong following your heart, never!" He stomped back on the gas pedal, shooting rocks behind them as they took back off heading into the Big Bend National Park.

Chapter 16

C ap slowed and pulled over to the side of the road, dialing a number on his cell phone. "This is James Garret with the Border Patrol. Do you have time to meet? Yes, we are in the area. OK, give us 10 minutes." He hung up. "We are going to meet with this militia group."

"They're not a bunch of crazies?" Sweeny asked.

"I don't think so. But Chief didn't have a clue what they are doing in Big Bend Ranch." Cap turned off the pavement onto a dirt road heading south toward the border, the mountainous terrain surrounding them with a dry underbrush that was subject to fire. A cloud of dust formed behind Cap's truck while he dodged potholes along the dirt road.

"Why in the world are we meeting out here?" Sweeny asked.

"I don't know—they wanted to show us something."

"Are you sure? Kinda strange that they would call us out in the middle of nowhere."

"Nowhere is where we work."

Coming around a bend, they spotted three trucks with all-terrain vehicles being towed by each truck. Five men stood around one of the trucks cloaked in camouflage, all wearing tactical sunglasses. "This is a volunteer group?" Sweeny asked, not sold on their safety.

"Yep. You seem nervous. I wouldn't have brought us out here if I didn't trust the situation. Haven't you learned that?"

"I trust you, I just don't trust them." Their trucked rolled to a halt, and the two border patrol agents stepped out.

"Afternoon," Cap offered a greeting in his raspy voice. "Agents," one of the men answered.

"You boys are a long way from your normal stomping grounds," Cap replied.

"Nope, we are on a mission."

"What's that?" Sweeny asked.

"You familiar with the term 'rape tree'?" the man asked.

"We are, haven't encounter any in our area," Cap answered.

"You got one now. Can we show you?" The man pointed at their ATV's. Cap nodded and walked back to his truck opening the back glass for Valentine to climb in and out of the truck, and after filling a bowl of water, he commanded her to stay. Sweeny strapped his M4RIFLE to his back and climbed on one of the ATV's. Dust rolled out from the tires as the five all-terrain vehicles barreled toward the border.

As they came around a shallow bend, a tree in the distance came into focus with something hanging off most of the branches. Sweeny cocked his head, trying to figure out what the tree was littered with and edging close, he realized it was women's undergarments. The tree, with its ornaments, gave an eerie vibe. One by one the ATVs turned off.

"I never expected we'd see one around here," Sweeny replied.

"We came across a large group of aliens last week. One of the Mexican was a 10-year-old girl. She explained that she was brought across last year in this area and raped at a tree by a coyote. He hung her panties on the tree as a trophy," one of the men said.

Another man approached the tree and pointed to a pair of panties. "I would say these belong to the little girl, but if you look close, you'll see there are 10–12 panties that would only fit children."

Sweeny stood silently in shock. He was familiar with rape trees in southern Arizona, but this was his first, and to imagine children being raped made him sick to his stomach. One of the volunteers walked off to the side and threw up. "Sorry. I just can't handle this," he apologized.

"No apologies needed," Cap replied.

"There is no doubt they'll come back to this tree. Out of pity for the little girl, we want to take these coyotes down," another man of the group said.

"A man by the name of Jose Emmanuel was with the three coyotes before they crossed," one of the men added.

"Jose Emmanuel knows about this?" Sweeny asked.

The man nodded his head. "Yes, you guys know the name?"

"We know the name," Sweeny answered.

"This little girl's family paid $10,000 the first time they were smuggled over and caught. This time they paid $15,000. These coyotes are cleaning up," the man commented.

"We figure the average pay of smuggling is $5,000 a person and $10,000 a family. Most of the time Jose's men will leave them for dead in the mountains," Sweeny said.

"Fricking savages!" another man replied.

"We'll have agents set up here. We'll catch 'em," Cap reassured the men.

"We know you boys have an endless job; we're here to help," the man replied.

Sweeny's guard went down. "We'll catch these low lives!"

***

Lawson finished his shift at the border crossing and drove back toward his house. *I wonder if she would mind me stopping by?* he thought about Lia. *Things went pretty good at the pizza place the other night. Maybe she was busy the first time?* He swerved into the right lane and turned back, heading to the pharmacy. Dust from Lawson's truck hovered in the air before a wind took it from in front of the pharmacy. *Here goes everything.*

An electric bell tone sounded as he walked in, finding Lia standing behind the freshly stained soda fountain bar. She was entranced with something behind the bar, and Lawson wasn't sure she knew it was him that walked in. "The bar looks great," he commented.

"They finished yesterday, and you will be the first to try this." She didn't look up. Lawson walked closer to see what she was working on, and she set an old-fashioned glass with a root beer float on the bar.

"Try it and tell me what you think?"

He sat on one of the red top bar stools that was fixed in place and pulled the glass toward him. Lia watched as if she had created a masterpiece. "Well?" she asked.

Lifting his eyebrows and nodding his head, he replied, "It's good, really good."

"You're not just saying that?"

"No, honestly it's good." He scooped out another bite.

She reached down and set another half-eaten float on the bar. "I thought so too, but I needed another opinion."

"What else do you need sampled?" He smiled.

"Well, let's see." She started looking around the bar.

Putting his hand over the bar, he said, "I was just kidding," stopping her from looking.

She smiled and grabbed her float. "So Sweeny's daughter is cute and not scared of much. What's their story?"

"His wife died a few years back. He was working near Del Rio at the time, and after the accident, he moved up here to join us."

"That's sad. He seems like a great father."

"He is," Lawson said. There was an awkward quietness as they both scooped out a bite of root beer float. "There is a professional rodeo at the fairgrounds next Saturday," Lawson bravely asked. "Would you be interested in going?"

She was quiet for a moment, giving Lawson the impression that he was about to be shot down again. *I know my father would never approve of this*, she thought, *but he's not here!* "I would love to."

Chapter 17

The following day, the team decided to take advantage of their slow day and spend an hour cooling off back at their swimming hole. Cap was sitting at his usual perched position with Valentine tucked behind him under a ledge. Sweeny took off running and leaped off the edge of the already wet rock, aiming toward Terry, who was trying to keep his phone above the creek, and missing him by only inches. Terry scrambled to dry off his phone. "Sweeny, you ass!" he yelled as Sweeny emerged.

Flipping his wet hair to the side, Sweeny grinned. "You shouldn't be texting in the water." Terry gave him a dirty look.

"Hey, you guys want to cook ribs next Saturday?" Sweeny announced.

"Next Saturday is the rodeo, what's wrong with this Saturday?" Lawson asked.

"It's three days, you can go Sunday. Vicky and I are going to Marfa this Saturday."

"I already made plans to go Saturday." He answered and immediately wished he wouldn't have said anything.

Everyone got quiet and Sweeny looked at him, "Plans?"

"Well I was thinking about going that evening." He looked down.

"You're taking pharma, aren't you?"

"Her name is Lia."

Sweeny started laughing, "So you have an eight year old pave the path for a date?"

"I didn't…."

"It's ok, whatever it takes to get a date." Sweeny interrupted. Lawson didn't answer knowing he would never win with Sweeny giving him a hard time. "You'd hear that Cap? We've been sold out."

"She's prettier to hang out with than you knuckle heads." Cap responded.

Sweeny made his way to calf deep water exposing all, "Prettier than hanging with me?" Dale and Terry threw clumps of mud at him. "You girls are just jealous." He laughed taunting them.

"Girl, there has been a hell of a lot change in the last 25 years." Cap said to Valentine blocking out the vision of Sweeny. She took his conversation as an invitation to join the agents swimming and ran to the edge of the rock ledge.

"Come on, girl," Dale yelled at her. She sprung from the rock landing in the cool water that was flowing from the mountains. Cap just watched thinking that he didn't have a towel to dry her off and she was going to ride with Dale and Terry. Realizing he was out of tobacco, he climbed down and headed toward his truck. Valentine swam to shallow water and chased Sweeny up and down the bank. Lawson noticed Cap fishing for something in his truck and made his way toward his truck that had country music blaring from the open doors.

"You run out of tobacco?" Lawson asked, drying himself off.

Cap held up a large coffee can, "Nope." He opened the can and filled his leather pouch.

Slipping into his tactical issued pants Lawson grabbed his shirt and followed Cap back up the rock face to his perch. "Here." Cap held out his hand to give Lawson a pull for his final step. Standing on the rock ledge, Lawson buttoned the last two buttons on his shirt and sat against the rock wall.

"Did you ever think you'd be putting up with this?" Lawson asked, nodding toward the team swimming in their boxer briefs, except Sweeny.

"Huh!" Cap replied with a half grin, rolling the paper tight against the tobacco and licking the edge to seal his cigarette. "No, I can't say I did." Closing his Zippo, he took a long steady draw and blew the smoke into the clear sky, "So, you taking the pharmacy girl on a date?"

Lawson looked down at Sweeny chasing Valentine back into the water. "I wouldn't call it a date."

"What would you call it?"

"We're just going to a rodeo."

"Back in my time that was called a date. You boys have a weird terminology when it comes to girls. Either that or you're scared of girls and commitments."

"I'm not scared of girls or commitments."

Cap brushed his grey hair out of his eyes and rolled them toward Lawson. "Your generation would rather text each other than talk. And Lord forbid if any of y'all have ever written   a handwritten letter. When I was your age we would throw pebbles at a girl's window until she opened it to talk face to face."

"This isn't the 50s," Lawson laughed.

"Have you ever asked a girl to go steady?"

"That really doesn't happen anymore," Lawson replied, still chuckling.

"Then how in the hell would you know if the girl you're with is yours?"

Lawson just laughed. "You just know."

"BS... and y'all call it 'talking to each other.' It's called *dating*. Scared of commitment is what y'all are!" He took another drag of his cigarette. Lawson didn't argue back; he knew once Cap got on his soap box, there was no winning. "But, I'm glad you asked her out," Cap added.

Valentine made her way up the rock ledge and shook off in front of Lawson and Cap. Lawson held up his hands to block the water as Cap hid his cigarette from getting wet. Valentine stopped and drew attention to Lawson. He looked at Cap then back to Valentine, asking "What's the matter, girl?" Her upper lip lifted, showing her teeth, and a low, evil growl came from her clinched teeth. "Valentine!" Lawson said, shocked.

"Don't move, compadre!" Cap said, holding his cigarette with his teeth and reaching for a large stick he had left on the rock for whittling. Lawson gave him a funny look too. Valentine made a step toward Lawson. "Stay!" Cap ordered in a loud command, and with the stick, he jabbed at Lawson's back. A six-foot rattler slithered from behind Lawson, and he could feel the scales slide against the small of his back.

"Holy—" Lawson started to say without moving. Once the snake made its way out of striking distance from Lawson, he jumped back with a loud, high pitched-scream. Everyone swimming below stopped as if they had been shot and looked up. Valentine's teeth vanished, and she cocked her head sideways at Lawson's scream. Cap also gave him a funny look. Lawson didn't care at the time that he sounded like a five-year- old girl. With everyone looking up, Cap flipped the snake on the stick and flung it toward the creek below. Sweeny, Terry, and Dale all screamed as they rushed to the bank like a shark was after them.

"I swear! A bunch of half-naked, girl-screaming boys!" Cap said in a low, exasperated tone. "It's a wonder you girls ever get through a day!" he said in his raspy voice.

Chapter 18

Back at the station, Lawson couldn't help thinking about the rattlesnake that had curled up behind him. He wasn't afraid of much, but snakes were a different story. He left the station heading home to catch up on some much-needed cleaning around his small house. Turning onto the highway that Lia's pharmacy was located on, he could see it in the distance, and as he got closer, he noticed someone outside. Lia lifted a cardboard box and set it in the back of her jeep then reached up to close the hatch. Her long black hair fell to the waist of her navy shorts, and her dark-complexioned legs caught the attention of the agent. *Wow, she is beautiful!*

She turned to walk in and caught sight of Lawson's truck. With a small wave, she lured him into the parking lot. "Were you going to pass without stopping?" she smiled.

"I didn't want to bother you," he said with both forearms on his rolled-down window.

"Yeah, we're really busy." She pointed to the empty store.

"Your soda bar not bringing in business?"

She shook her head, "No, I got to figure out a way to advertise to the school."

"Sweeny and I are good friends with the principal. Maybe he'll let you put up some flyers."

"I might have to take you up on that." She paused for a moment. "Are you busy at the moment?"

"No. Just got off duty and heading home to clean."

"Would you be interested in riding with me on a delivery?"

He looked at his clock. He wasn't sure why, since he didn't need to be anywhere. "Sure."

He rolled up his window and locked his truck, *I'll never hear the end of this if the guys see my truck parked here.* He followed Lia into the store, and Erika walked from the office. "You're becoming a regular here."

"Just making sure y'all aren't breaking any border laws," he joked, but only received a funny look from her.

"Do you mind staying here? Lawson is going to ride with me to make these deliveries," Lia asked.

"Not at all. Let him get terrorized from your driving," Erika replied.

"I don't drive bad!"

Erika looked at Lawson making a *yes* gesture by nodding. "Good luck," she said. "And don't be late—I have to be somewhere this evening."

Lia picked up another sack and headed back outside with Lawson following. As he looked back while closing the door, he saw Erika texting on her phone. Without saying anything, Lia climbed in the driver side of her jeep and started the engine. Lawson looked again at his truck with the same thought as before, then climbed in the passenger side. He pulled the seat belt across his chest just in time to grab the dash as Lia slammed the jeep in reverse. After his head came back to a rest, she stomped on the gas, shooting rocks across the parking lot. *Is she joking?*

"Thanks for riding with me. I have a delivery to a man that freaks me out. Erika normally goes with me, but I hate to close the store for one delivery," she said, leaning into the corner she was taking.

Lawson held onto the handle with wide eyes. "No problem." A car swerved out of her way, and Lawson pointed and tried to say something.

"So, how was your day?" she asked, unaware of the car and most of the other people on the road.

"It was—" He stopped and held his breath as she shot through an intersection. "You know, you might want to slow down and stop at the stop signs."

She smiled, "Are you scared too?" He didn't want to answer the question. Before long, they were out of town and jetting south toward her first delivery.

"So, Mr. Lawson Cain, what's your story?" she asked.

"I don't know if I have a story."

"Everyone has a story." She looked over at him. Her brown eyes baited him to answer her question.

"Just a typical Texas story. Played football in high school and joined the profession of my father and grandfather." He started.

"They were Border Patrol?"

"No, deputy sheriffs. I am the first to join the Border Patrol. Moved here after academy." He looked down at her radio, noticing that it was tuned to the same country station he normally listened to. "You like country music?"

"It's all I can pick up. I have been thinking about getting a satellite radio."

"Cap just put one in his truck. 80 stations and he only listens to one." He put his hand on the dash to prevent himself from being pinned to the windshield as Lia slammed on the brakes. She took a hard left, turning onto a dirt road, the same dirt road that led to their favorite swimming hole.

"Have y'all been back to the creek?" She blushed, thinking back to when they first met.

"Yeah, but we're gonna have to find another one since you girls found us," he joked.

The jeep rolled along a half-beaten path that led to an old rustic shack with a few rusted cars in the front. A man sat on the front porch wearing only a pair of pants and a large straw hat. He looked up at Lia's jeep and stood to his feet, approaching the jeep as she stopped only a few feet from the structure. The man's leather skin face was dark and mysterious, and Lawson thought he looked a little scary. He couldn't believe Lia brought this man's medication to him.

She rolled down her window, saying *"Hola*, Senor Delachona."

"Hola, who is this?" the man asked, pointing to Lawson.

"This is my friend, Senor Cain." She smiled at Lawson.

He pointed at Lawson. "I know this man." He stepped back, making Lawson uncomfortable. "He is a good man."

"He is, here are your meds. One in the morning and one at night. I'll come back in two weeks." The Jeep started crawling.

"Gracias." He pointed at Lawson again. "He is a good man."

Lawson wasn't sure how to responded and waved, "Thank you."

"So, Senor Cain is a *buen hombre*," she smiled.

He nodded, "I'd take his word for it."

The Jeep fishtailed leaving the path, and heading back toward the highway, Lawson was wondering if she would get upset if he asked to drive.

"You want some good Mexican food?" she asked.

Surprised at her invitation, he answered, "I could do with some Mexican food."

"I know this really good place." She pulled her phone out and texted Erika.

The Jeep swerved into the oncoming lane, and Lawson couldn't keep quiet any more. "Lia! You want me to drive?"

"I'm good," she answered, clueless of his nerves.

They pulled up to a restaurant that Sweeny and Lawson frequented on the weekdays. Walking in, they were greeted by a young girl. "Two?" she asked. Lawson nodded, and she led them to their table.

Lia's phone sounded with a text. "Dang it!"

"What's the matter?" Lawson asked.

"Nothing. Erika is leaving early. Oh well, it wasn't like we were busy today." She ordered a water with lime and began eating the chips left in a red basket.

Chapter 19

The following day, Lawson sat at his desk with his feet propped up and playing with a rubber band; he wasn't sure why Lia intrigued him the way she did. He hadn't had a serious girlfriend since high school. Dale sat across from him engrossed in a report he was finishing for Sweeny and Terry. It seemed that 10 minutes of actual field time took hours to write. Sweeny, who had been outside filling his truck for the day, sat down on the edge of Lawson's desk.

"So, what did you do yesterday after work?" he smiled.

Lawson held the rubber band. "You know where I was," he groaned, knowing that Sweeny was going to ride him about this.

But to his surprise, Sweeny sensed Lawson's annoyance and replied only with "That's cool. Get in good with her so I can get free root beer floats." "Probie," Sweeny turned his attention to Dale, "how's that report coming?" He left Lawson's desk.

Lawson watched as Sweeny leaned over the shoulder of the rookie and helped him correct a few minor errors. Sweeny's talk with Cap had him perplexed. He had lived with the thought of being responsible for his own wife's death for so many years, it was going to take more than one afternoon with Cap to alter his mind. Lawson had taken notice that something was on his mind; they had spent the last five years together and knew each other's quirks.

A call came over the radio from a BORSTAR team out of Marfa: The team had been called to the Chisos Mountain range, and Lawson's group froze in place listening as the BORSTAR agents spotted a large group of immigrants near a ubiquitous area called Elephant Tusk. Knowing where the location was created, there was no doubt that coyotes were leading people to nowhere, a typical pattern of Jose Emmanuel's men.

A familiar voice came over the airways calling for the Presidio Station. The voice belonged to one of the agents they had previously met with in Marfa. Cap set his coffee cup down and answered the call, "Go ahead."

The agent asked for any available help with the tracking of a few lost illegals that had fallen behind the day before. Lawson's team burst out through the door like a fire department headed to a fire, with Valentine leaping over the tailgate of Cap's truck and vanishing through the open back window. One by one, the patrol trucks sped out of the yard behind the station and barreled down the streets of Presidio, heading south back to the Big Bend National Park.

Once out of town, Sweeny toyed with Lawson, who was in front of him, by trying to pass him on the outside. Lawson swerved into his lane, cutting him off. "You two knuckleheads cut it out," a raspy voice sounded over the radio. Lawson glanced in his rearview mirror to see Sweeny giving him the middle finger and laughing.

Having arrived, they were now in territory they knew, and Lawson was a little confused that BORSTAR hadn't called them at the beginning. Parking their trucks near the others, they watched as the BORSTAR team led out 20 to 25 illegal aliens from the harsh terrain. A few small children were mixed in the bunch, with one woman carrying her infant. "Damn! They wouldn't have lasted two days out here," Sweeny said, closing his door.

One of the agents, who belonged to the familiar voice on the radio, walked toward Cap. "We think there are 8 left, probably 2 or 3 hours south of here. I've called in air support."

"Unload these 4-wheelers and get up there and pick up their tracks. I'll stay behind," Cap ordered his team. Within minutes Lawson, Sweeny, and Dale had their ATV's unloaded and their gear tied in place. Lawson gave Cap a halfhearted salute and flung dirt and rocks taking off toward the tracks. They passed three other agents briskly leading two handcuffed Mexican men out of the terrain—the coyotes that had led the group astray.

"I just don't see how they can be so brutal to plan on leaving all those people out here to die," Dale yelled above the engine.

"We're dealing with a different breed of people," Lawson yelled back.

Once on their tracks, the three ATV's headed south weaving in and out of sage brush and smaller trees. Lawson gave the lead to Sweeny, who was their best tracker and followed with Dale pulling up the rear. Dale fought with the dust from the tires ahead waving his hand in front of his face and casually wiping his glasses. Climbing over a steep ridge and coming to a stop, Sweeny pointed off in the distance. "That's them there."

"Where?" Lawson squinted his eyes. "300 yards past that creek."

Lawson shook his head. "You got eyes of an eagle."

"We'll head north toward that lower area of the creek," he pointed. "Probie, call Cap and tell him we've spotted them."

Dale gladly hung back long enough to call Cap and let the dust settle before catching up with them. Coming down the ridge, Lawson pumped the back of Sweeny's ATV, and Sweeny swung around and gave Lawson a dirty look.

"That's for flipping me off," Lawson smiled. Sweeny grinned and aimed toward the creek. Dale caught them before they crossed.

"*Patrulla Fronteriza!*" Lawson yelled at the abandoned group, announcing who they were. A corpulent woman fell to her knees sobbing. Lawson wasn't sure if it was from being caught and losing the money they paid the coyotes or out of joy from being rescued.

An elderly man held out his hands, asking "*Agua?*" Sweeny quickly un-mounted from his ATV and pulled out six bottles of water, handing one to each person. A little boy sat beside the old man and downed his water. The small, deserted group had a sign of relief as if they knew their outcome wasn't good. One of the six was a little girl, no older than Vicky, who clung to her shirt, holding it on her shoulders. Sweeny noticed it was badly torn and barely covered her.

"*Estas bien?*" he asked her. She looked down, drinking her water and ignoring him.

"Da fat guy... he have him way with her," the elderly man said.

"One of the coyotes raped her?" Sweeny asked, barely able to say the words.

"*Ce.*"

Sweeny thought back to passing them before tracking the group. Only one of them was overweight; the other was little and scrawny. He unbuttoned his shirt and wrapped it around the little girl, and she peeked briefly at him from under her bangs with tears in her eyes. "Don't worry, sweetheart, no one will hurt you," Sweeny told her, evil thoughts of the rape tree racing through his head as he planned his greeting once they got back to the trucks.

They loaded everyone on their ATV's and slowly drove out to the road leading back to the trucks. Lawson managed to radio ahead and let them know they were heading out with the six. The elderly man's words echoed repeatedly through Sweeny's thoughts, and he was glad he was wearing sunglasses so the others couldn't see his watered eyes.

After what seemed like a half-day ride, the team pulled up to the trucks and other agents. A paramedic met Sweeny and took the little girl from his arms. "I'll get her a shirt and give you back yours in just a second. I imagine you'll want your badge back," the man grinned.

"Not right now," Sweeny said under his breath as he briskly walked toward the two men still handcuffed and on their knees. Before anyone could react, Sweeny bent down and uncuffed the larger man and pulled him to his feet.

"What the hell are you doing, Sweeny?" One of the agents asked. Lawson and Dale looked up to see Sweeny standing in front of the man.

"Sweeny!" Cap hollered, aware of what was transpiring.

Sweeny drew his pistol and shoved it into the mouth of the trembling man. The coyote tried to back away, but with Sweeny's death grip on his shirt, he couldn't break free. Two other agents drew their weapons and aimed at Sweeny. "Put down your guns!" Cap stepped in the way and turned to Sweeny. "This ain't the way, compadre," he said in a low tone. The supervisor of the BORSTAR team immediately made his men holster their guns, and Cap could hear him reprimanding them for drawing their weapons on another agent, no matter what the cause was.

"This low life son-of-a-bitch raped that little girl. I'm going to send a message back to all these coyotes!" Sweeny clenched his teeth.

"Not this way. Think about it: Do you want to do fricking time for this guy? What about Vicky?" he whispered in Sweeny's ear. Sweeny took a deep breath and lowered his weapon. A sigh of relief came over the agents. Without a warning, Sweeny smashed his pistol into the face and forehead of the man, sending him to the ground. He was unconscious before he hit the dirt.

Sweeny spit on him and looked at the other man. "If you get back to Mexico, tell every coyote that I will shoot them dead in the brush when I find them. Understand?" he yelled. The Mexican nodded his head, fully understanding the warning.

"Damn, Sweeny," the supervisor replied.

Cap cut his eyes toward him, "I believe he fell."

The supervisor nodded his head, "Yeah, I think so too." Sweeny stormed off toward the ambulance to retrieve his shirt.

"Make sure he calms down," Cap looked at Lawson.

"Yes, sir."

Chapter 20

It had been a rough few days with the team decompressing from the heartache of the previous situation with the little girl they had found. Sweeny repeated his promise of killing any coyotes who raped another person, but his true intent was to kill Jose Emmanuel and end this horrifying nightmare that the Mexican people were going through. He had left work early the following days picking up Vicky from school. The emotions he felt were relatively close to those of losing his wife.

With the high school game away for Friday night, Lawson grilled himself a burger and stayed up late catching up on his favorite sitcom. He had fallen asleep on the couch only to wake up close to sunrise and stagger into his bedroom, curling up in his warm bed. A noise caused him to sit up in bed. *What was that?* He lay back down, reasoning with himself that it was a noise he dreamed. Just as he got comfortable again, the noise reappeared, this time in the form of a knock at the door. *Who in the world could that be?*

Pulling a shirt over his head, he looked out the window, and not seeing a vehicle in the drive, he paused. This time the knock was louder and more persistent. He thought for a second—there had been reports of agents being ambushed at their homes by coyotes, but that had happen only in southern California. Then a figure walked past the window, and he stood to the side and bent the blinds enough to see who was outside. Lia.

He quickly opened the door, catching her walking down the steps of his porch. "Hey."

She turned and replied, "I didn't mean to wake you."

He looked at his watch to see it was 8:15 a.m. "Didn't want to wake me?" he smiled.

"Well, I remembered you said you were off today, and I was wondering if you would ride with me to Ojinaga to pick up a few things for the store?"

"Sure, but I need coffee first. Come on in while I get dressed and make some." He stretched. She followed him in, anticipating his house to be the typical bachelor pad, but to her surprised it was decorated with a southwestern flare. *Surely there was a girl involved to have decorated this nice, a single guy?* she thought. Lawson caught her staring into the living room and studying the pictures on the walls.

"You have a nice place," she commented.

"Thanks, between my mom and Sandra it's turned out nice," he answered, clueless about her thoughts. The coffee pot started percolating. "I'll be right back." He disappeared into his bedroom to change.

"So Sandra has adopted all you agents?" she yelled, looking around the kitchen.

"Yea, pretty much. All except Terry—he's pretty much quiet and has a family here." He walked into the kitchen pulling a shirt over his abs, a familiar sight Lia hadn't forgotten. "So you're a morning person?" he asked, reaching for cups.

"I don't sleep much; I read a lot at night."

"What do you like?"

"Everything, mostly indie books. I'm reading a funny book about the elderly going to a camp right now." After the coffee was ready, Lawson poured it into two travel mugs, gave one to her, and then followed her outside.

"I'll drive," he said.

"I don't mind," she giggled.

"They know me at the border, so it'll be faster," he replied, not wanting her to drive.

Having arrived at the border, Lawson ducked in line with the other cars and awaited their turn to talk with the agents. As they pulling under the canopy, a Mexican agent approached with his rifle in hand. Lawson gave him an uneasy glance. "*Hola*. What's up with the assault rifle?"

"A lot going on today. Who is this?" he asked.

"Lia, a friend. We're going after some drugs," he smiled.

"Very funny." He signaled for them to pass through.

"Drugs?" she asked.

"You are a drug dealer," he laughed.

Crossing into Ojinaga, Lawson instinctively scanned the area for anyone out of place. The last thing he wanted to do was to put Lia in danger. She gave him a few directions to a store where she purchased most of the décor in her pharmacy, and with the soda bar finished, she had just a few last things to add. Lawson put the Jeep in park and climbed out, meeting Lia in front of the vehicle. Someone called her name, and turning, she saw her father and brother approaching. *Damn!*

"*Quien es este?*" her father asked with a stern voice.

"This is Lawson," she pointed to him. Lawson wasn't sure who was standing in front of him until she turned to him, saying, "This is my father and brother, Carlos."

Lawson stuck his hand out. "It's nice to meet you," he said in English. Her brother gave him an uneasy grin, making it apparent that he wasn't welcome.

"So, Mr. Lawson what do you do?" her father asked with his arms folded across his body, not shaking his hand.

At his side, Lia answered, "He's with the border patrol."

"And you're just helping my daughter across the border today?" her father asked.

Lawson noticed the black handle emerging from her brother's waist, "Yes, just helping her pick up some items for her store," he answered.

Her father smirked and nodded, "Friends?" He turned to Lia, adding "Make sure you see your mama."

"I will call her," Lia answered with a more forceful tone. Her father turned and walked away with her brother, Lawson watching as Carlos turned to look at him several times.

Lia pulled him into the store and took a deep breath. "I'm sorry. My father is...."

"Protective?" He finished her sentence.

"Concerned," she replaced his word.

"Why was your brother carrying a pistol?" he asked.

"I didn't know he was, but it wouldn't surprise me. He's not the greatest brother and has got into a lot of trouble. But he's my dad's favorite. Enough about them. Help me pick out wall décor for the soda bar." She turned her attention to the pictures and iron works hanging from a makeshift display.

***

"He is an agent. The last thing we need around our family," Carlos replied to his father.

"I will talk with her," her father replied.

The two of them walked past the once grassy square that held many town festivals and dances. Carlos pulled open a door leading into a staircase for his father. "If any of these coyotes around here learn that my sister, your daughter is seeing a border patrol agent, they will hunt us down," Carlos added.

"And I said I would take care of it. Now drop it," his father demanded.

Chapter 21

The weekend had flown by before Lawson realized it. Saturday had started out bizarre with the uncomfortable greeting from Lia's father and brother. Lawson wondered if that was her hesitation for accepting his invitation to coffee. He had gotten home early that afternoon and tried to catch Sweeny and Vicky, but they had already left for Marfa. Sunday morning the team had congregated at the basketball court for their Sunday morning game, but Lawson had secretly brought nicer clothes with the intention of going with Lia if she showed. After the priest asked the men to join them and received his normal "No, thanks," he pulled the doors shut, at

which Lawson decided to stay with their game.

The following day, Lawson was almost out the door on a bright Monday morning when his cell phone rang from his back pocket. "Good morning," he answered Cap's call.

"Chief wants to see us today."

"I'm heading in now. Marfa?"

"Yes," Cap answered, then hung up.

Lawson checked his wallet to make sure he had enough cash for lunch. There was a bar and grill in Marfa that Cap like to go to when they were at headquarters. Driving in, he passed the pharmacy and noticed Erika outside talking with two Mexican men. Lawson honked, receiving a big wave from her. *I don't see Lia's Jeep.*

Pulling in the gates to the station, Lawson found Cap standing outside smoking. "You're driving," Cap commented as Lawson rolled down his window.

"Where's Valentine?"

"Sandra's got her today. Sweeny and Dale just left to patrol north of here." He flung his cigarette before closing his door.

***

Sweeny and Dale headed north on Hwy 170, the morning bright and unusually hot for the time of day. Dale was engrossed with his phone, while Sweeny thought back to the little girl they had rescued last week. He was struggling with letting go the thought of her precious face and the tears that had fallen to his shirt. The team had dealt with rape before and even the abuse of children, but for Sweeny there was something different about this little girl. He glanced over at Dale, seeing him study the screen of his smart phone.

"What are you doing?" he asked.

"Fantasy football league," Dale replied.

As Sweeny pulled off the highway and onto what appeared to be an endless dirt road, Dale looked up, asking "Where are we going?"

"Lawson and I found this spot last year," Sweeny explained. "Coyotes bring over illegals by raft."

Dale returned to his screen, and the highway disappeared in the dust from their truck as the dirt road opened to a dried prairie abundant with scorpions and rattlesnakes. Sweeny turned off the dirt road and drove toward two giant rocks resembling a gate that stood up from the earth as if placed on their ends. A large mound rose from the prairie just inside the rocks. Sweeny drove around the rocks as Dale looked up, asking "What is this place?"

"I don't know for sure. We think it was a fort, probably from the mid-1800s."

Dale examined the large mound of earth pushed into a square close to the size of four football fields. "What's over the hill?"

Sweeny stopped the truck. "Let's walk over and see." They climbed out of the truck and waved the lingering dust out of their faces. Once they were on the mound, the inside looked the same as the outside—dried shrubs and sere grass.

"Pretty good view of the Rio Grande," Dale said, looking down on the muddy river and the farm land that bordered the Mexican side of the river. Sweeny was sitting on the ground throwing a few rocks down the hillside when a small blue truck materialized on the opposite side of the river. Dale pointed to the lone man getting out of the truck and looking across the river with binoculars. "I guess we messed up his day," Dale observed.

The man spotted the two agents sitting in open sight, with Sweeny smiling from ear to ear and his middle finger sticking up, "Yep, Probie, I believe we did." The man quickly entered his truck, leaving a trail of dust. "Well, nobody's crossing here today. Let's get lunch!" He dusted off the seat of his pants and walked down the hill.

The rear end of their truck swung around as Sweeny gassed the 8 cylinder engine, throwing rocks toward the Rio Grande. They raced down the beaten path that led back out to the highway and without stopping, turned onto the blacktop heading toward town. Sweeny's dash was littered with pictures of Vicky, some of dance, some of him and her, and one in the middle with her holding flowers she had picked last Easter. Sweeny straightened the center picture from where it had slid out of place in his sudden turn onto the blacktop.

In the distance a dark cloud formed south of Presidio over Big Bend National Park, teasing the area with rain and cooler temperatures. Dale turned down the radio as they pulled into the diner parking lot and asked, "You want to call Terry and see if he wants to eat?" Sweeny silently pointed at Terry's truck tucked around the corner of the restaurant, but noticed Terry sitting in the truck looking at something behind him.

Sweeny picked up the mic to his radio, "What are you looking at?"

Terry's head suddenly shot up and scanned the area looking for Sweeny, "This white Toyota four door truck behind me. After getting out, they saw me and quickly got back in their truck. Suspicious."

"Knock on their window," Sweeny answered. Before Terry had time to answer, Sweeny jumped out and made his way across the parking lot. The three men stared at him as he approached and motioned for them to roll down their window. "*Hola*. Do you guys need some help?"

"No, Senor," one of them answered.

"Y'all from around here?" Sweeny asked as Dale and Terry walked up.

"We are from Del Rio," the man answered.

"You mind if I see some IDs?" Sweeny asked. The three men dug in their pockets and one by one presented driver licenses and citizenship papers. "Long way from Del Rio?"

"We are visiting friends. Have we done something wrong?" the man answered in an elevated tone.

"No. You have a good day." Sweeny returned their IDs, and the man rolled up his window and started pulling away. "Let's follow them," Sweeny said as he walked past Dale. Without arguing, Dale climbed back in the passenger side and pulled his seatbelt across his chest. They watched the white Toyota take a right turn off the main road and quickly sped to the intersection. The truck wasn't in sight.

"They're on 2nd," Terry's voice came over the radio. Sweeny drove to a street three blocks from 2nd in hopes of finding them again. The Toyota came in sight again and turned into a dual complex parking in front.

"Hang back," Sweeny said on the mic while watching the three men, who were oblivious to the agents watching. They walked up to one of the units and were met by an older man. They talked for a minute, then disappeared inside with the man.

"Well, nothing really suspicious about that. Let's go eat," Terry said over the radio while sitting in his truck just down the road.

"Maybe we should wait," Sweeny answered.

"Come on, they haven't done anything," Terry persisted.

"OK," Sweeny answered. Turning to Dale, Sweeny said, "He's kinda acting strange," referring to Terry.

Dale shrugged his shoulders. "Probably just hungry."

The old man return to the door and looked both directions, then pulled it closed. "What are you looking for?" one of the men asked.

"You can never be too sure," Jose Emmanuel answered him.

Chapter 22

The sound of an incoming text chimed from the front pocket of Lawson's pants. "I know its short notice but would you like to go to my sister's wedding this weekend?" Lia's message read. Lawson looked at the phone, shocked with the invitation.

"I don't think your father and brother would approve of me," he answered.

"They will be fine," she replied.

Lawson thought for a moment: *What could go wrong?* "I'd love to," he answered. "Swing by the store Friday afternoon around 4. Dress casual." *Casual?*

"You two meet me in the conference room," Cap said, catching the attention of Lawson and Sweeny while pouring a cup of coffee.

"Conference room? What did we do?" Sweeny asked with his feet kicked up on his desk and folding a paper airplane, then flying it across the office. Cap snatched it out of the air and crumpled it up.

Sweeny raised his eyebrows at Lawson, "OK?" and followed them to Cap's office.

Lawson pulled the door closed behind them. "You boys still have that informant in Ojinaga?" Cap asked in his raspy voice.

"Which one?" Sweeny asked.

"The little squirrelly man."

"Yes sir," Lawson answered.

"Ask him if he knows anything about a shipment of marijuana. If not, tell him to keep his ear to the ground."

"You know we'll have to go to Ojinaga to ask," Lawson replied.

"Whatever." Cap wasn't interested in learning more than he needed to.

"We'll take my truck," Lawson said, walking out.

They headed home, changed into normal clothes, and got Lawson's personal truck. There were times they entered Mexico undercover and investigated coyotes they knew were smuggling people into the US. Sweeny had arrested a man last year who took a deal to become an informant instead of having a record with the Border Patrol. Sweeny never trusted him and still wasn't sure he wasn't smuggling a few people himself, but the information he gave always led to a big arrest.

"You want to stop?" Sweeny asked, seeing Lia's Jeep parked in front of her pharmacy.

Lawson cut his eyes at him. "She doesn't need to know about this."

"I wasn't going to tell her we working undercover," Sweeny replied.

"She knows I'm working today. I'll stop later."

"You getting serious with her?"

"Just talking."

"You know, the high school is having their fundraiser concert tomorrow night. You should ask her," Sweeny commented.

"We'll see," he replied, having already asked her.

The boys pulled in the inside lane at the border and waited their turn with the Mexican agents. An agent with dark sunglasses approached Lawson's truck. "Act like you're driving off when he knocks on your window," Sweeny said, grinning.

"He knows my truck," Lawson said, rolling down his tinted windows.

"Senors," the agent greeted them.

"Agent," Sweeny mocked his
seriousness.

He gave Sweeny a dirty look. "You crossing on business or personal reasons?"

"We're smuggling hookers and personalities. We'll bring you one of both," Sweeny said.

"Don't listen to him," Lawson said, cutting his eyes at Sweeny.

"Yeah, easier said than done. Be careful." The agent signaled for the gate to be lifted.

"You don't have to be a jerk," Lawson said to
Sweeny. "To Mr. Serious? He needs to be broke in."

Lawson pulled out a phone from his console and texted the informant. Both Lawson and Sweeny kept a spare cell phone for their undercover work and communication with informants. A few moments later, his phone sounded with a returned text. He typed in another message and waited. After the reply, Lawson reported, "He'll meet us at the corner of Independence and Retes at La Joya."

"Ha! A party supply store," Sweeny laughed.

Many of the streets and sidewalks were deteriorating with old age and neglect, and many people who were jobless littered the area. Stucco crumbled from the buildings onto the sidewalks and became part of the path with no one to clean it up. Lawson turned onto Retes and proceeded west to the corner where their informant had agreed to meet. Sweeny pointed ahead to a small, squirrelly man sitting on the sidewalk with his feet in the street. He stood and walked beside a colorful yellow and pink building with a wraparound awning. Lawson slowed and pulled to the side.

"*Hola*," the man sheepishly greeted them.

"*Como estas*," Sweeny answered. The man pointed to a set of stairs leading up to the second story. "What can you not tell us here that you have to tell us in there?" Sweeny quizzed him.

"Too many eyes here," the man replied.

Lawson shrugged his shoulders and followed the man up the staircase. Opening the door, they entered an air-conditioned room with tile floors and windows that wrapped the building. Lawson scanned the room for anyone else.

"It's just us," the man replied.

"What do you know about a shipment of marijuana crossing tomorrow?" Lawson didn't give him any time.

"I might know of something. But you know my children need school supplies and clothing...."

"Have we never not taken care of you?" Sweeny interrupted.

"*Ce*. Word on the street is a large shipment is going to be rafted across and loaded into a horse trailer. Near El Mulato. A big shipment." He rubbed his fingers and thumb together with a grin.

"It could be bigger if you tell us how you know this," Lawson said.

The man looked down in thought, "Senor, my family—"

"What is the word on Jose Emmanuel?" Lawson interrupted him.

"Not much. He hasn't been around lately. I do know they are crossing north of Presidio near the square mound this week."

"Dale and I were just there," Sweeny said.

"There is a bar just west of here on Benito Juarez. Some of his coyotes have been working out of there."

"I could go for a beer," Sweeny said.

Lawson handed the man a wad of cash. "Are you staying clean?"

"*Ce*, Senor." He thumbed through the cash. "Gracias," he said, and then added, "If you will wait a few minutes after I leave. No offense—we don't need to be seen together." The man quickly vanished out the door.

Lawson walked to the window and watched him jog across the street and disappear around the corner of a gas station. The streets were busy with traffic and people walking the sidewalks. "Do you find it odd that he left so quickly?"

"Nah, he's a strange little guy. Let's get a beer."

Leaving their truck in the same place, they walked a few blocks west and stopped in front of a white building with an arched entry painted with ivy vines and flowers—not the typical entry to a bar in Old Mexico. Sweeny pushed open the large wooden door that had iron décor and a small barred window in the center. After their eyes adjusted to the darkness and smoky room, they made their way to a small table with four wooden chairs surrounding it. The bar had a couple   of Mexicans sitting at the bar hunched over their mugs and another man negotiating pricing with a prostitute.

One of the men at the bar looked up at Sweeny and asked for a light, but Sweeny held his hands up, insinuating he didn't have one, and ordered two beers. The bartender set two frozen mugs on the old wooden bar, and Sweeny paid him and returned to the table. "Not much going on here," he observed to Lawson.

"Let's give it a minute or two," Lawson replied seconds before the door swung back open, flooding the room with sunlight. Four Mexicans walked in and headed toward the back without scanning the room. "Those guys are in a hurry to get somewhere," Lawson commented.

Sweeny took a huge gulp and stood up. "Let's find out where they are heading."

Before Lawson could stop him, he made his way through an opening that was divided by a dusty hand-woven blanket hanging from the header. It was hard to see who was most surprised, the four men that were standing in the room or Sweeny, who didn't expect them to be congregated only feet from the opening. "*Hola!*" Sweeny shouted, acting drunk. The men gave him a dirty look, and he noticed the bathroom on the opposite way. Not waiting for an answer, Sweeny shot toward the door leading to the bathroom that looked like it hadn't been cleaned since the bar moved in.

Sweeny waited a few minutes, then walked back out to find the men seated around a table across the room from Lawson. "What did I miss?" he asked.

"They sat down after you busted up their meeting," Lawson replied with the mug blocking his mouth from the room. Sunlight invaded the room with the door swinging open again. A lone man entered, and giving himself some time for his eyes to adjust, he scanned the area, then joined the table of men. "Damn!" Lawson whispered with his head down.

"What?" Sweeny asked.

"It's Lia's brother," Lawson answered, then looked up to see him talking with the other men. "We need to go."

"He'll see you if you get up," Sweeny replied, looking around the bar. "Let me cause a scene and you slip out."

"You sure?"

Sweeny smiled, giving Lawson an uneasy feeling about the scene he was going to create. He stood up and walked toward the bar. "Bar tender!" he shouted, gaining the attention of the room. Lawson, staying low, slipped out to the door and quickly exited, hearing Sweeny demanding a refund on his lukewarm beer. Minutes later, Sweeny walked out with a big grin, calling to Lawson, "We might want to run!"

As they disappeared around the corner, Lawson caught a glimpse of the bartender coming out with a sawed-off shotgun. Sweeny was still wearing a grin, leaving Lawson wondering what he did in such a short time.

Chapter 23

"Are you sure your man said they were moving drugs here?" Terry asked with a pair of binoculars glued to his eyes. Terry, Dale, Cap, Lawson, Sweeny, and five other agents lay in the dirt looking over a small mound and Hwy 170 toward the Rio Grande.

"He hasn't led us astray yet," Sweeny replied without looking up.

"We've been here half the day. This might be that one time," Terry grumbled, aggravated from lying in the dirt in the heat of the day. Sweat rolled off his forehead and onto the binoculars. "Lawson, let's wrap this up and get out of here," he tried to persuade him.

"Nope. Here comes a trailer," Sweeny said, looking down the highway. The men watched as the Ford F250 pulling a four-horse aluminum trailer slowed down and pulled off the blacktop onto a dirt road leading to the border.

"Crap!" Terry replied.

"You disappointed?" Sweeny shot him a stare.

"Look alive, boys," Cap echoed into his hand-held radio. The truck and trailer vanished over a ridge, leaving a cloud of dust hovering over the road. Valentine's head popped up hearing Cap, who had not spoken much of the morning. "Stay down girl," he added. She laid her head back on the dirt, looking up at him with her brown eyes.

A voice came over the airways. "They are stopped just beyond the tree line from me. Wait." There was a pause. "Two trucks just pulled up across the river." Another pause. "Yep, they have rafts and are loading bushels of what looks like marijuana. There are five men on the Mexico side and three over here."

"Let us know when they are loaded," Cap answered.

"Yes, sir," the voice replied.

After a short time, the observer reported, "OK, they're loaded and coming out."

"What do you think?" Cap looked at Lawson.

"I say take them here."

Without warning, Cap stood up, saying "Let's go." All the men ran to the five trucks that were parked out of sight on the dirt road. Lawson and Sweeny reached their truck first and pulled out with the four others close on their tail. A storm of dust and border patrol trucks poured out onto the blacktop only yards behind the white F250 and aluminum trailer. The engine of Lawson's truck roared as he floored the gas and pulled along the side of the truck and trailer. The eyes of the men inside the cab grew wide as Lawson pulled in front of them with lights flashing and slowed, causing them to stop.

Sweeny ducked out of the passenger side with his M4RIFLE aimed at the driver. "*Manos arriba!*" he shouted. Hands quickly went up in the truck, and Dale and Terry approached from the driver side with the other agents joining Sweeny on the passenger side. The driver door swung open, with the driver dashing toward the dirt road that led back to the Rio Grande. Valentine pinned him to the blacktop within feet from the truck, and he screamed in fear with her mouth wrapped around the back of his neck and her teeth piercing his skin.

"Val!" Cap yelled. She released her grip, but kept her front paws on the back of the man.

"That was stupid," Sweeny said, pulling the driver's hands to the small of his back and cuffing him. Dale and Terry cuffed the other two men while Lawson, Cap, and the other agents inspected the trailer.

"Holy crap!" Lawson shouted.

"Big?" Sweeny asked with his knee in the center of the man's back.

"I'd say. It's full."

"You better call the DEA in Alpine," Cap said. A border patrol truck with a metal cab on the back pulled up, and Sweeny and Dale loaded the three men into the small enclosed prison.

Sweeny reached up and gave Dale a high five. "Now that's how you do it!"

"I bet there's more than a thousand pounds here," Lawson said with a grin, knowing it was a bigger bust than they had expected.

"I guarantee you it's going to be close to a million dollars in street value," Terry said, having experienced many drug busts. "Only problem now is we're gonna have to wait for DEA in Alpine to get here."

Lawson looked at his watch. *It's already 3 p.m. Dang,* he thought, *it's going to be a couple of hours before DEA gets here.* "Cap, can I speak with you?" Lawson motioned to his truck.

The two of them walked to Lawson's truck with everyone wondering what the big secret was. "Hey, I know I need to hang around for DEA, but I told Lia I would go to her sister's wedding, and I need to be there in an hour. Can I leave?"

With a smirk, "Wedding? I thought you said her father didn't care for you," Cap replied, lighting a cigarette.

"Well I don't think he cares a whole lot for any white boy seeing his daughter."

"You're messing up if her dad doesn't approve. But that's your business. Let Dale fill out the report. He needs some experience."

Lawson waved Dale over to their conversation. "I'm leaving you to fill out the report; if you have any questions, Sweeny can help."

"You're leaving?" Sweeny yelled.

"Help Probie with the report," Lawson yelled back.

"Where are you going?"

"I'll tell you later." Lawson tried to drop the conversation that was being shouted over all the agents.

"You're going somewhere with Lia, aren't you?" Sweeny yelled back.

***

"Papa, we are just friends. It's nice to have someone," Lia spoke into her cell phone.

"I don't care for him. He is not welcome here!" her father's voice rang out from the other end.

"It's too late—I've already invited him."

"Un-invite him! My word is final!" The line went dead.

Lia had grown up in a small town with small town and old school rules. Her father was a loving man, but at times seemed to have a dark side. He wasn't subject to change and was hell bent on not letting his family change either. Lia had always respected his demands when she lived at home, but now that she was out living on her own, that had changed.

Well, crap! What do I do? she wondered.

Lawson sprinted into his house and quickly slipped out of his uniform. Running to the bathroom, he pulled over a button shirt and grabbed a pair of socks. *I am so late!* He sprayed body spray over his shirt and raced to the kitchen. *Where is my belt?* Digging through a white basket of dirty clothes, he pulled a brown leather belt out of the loops from another pair of jeans. Downing a cup of water, he pulled the door to and dashed to his truck. *I'm going to make it.* Rocks and dust flew up from under his tires as he aimed for the pharmacy. As he turned the corner, Lia's pharmacy came into sight, and his first thought was *Where's her jeep?*

Sliding to a stop in front of the vacant store, he asked himself aloud, "Did she leave without me?"

Crossing the border, Lia's cell phone rang. "*Hola*, Papa... No, he is not with me. I'm on my way." She hung up. *Lawson, I'm sorry*, she thought to herself.

Chapter 24

"Hey, y'all still going to the high school's fundraiser tonight?" Lawson asked Sweeny on the phone.

"Yea, I almost forgot about it. Why did you leave so early today if you're wanting to go with us?"

"I'll explain later. Where is it?"

"El Pasadita Bar and Grill. Swanky place, huh?"

Laughing, Lawson replied, "Yea, it's for a good cause. Vicky coming?"

"If I can get her out of her gym shorts and tee shirt," Sweeny answered, cutting his eyes at Vicky, who was pouting with her arms crossed and sitting on the couch. "Please put on the dress," Sweeny asked, covering his cell phone with his hand.

"Good luck—see you there." Lawson set his phone down on his kitchen counter. He couldn't decide whether to text Lia or let it go. Turning on the TV, he caught the news story of the day about $959,040 being seized today by the DEA in Alpine. *Dang, Terry was close on his figures.* Lawson sat on the arm rest of the couch and listen to the story. Not much was mentioned about the Border Patrol agents, which was the way they preferred it. Cap always reminded them that no press was their best press.

He walked back in the kitchen and fixed a sandwich and chips, grabbed his phone and returned to the living room, where he listened to the local sports report and ate. *Should I text her or just let it go?* His mind started racing. *Maybe she's sick or injured?* A news report came on the TV about a wreck just outside of Presidio involving an 18-wheeler and two teenagers. He picked up his phone. "You OK? I'm sorry if I messed up the time or something. Just checking on you." He sent the message.

***

Lia's father stood proudly at the head of the makeshift aisle with chairs on both sides lined with magnolia flowers and white ribbons. To his left was Lia's sister, dressed in a short white dress with a small veil covering her face. At the sound of the band, they began their march down the aisle, stepping carefully on the bunched-up red carpet that lay on the rocky ground. Lia and two of her sister's friends stood on the opposite side of the groomsmen and the groom. She smiled with a tear in the corner of her eye, happy for her older sister's big day.

I hope he's not pissed at me. I should have called him. Damn it, I hate this. I should be able to date who I want and not worry about my father's approval. Crap! We're not even dating. I should have brought him. The priest spoke up, catching Lia off guard on where they were in the wedding.

As her sister kissed her new husband, white doves were released into the air, and then her sister shot a quick glance at her brothers, who were pulling their guns to fire in the air. "No!" She shouted. They honored her wishes and put them down, with the audience laughing at her persistence. They had begun their walk back down the aisle when a single shot rang out, scaring everyone, and her sister turned to find her younger brother smiling with his pistol in hand.

The family quickly turned the ceremony into a reception by bringing out tables, food, and drinks. Within minutes, the mariachi band started up, and the party began. Lia ducked in line to hug her sister's neck and congratulated them, then turned to find Erika, who was already holding a plate of food and balancing a drink. Lia pointed at a table and collected a plate, but Roberto cut her off with a laugh. "Gotta be quicker, little sis."

"Come sit with us. I need to talk to you," she asked him.

They loaded their plates with homemade tamales wrapped in banana leaves and corn tortillas. Lia set her plate down and marched to the bar, where Roberto cut her off again. "Dang it, Roberto, if you knew my day, you'd have some sympathy."

"Bad day? Here!" He handed her a shot glass of Jose Cuervo. "This should help." She didn't disagree, and together they slammed their shots and walked back to the table with Erika.

"What about me?" Erika asked, seeing their
salutes. "Trust me, there will be more," Lia replied.

"That doesn't sound like my little sis," Roberto commented, unwrapping a tamale.

"It's Papa," Lia started.

"No, it's Lawson," Erika interrupted.
Roberto looked at both girls and asked, "Who's a Lawson?" "A friend. But dad is throwing a fit about me hanging
around him."

"Friend? Or boyfriend?"

"Friend," she answered, defending herself.

"OK, OK. Don't get upset with me. You know Papa and his thoughts about marrying outside of his Mexican heritage. I'm sure if you explain to Papa, he'll understand."

"That's just it. He saw me and Lawson in town the other day, and he assumes we are together." Erika left the table and joined few guys before walking toward the bar.

"My advice. Find a Mexican man." "I
might just never date," Lia replied.

"Never date! I can find you someone," Carlos stumbled to their table and put his arm around Lia.

"Carlos!" She pushed his arm away that was greasy from his hair. "You're already drunk?" He held up a bottle of whiskey and stumbled to the next table. "This party is not going to turn out good," she said, looking back at Roberto.

"Always interesting around here," Erika said, setting down a bottle of Patron Silver. "Might as well drink in style." She poured everyone a shot.

The band made their way in their direction. "Date who you want, just keep it quiet around here," Roberto smiled.

***

"Don't be mad. I can explain, but I understand if you don't want to hear it," said Lia's text. Lawson read it sitting at a table with Sweeny, Dale, and Vicky listening to a country band play on stage. The high school had sold tickets to the concert for a fundraiser to help with the purchase of new computers.

Vicky leaned over to Lawson while he read the message and asked, "Is that from her?" She smiled.

"It is," Lawson smiled back.

"I like her. Have you asked her to be your girlfriend yet?"

"I'm taking my time. No reason to rush into things." He leaned down and playfully touched her nose.

"You better ask her before someone else does. Happened to my friend Sara," Vicky said, looking back at the band on stage.

"I'll keep that in mind," he answered, sitting back in his chair.

The band started playing a George Strait song, *I cross my heart*. Couples flooded the dance floor and began two stepping to the music, and Sweeny held his hand toward Vicky. "Should we show them up?"

"Yep!" She jumped up and pulled her father to the dance floor. Couples that were already on the floor stepped to the side as Sweeny led his eight-year-old daughter to their favorite song. Lawson sat watching them, wondering if that would ever be him. He figured at the rate he was going, Vicky would be married before him.

He held his beer up to Dale. "Good bust this morning, Probie." Their bottles clanged.

"Dad?" Vicky motioned for Sweeny to duck down to talk in his ear.

"Yes."

"When are you going to get a girlfriend?"

On a normal day, Sweeny would laugh and make up something funny, but since his conversation with Cap the other day, his thoughts about never dating were wearing thin. "I don't know," he answered, hoping it would be dropped.

"Well, I hope soon," she said, looking down at her feet and trying to match her father's footsteps.

"What's the rush?"

"No rush. Just the other girls at school all have moms at home. And, I don't know, I kinda don't want to be the only one."

Sweeny felt a pain in his throat, like a knife was jabbing at his jugular. "All I can tell you is, when the time is right."

"Cross your heart?" She looked up into his eyes.

"And promise to give all I've got to give, to make all your dreams come true. In all the world you'll never find a love as true as mine," he sang back to her with the lyrics of George Strait in the background.

She motioned him back down to her level. He leaned over expecting another question, but felt her sweet soft lips planted on the side of his face.

Chapter 25

"You know, if you turned that down, we'd probably catch something," Lawson said, pointing to Sweeny's Bluetooth speaker in the corner of their boat. Lawson and Sweeny had decided to spend their morning fishing.

"I don't think it matters either way. Can you hear underwater?" Sweeny set down his longneck bottle of beer and cast toward the shore with a white spinner bait. The boys had been out since 10 a.m., and with it getting close to noon, they hadn't had a bite and their eighteen-pack was dwindling.

Sweeny had promised not to mention anything about Lia leaving Lawson the day before when they had decided to go fishing—but that was seven beers ago. "So why do you think she left you?" Lawson pretended not to hear the question. "You can't ignore me," Sweeny added. "We're in a boat." He laughed and sang out a few lines of a rap song about a boat.

"I told you I wasn't interested in talking about it."

Sweeny dropped his rod and reel trying to cast out. Picking it back up, he slurred out, "Hell, it was only a date. Not like you were married or something."

Lawson considered himself a rough, tough guy, but wore his emotions on his sleeve. His mother would often say she didn't know where he got his sentimental manner. Lawson had been hurt one time in his life, and it was back in high school. For most young men in their 20s, high school sweethearts were a thing of the past, but when it's love, there is no past.

Oliva Caldwell was a beautiful 18-year-old cheerleader and dating the star linebacker for their football team, Lawson Caine. The two had been a couple since their senior year had started, but had been on a few dates before then. There wasn't a day that went by that they didn't see each other, and with Oliva's dad a graduate of Paris High School and an alumni football player, Lawson was a star in his eyes too. Lawson spent many nights at their supper table, talking with her father about the good old days of football and music in the 70s.

It seemed like it was only yesterday that Lawson was in Oliva's bedroom supposedly studying. Sitting on her bed, she wrestled him to his back and sat on top, pinning his arms on each side of him. She leaned over with her brown hair falling to both sides of her face, "Lawson Caine, when are you going to ask me to marry you?" she said in a thick east Texas accent. "I'll marry you right now," he replied. She smiled and planted her lips on his.

"How's the studying coming?" her mother asked through the closed door.

"We're doing fine," Olivia smiled, still straddling Lawson on the bed.

Marriage was on Lawson's mind, and why not? They had dated most of their senior year, but during a party at a friend's house, he lost Oliva.

"Have you seen Oliva?" he asked a friend.

"I think she's upstairs," his friend pointed, holding a red Solo cup. Lawson pulled himself up the stairs faster with the help of the banister and opened the first door he came to.

"Sorry," he apologized to the couple he had stormed in on. He pulled the next door open, and it was then that his high school love crashed in front of him. Finding Oliva in bed with another guy was the sharpest pain he had felt. Fighting didn't cross his mind—just the humiliation and time wasted on someone who had just a few days earlier was talking about marriage. He spent the next two months with his head down and as little time at school as he could. They never spoke, and after graduation he parted ways with many of his friends. Later in academy, he heard that Oliva had gotten married, pregnant with someone's baby. He never asked. It was a story he never shared with Sweeny or any of his team, wanting to forget and erase it from memory, but emotions are hard to erase.

"You're not planning on marrying her?" Sweeny asked, trying to cast his bait and hold the rod at the same time.

"What?" Lawson replied, coming out of his thoughts.

"Lia! Drink another beer." Sweeny threw an unopened bottle. "Here's to us guys." Sweeny held up his bottle and swayed with the boat. Lawson twisted open his bottle and was taking a huge swig when Sweeny's pole doubled over with a hit. "Holy sh—" Sweeny couldn't finish as his pole jerked out of his hand and landed in the bottom of the boat. Both guys looked at each other, dropped their beer, and dove after the pole dancing on the floor of the boat.

"Grab it! Reel!" Lawson yelled with Sweeny under him trying to hold on to the rod and reel in the large fish on the other end. Their boat turned sideways with the tight tension of the line. "Reel, Sweeny!" Lawson cheered.

"Where's my beer!?!" Sweeny yelled, trying to gain his

footing. Just as the boys stood up, the fish darted to the port side, pulling the boat around and sending Lawson and Sweeny back to the floor. One of their bottles rolled into Sweeny, who picked it up and took a big gulp. Lawson caught the pole as it slipped from the Sweeny's distracted grasp. "I got this," Sweeny assured him.

"Reel!" Lawson shouted back.

Sweeny started laughing and stood back up, only to fall over Lawson and drop the rod. Both boys crawled to the side of the boat to watch Sweeny's casting rod disappear into the brown water. "Damn, Sweeny! That was a good pole," Lawson complained.

"Hell, that was a good fish," Sweeny responded. They leaned back on the side of the boat sitting in spilt beer and pond water and laughing. "I want to get a tattoo," Sweeny said.

Lawson gave him a funny look. "Tattoo?"

Standing up, Sweeny insisted, "Yep, lets head to that tattoo place down from the school."

"What in the world has got you wanting a tattoo?"

"I don't know—it just sounds like a good thing to do."

Pulling up to the dock, they tied the boat and stumbled to their truck. An elderly man who was sitting on the bank fishing turned on his bucket and looked toward the two young men. "You boys look like two monkeys on a football out there. That pond isn't four feet deep; you gonna leave your pole?"

Sweeny looked at Lawson, then back to the old man. "I can't swim," he said, still laughing. The old man gave a dirty look, waved them off, and went back to fishing.

Lawson pulled up to the tattoo parlor. "You sure about this?"

"Yep." Sweeny slid out of the passenger side.

Lawson flipped through the examples of tattoos as Sweeny lay on his chest and the artist carefully gazed at his shoulder and then at the paper Sweeny had brought in. "You want one?" a young girl asked Lawson. She had two sleeves of ink, a nose ring, and two more in her lip.

Lawson paused, looking at her. "No, thanks."

"He's scared," Sweeny said without looking up.

"I can take that fear out," she said, looking him up and down.

Lawson didn't know what to think. "I'm good."

Chapter 26

“What's wrong with you?” Erika asked Lia, who was throwing boxes at the back door.

“Nothing!” she snapped back.

“OK? Did I do something?”

Lia stopped and blew her hair out of her face. “No, it's not you.”

“You know he's playing basketball with the other guys right now. Just go over there and talk with him.”

“What am I supposed to say? ‘Sorry for leaving you last Friday, my father hates you.’” She kicked an empty box out of her way.

“Yes. It's not like y'all are a couple. Or are you?”

“Just help me clean up back here.” Lia crushed a box with her foot. She knew Erika was right and what would it hurt to catch up with Lawson and the other guys. She heard the front door open and looked up to find Erika was gone. *Surely she isn't going to the basketball courts? By all means, don't help me!* Looking out the front windows, she could see Erika talking with a few men in a blue two-door truck.

"Who was that?" Lia asked when Erika walked back in the store.

"Just a couple of friends. You going?"

"No, I don't want to cause a scene." She looked up and Erika was gone again. *Good grief!*

The sound of the front door opening came again. She waited a minute, thinking that Erika had left again. "By all means, let me do this by myself!" She bent over and shoved a wad of packing papers into a garbage bag.

"I'll help," a voice came from the doorway. Lia looked up to find Lawson leaning on the door frame.

"Sorry, I thought—"

"She's yelling at me," Erika pushed past Lawson. "I'll do this."

"I don't—" Lia began.

"*Go.*" Erika mouthed to her and pushed her toward the door.

"Would you walk out front with me?" she asked Lawson.

He looked back at Erika. "Have fun," he added, and followed
Lia out.

Lia took a deep breath walking out the front door, hoping this conversation would go well. Turning, she found herself hypnotized by the warm smile he gave. *Why are you so freaking nice?*

"I'm glad you stopped by," she
started. "I'm glad you texted me."

"Text?" She cocked her head.

He pulled out his phone and looked at the message that read, "Can you come by the pharmacy this morning, I need to talk to you."

Lia looked over his arm and saw the message. *Erika!*

"You did text me?" he
questioned. "Yes," she lied.

He leaned against his truck, waiting for her to start the conversation that was so urgent. She looked over his shoulder and saw the rifle barrel sticking up from the passenger side. He turned to see what she was staring at. "I've got to shoot this afternoon."

"Oh." She looked back at him.

"Have you ever shot before?" he asked.

"No," she answered unsure, if it was an invitation.

"Want to go?"

She looked back at the store and knew Erika wouldn't stay around if she left, but she had already left him once and turned him down another time. *Say no this time, and that will be it.*

"Yes." A smile formed across her face.

Lia told Erika her plans were and begged her to stay, knowing that wasn't going to happen. On the ride to the rifle range, that wasn't much more than a bench and a few targets, Lia laid her arm on the window seal and let the warm air blow her hair from the back of her neck. As she took a deep breath through her nostrils and exhaled, a sense of peace overcame her. She looked at Lawson. "I'm sorry."

"About?" He knew.

"My father isn't crazy about me dating outside of our Mexican heritage. And when I told him I was bringing you as a friend to the wedding, well, he didn't like it. I'm sorry."

"I understand," he answered.

"I don't. He's so old school and—"

"Listen, I don't want to start anything with your father. Can't we just be friends?"

Friends? She looked forward, not saying anything. She turned up the music to drown out the wind blowing through the truck and watched as the bare lands of west Texas pass by in a blur. She thought about her father and his orders not to date outside of their nationality and the complication of him finding out that she was with Lawson. The truck slowed and turned into a pair of open red gates that bore the sign *Border Patrol Range.*

"You ready?" Lawson asked after putting the truck into park.

"Lead the way."

Lawson pulled his M4 rifle out of the cab by the straps and slung it on his shoulder, grabbed a duffle bag, and walked to a wooden picnic table. Fumbling through the bag, he handed Lia a blue pair of ear protectors and a clear pair of shooting glasses. She smiled and took the items. He set his rifle in a set of shooting vises and walked back to his truck. Reaching over the back into his tool box, he pulled out another case with a black synthetic .270 cal. rifle inside.

"How many guns do you have?" Lia asked.

"Here? Or in general?"

She gave him a funny smile, "With you?"

"Just these two. Plus my service pistol." He thought a moment. "And the revolver in my cover compartment and the

.38 under my seat," he smiled.

After placing a couple of targets down range, he picked up his M4 and inserted a loaded clip, "You interested?" He looked at her with one eyebrow higher than the other.

"Sure." She reluctantly reached for the weapon. He showed her the safety and the bolt to chamber the first round. Pointing to one of the targets, he stood behind her and gave her room. She pulled the cold stock to her cheek and studied the target for a moment worrying about what he would think of her if she couldn't hit it. The gun jumped in her arms with the squeeze of the trigger, scaring her and leaving her not sure where that round went.

"Go ahead and shoot a few more times," she heard Lawson's instructions from behind. Squinting her eyes, she pulled the trigger three more times, and each time the sound rattled through her head. She pulled the rifle down and looked at the target. *There's no holes.*

"Maybe if you sit on the bench and use the vise it will help," Lawson commented. Embarrassed, she turned and handed the rifle back to him, saying "I don't think this is for me."

"Nonsense. Have a seat." He pointed to the bench. He caught a glimpse of the disgusted look on her face as she sat. "It's OK," he assured her.

"Why don't I watch you?" She tried to get out of shooting.

"Here." He sat behind her, straddling the bench. She could feel his body scoot up tight to hers, and chills ran up her neck as he reached around her with his left arm.

OK, never mind. Maybe I will try this shooting thing.

With the rifle resting in the shooting vise, he said, "Lean over and rest your cheek here." He tapped on the stock of the gun. She gently placed her face against the gun that was still warm from the four shots earlier. He pulled himself tighter against her back and placed his right arm under her right arm. She felt her heart skip a beat.

"Close your left eye and look down the barrel with your right eye," he instructed her, looking over her dark hair. She could feel the warmth of his breath on her ear as he continued to instruct. "OK, take it off safety and slowly squeeze the trigger." She began gently pulling the trigger with her index finger while Lawson held her tightly in place. The shot rang out, surprising her, but not scaring her. She felt safe with Lawson cuddled up behind her.

"Good shot," he replied, but stayed frozen in the same position. "Try another," he said.

I could do this all day!

After three more shots, she looked over her left shoulder and found herself inches from Lawson's face. His warm smile sent another round of chills up her spine. "I think you have the hang of it," he commented.

Maybe you should show me a couple hundred more times.

The afternoon flew by as Lia sat behind Lawson observing him practicing with both rifles. She couldn't help but notice that as he leaned over to shoot, his t-shirt would tighten on his back and shoulders, defining every muscle. Lia shook her head every time. "I'm going to have to go to confession!" she giggled.

Chapter 27

A white four-door Toyota truck pulled up to a two-story apartment complex and parked. The three men inside climbed out and walked to one of the apartments, scanning the area as they walked. A door opened on one of the downstairs units with an older man standing in the doorway. He was dressed with a white tank undershirt tucked into his black slacks and a silver cross that hung from his neck.

"If anyone followed you, we'd know by now," he said.

"I've been nervous ever since those patrol officers questioned us the other day," one of the men replied.

"You should be," a voice replied from behind the older man. Carlos Gonzales presented himself in the doorway with his black handled Smith and Wesson tucked in the front of his jeans.

The men stopped short of the front porch, looking at each other in surprise with Carlos standing before them. "Well, come in before everyone knows we're here," Carlos ordered, walking back into the room.

The three men reluctantly entered, each thinking of the reputation Carlos had with the coyotes in Mexico. Carlos had killed a coyote earlier in the month for questioning his loyalty to Jose Emmanuel.

"We started a crossing north of here, and the agents must have known because they were waiting on our scout," one of the men started.

"Dumb luck!" Carlos replied.

"Maybe. However, they were there."

"Your sister owns the pharmacy store?" another man asked. "And?" Carlos shot him a glare.

"Can she help?"

Carlos shook his head with a smirk. "No. She would turn us over in a heartbeat."

"Well do you—"

"I said leave her out and alone! Clear?!" Carlos's voice grew intense.

"*Ce*," the man replied, cowering down.

***

Lia's jeep crept through the dirt parking lot in search of the Border Patrol trucks that were parked beside each other. She peeked at the radio that displayed the time and then out through the dust that had risen from other cars and trucks parking for the last night of the rodeo. "There's your knight in armor over there," Erika pointed to Lawson, Sweeny, and Dale, who were sitting on their tailgate. Lawson pointed to a spot that was beside their trucks for her to park.

"Did you save us a spot?" Lia asked, opening her door.

"Had to fight off three car loads of pissed-off cowboys who

wanted the spot," Sweeny replied.

"Cowboys in cars?" Lia asked with a snicker.

"Funny," Sweeny replied, matched with his comment.

"I figured you boys would be out here turning up a few beers before the rodeo. What's with the uniforms?" Erika asked.

"Our chief patrol agent thought it would be good PR," Lawson answered.

"Political Bull—" Sweeny started before being interrupted by Lawson.

"Good PR." He shot Sweeny a look.

"We'll be turning up a few after this," Sweeny said, looking back at Lawson.

The five of them merged into line with the other fans and approached an elderly man who was taking up tickets. Sweeny and Dale walked past the man, who was clearly allowing the agents in for free. The old man looked at Lia and Erika. "Are these young ladies with you?" he asked Lawson.

"They've jumped the border so many times we have to keep an eye on them," Sweeny said from inside the gate.

"Funny," Lia returned the comment.

"Yes, sir, they are," Lawson replied.

"Why, you're the young lady that owns the pharmacy store," the man smiled.

She returned the smile, "Yes sir, I am."

"Well, I took your idea you gave me the other day while I was picking up my meds, and it worked," he said in an excited tone.

"I'm glad I could help."

He stepped out of her way and waved her and Erika past the gate. Catching back up with her, Lawson asked, "What was your idea?"

"Patient confidentiality," She grinned. "You don't want to know," she added.

A couple of kids stopped Dale and asked him about his service weapon and how many bad guys he had killed. Sweeny left him with his fans and headed toward the concessions while Lawson, Lia, and Erika watched as Dale entertained the boys with a story of their Border Patrol dog chasing down a bad guy last week.

"Sounds pretty good when he tells it," a raspy voice came from behind the trio.

The three turned to find Cap, Sandra, and Vicky. "Hey Cap, glad y'all made it," Lawson said.

"Yea, the Mrs. can't go long without making a rodeo."

"Just something about cowboys," Sandra laughed, looking at Cap. "I hope these young men are treating you girls well."

"Yes, mama," Lia replied, then turned to Vicky. "And how are you doing?"

"Good," she replied with a big smile.

"Enjoy the show." Cap led the girls in Sweeny's direction.

"They are so sweet," Lia said.

"So sweet," Lawson chuckled. Vicky turned twice walking off and waved at Lia. "I think you have a fan," he said to Lia.

"She is precious."

Sweeny joined them in the stands with a couple of corn dogs and a drink. Scooting past the other girls, Erika took a bite out of one of the corn dogs. Without seeing it happen, Sweeny placed his drink by his feet and opened a package of mustard. "What the?" he said, dumbfounded at the one corn dog with a bite taken out of the side of it.

"What's wrong?" Erika asked.

"They gave me a corn dog with a bite out of it," he answered.

"Here, I'll eat it while you go get another one," she said.

"You can have it." He handed it to her.

Lawson shook his head with smile, thinking Sweeny might have met his match with Erika. She finished the corn dog by crunching the last little bit on the stick in time to stand for the national anthem and prayer. Dale's radio fell from his belt and clattered down the aluminum steps, and Sweeny shook his head, embarrassed as half the crowd turned toward the noise. "Sorry," Dale quietly said, picking it back up. He set it beside his seat.

"Where's Vicky?" Lia asked.

Pointing in the direction of Cap, Sweeny answered, with a mouth full of corndog, "She's with Cap and Sandra."

During the barrel racing and halfway through the rodeo, Lia brought up yesterday evening. "Thanks again for taking me shooting."

Sweeny peered at Lawson. "Shooting? You didn't tell me you had company."

"I wasn't aware I had to... Dad," Lawson replied out of the corner of his mouth.

"You two act like y'all are dating," Erika said.

"I think they are," Dale piped up.

"Shut-up, Probie," Sweeny said, then turned to Erika. "Maybe they are."

"It was fun—we need to go back soon," Lawson answered staring at both of them, insinuating for them to be quiet.

Yes, we do, Lia thought with a smile.

"I'll be back," Erika said, standing up with her purse.

"Where are you going?" Lia asked, looking up at her squeezing past the group.

"Bathroom... Mom," she answered.

The announcer's voice grew with excitement as he introduced the next cowgirl, who was entering the area on a big stout bay horse. Inhaling her first barrel a voice echoed over the speakers, "Y'all let the Georgia girl hear you!" The crowd began cheering louder as she turned the third barrel and headed out the alley way.

"Hey," Lia whispered to Lawson.

"Yeah?" he answered, watching the next cowgirl start her run.

"Would you want to go with me tomorrow to see my grandmother?" Her voice was still low enough for only Lawson to hear.

He grinned. "You're not going to leave me again if I'm not on time," he picked at her.

He felt the jolt of her elbow in his side. "No."

"Yes, I would like to," he whispered back.

After the last bull rider was bucked off, the announcer thanked everyone for coming and said good night. The stands rapidly began to empty with the patrol agents shaking the hands of several of the crowd thanking them for their service. The five of them hiked to their vehicles that rested in the cloud of dust created by the mass exodus of the fans. Dale felt his side, looked down, then shot Lawson a look. "My radio!"

"You set it beside you after the anthem."

"Wait on me!" He turned and jogged back to the stands.

"I think he'd forget his right arm if it wasn't attached," Sweeny replied.

"Lia, we better go. I'm not feeling so great," Erika replied.

"Told you not to eat that corn dog," Sweeny said, still unaware she was the one who took a bite out of it.

"Ok," Lia answered. "We... I had a great time. Thanks for saving us a spot." She pointed at her jeep.

"I'll text you after a while," Lawson answered.

The girls climbed in the Jeep and started out of the parking lot when Erika's purse fell to the floor board, making a loud thud. "What in the world are you carrying?" Lia laughed at her.

"Nothing. That was my foot," Erika nervously replied, picking her purse up with Dale's radio stashed inside.

After the Jeep pulled out onto the black top, "Well, Probie?" Sweeny asked as Dale walked back up.

"No! I can't believe I lost my radio."

"Well, somebody had to pick it up. Hopefully it will turn up," Lawson tried to assure him.

Chapter 28

Sitting on the concrete steps that led to his front porch, Lawson scanned the street for Lia's Jeep. The morning started out warm and stale with little breeze, making him believe he should have worn shorts. The sound of a six-cylinder engine roared at the end of the street, and Lawson watched as Lia's Jeep came into sight. He winced as she slid to a stop with one wheel in the grass and the other three on blacktop.

Rolling down her window, she smiled. "You just gonna sit there?"

"Waiting for you to get out so I can drive," he replied.

With a grimace, Lia opened the door. "I'm not that bad of a driver," she said in a low tone.

Lawson hopped up from his porch and jogged to the passenger door. Lia stopped for a brief moment, confused about whether he was going to let her drive. Lawson opened her door and stepping behind her, helped her in. *OK, treatment like this I don't care who drives*, she thought.

Pulling the door closed, buckling his seat belt, and pulling out into the street, Lawson looked at her, asking "Where to?"

"South of Ojinaga," she answered.

They talked about the rodeo, work, Sweeny and Vicky, and her family as they drove across the border and through the diminished town of Ojinaga. Lawson slowed as a few stray dogs ran out in front of traffic, followed by two young boys chasing them. Picking up speed, they head west on Hwy 16 to a distant mountain range. Lia became quieter the closer they drew into the mountains, worrying about what Lawson would think about her grandmother. The one thing she didn't explain to him, in fear he wouldn't have come, was that her grandmother claimed to be a medicine woman.

"We are going to turn just past this ridge," she pointed.

Slowing down, Lawson took a hard right onto a dirt road that seemed to disappear into the distant mountain. After a few miles of dust, rocks, and potholes, he asked, "How far?" Before she could answer, a dilapidated old mud shack came into focus. Coming closer, he could see part of the front porch had caved in, leaving rusty tin lying on the ground and a small stream of white smoke coming from the chimney. *Kinda hot for a fire?* he thought.

Before he could put the Jeep in park, a leathery skinned old woman walked out on the front porch. Lawson stared in amazement at the woman, her straw hat, the band of hawk feathers lining her dilapidated bicep, and a string of rattlesnake heads hanging from her neck. Lia opened her door, then looked back at him. "I was afraid you wouldn't come if I told you my grandmother was a medicine woman," she admitted.

Lawson smiled at her, "I would have come." He stepped out of the Jeep.

"Abuela!" Lia said with excitement and hugged her aged grandmother. A blue heeler met Lawson and sniffed his shoes,

"That's Blue. She's harmless," Lia said with one arm around her grandmother. "Abuela, Lawson." She pointed at him.

"*Hola*," Lawson replied, nodding his head.

"So, you're the young man courting my grand-daughter?" the old lady asked. Lawson was shocked at her near-perfect English.

"We are friends," Lia grinned.

"HA! Me and your grandfather were friends and had 13 children. Come in before lunch gets cold." She waved them toward the front door. Stopping short of entering the threshold, she turned back to Lawson. "You're not allergic to cats, are you?" she asked.

Lawson looked at Lia, then back to her grandmother. "No, mama, their hair doesn't bother me."

"Hair! Who's talking about hair?" she laughed, walking in the old mud house.

Lawson froze in his tracks. "She's not cooking cat, is she?"

"I don't know." Lia gave him a devilish grin and followed her inside.

Lawson wasn't sure to follow them or get back in the Jeep with the many different animal furs hanging from the porch. But after he entered the small shack, Lia assured him that her grandmother was only joking. He studied the inside, finding it cozier than he expected. A thick old wooden table with four chairs centered the room, and the walls were lined with wooden shelves that matched the table. An iron rack straddled the fire lit in the fireplace, and steam poured out of the two cast iron kettles that rested on the rack.

"Do you know anything about carpentry?" the old lady asked Lawson.

"A little," he answered, unsure why she was asking.

"I could use some help with the porch." She enlisted him to help fix the fallen-in porch.

"I can't help but ask, you speak very good English," Lawson said.

Studying him for a short moment, she answered, "I attended Texas Tech in the 60s."

"Really?" he asked before he realized it sounded rude.

Looking back at the cast iron kettle, she added, "I studied animal science and worked in Austin for 30 years before moving back here." Lawson nodded his head, impressed. "Now, you two sit down and try my vegetable soup." She smiled at Lawson. "Cat!" She laughed again.

He was struggling with being impressed with everything, including the soup he was devouring. He spun the wooden bowl, looking at the age of it and wondering if it too had a story. The old lady sat down at the table with another bowl, her long grey hair lapping over the string of snake heads. Lawson watched her as she blew on the steam coming from her bowl, and she stopped and cut her eyes at him. Her facial figures changed from normal to concern under the many leather winkles on her face.

Lawson went back to eating, thinking it was strange that she was now watching him. Without warning, she grabbed his hand and turned his palm up. He looked at Lia, who mouthed the words, "Just go with it." The old lady put his hand back down and continued to eat. Moments later Lia spouted off, "Abuela, I almost forgot I brought you something." And without giving them a chance to say anything, she disappeared outside toward her Jeep.

The old lady grabbed Lawson's wrist and forced him to look here eye to eye, "Boy, you are headed to death!"

"I'm sorry?" He was shocked by her statement.

"Death is near."

"I don't understand. Me?"

"I cannot read death. Only that it is coming." Her old hand shook as she released his hand.

The door swung back open with Lia carrying a package. "It's a few things you asked for and a couple of things I thought you'd like," she smiled, proud to hand over the box of items from her pharmacy.

"Thank you, child." She stood and walked around the table to take the box. She suddenly stopped and shot a fiery glare back at Lawson, and everyone stopped moving in the room. The old lady looked back at Lia, then back at Lawson, then placed her right hand on Lia's stomach. "She is with child!" She looked at Lawson with widened eyes.

Lawson couldn't swallow—he just stared. *Pregnant? We haven't even kissed, pregnant?* He didn't know what to say. If she was pregnant, her grandmother would never believe it wasn't his. *Pregnant?* He was mortified.

"Abuela! Stop messing with Lawson. You'll never get him to fix your porch." Lia removed her hand and set the box on the table.

A loud, obnoxious laugh flooded the room. "Did you see his face!" the old lady said, opening the door. "Come, I'll show you the nails and tools." She laughed, walking out.

Lawson gave Lia a puzzled look. "I know, strange. But she means well," she said.

He followed the old lady as Lia cleaned what dishes there were. "That was funny," he said, trying to start a conversation. "I am picking on you," she replied, handing him an old milk crate of nails and a few tools.

"The death thing really did get me," he said.

She faced him and put her hand on his chest. "That I was not joking. You have death coming; please heed my warning." She walked back to the old mud shack with him still standing in place holding the crate.

Chapter 29

Sweeny convinced Cap to put out motion sensors around the mound north of Presidio in hopes that the scouts would return to pushing immigrants across the border.

A day after they had been placed, the sensors started taking hits and enough hits for them to stake out the area. During the first night watch that Dale and Terry had drawn, a couple of scouts drove the area on the Mexican side, but did nothing worth reporting.

The second night was Sweeny and Lawson's turn, and the first part of the night was quiet, but quickly changed when they received a call from a land owner just a few hundred yards north of their position.

"Sweeny! Hurry up. The land owner just north of here called in a large group of people crossing," Lawson yelled out his window.

Walking from behind the truck and zipping up his pants, Sweeny responded, "You can't rush pee. And land owner? Do they live on the property?"

"I don't know, but we have to check it out."

"Weird," Sweeny replied pulling his seat belt across his chest and lap.

The team had experienced unreliable phone calls in the past, mostly false leads that coyotes created to allow them to cross immigrants safely in other places. They had referred to the false calls as ruses and had adopted the word into their terminology. Sweeny had gotten good at figuring out the ruse calls before they could smuggle people across the border, but with just two of them tonight, Sweeny had no choice but to go with Lawson.

Their headlights swamped the bare land and sage brush that filled the area, and a few real coyotes eyes glowed red before they bolted for safety. The eight cylinders roared as Lawson floored their truck, aimed at the few structures on the farm north of the square mound they were located. The red glow of their tail lights had just disappeared when two coyotes ran out to the Mexican bank of the Rio Grande, motioning for 20 people to climb in the inflatable boats to cross.

"Lawson, I got a funny feeling about this call. I haven't seen anyone around this farm in a long time." Sweeny rolled down his window, scanning the area. No more than a few minutes after he made his comment, a call came over the radio that the sensors were going off back at the mound. Lawson slammed the gas and swung the F150 around, throwing dust and rocks across the sheds with a few vehicles under them. "I knew it!" Sweeny exclaimed.

Lawson called in for backup and air support. With the tips they had received and the activity on the sensors, he knew it could be a big crossing of people. The 17-inch tires boiled on the blacktop as they left the dirt road that led to the farm. Cap's voice came across the airways. "What is your 20?" his raspy voice echoed over the radio.

"We are less than a mile from turning back on the road that leads to the square mound," Lawson replied.

"10-4, on my way!"

Lawson shot Sweeny an apprehensive glare, "What if we are chasing what they want?"

"What are you talking about?"

"What if they know the sensors are there, and the ruse call was just to throw us off?"

"So, where are they crossing?" Sweeny asked.

Lawson slammed on the brakes, causing the truck to slide to a stop. "Back at the farm! The delivery trucks under the sheds. Why are they there?"

Sweeny caught on. "Go back!" Lawson spun the truck around and raced back to the farm.

"Hey Cap?" Sweeny called on their private channel.

"Go ahead."

"We have a tip that the real crossing is going down at the farm we just investigated."

"Who tipped you on that?" Cap asked.

Sweeny looked at Lawson, knowing if they said they had a hunch that Cap would be pissed. "Can't say."

"10-4, I'm turning on the dirt road leading to the mound now." Cap jetted down the road that still had a dust haze over the road from Lawson and Sweeny leaving earlier. He killed his lights and engine and rolled the last few hundred yards. Valentine, who was panting, ears perked up, craned her head over the dash, knowing they were about to get out of the truck. "Come on, girl," Cap said quietly, opening his door.

They walked swiftly down the remaining part of the road and into a section of trees that lined the Rio Grande. Cap crouched down and crawled to the bank with Valentine belly crawling behind him. Looking over, he saw three inflatable rafts filled with people paddling in place in the middle of the river. Watching for a few minutes, he noticed they were not approaching the US side of the river, "Well I'll be damned! This is a bunch of decoys," he said, looking at Valentine.

Lawson and Sweeny were rolling slowly down the road that led back to the farm when they received the call from Cap. "Boys, be careful—I believe your tip is right. Nothing but a bunch of decoys here."

"10-4," Sweeny said. "Pull to the back side of the barn." He pointed to an old hay barn. They got out and quickly jogged to the far shed that was closest to the river when Sweeny pulled on Lawson's arm. "The delivery trucks are gone."

"Where in the world did they go? We didn't pass anyone."

Sweeny pointed to the sky. "Listen."

In the distance they could hear the faint sound of truck engines to the north of them. Sweeny shined his light on the road. "Tracks. Shouldn't be too hard."

Lawson called again for air support, redirecting them to the north. "We should have them before long." Before they could get back to their truck, the helicopter buzzed over them with lights shining on the ground. Lawson picked up the tracks and followed the pursuit of the helicopter.

A voice of one of the pilots came across the airway. "We have three trucks stopped and all illegals out on foot."

Sweeny looked at Lawson. "Where they tipped that we were coming?

"I don't know. Weird for them to evacuate before anyone got there."

The pilot's voice came back over the radio, "There is probably 50 to 60 people hitting the river now. You guys will never catch them. Looks like a few kids too, but everyone looks like they're making it back across. A white Toyota has pulled up on the Mexican side."

"Same damn truck! How in the world did they know?" Sweeny said.

"I just don't know," Lawson said, pulling up behind the three parked trucks.

Across the river, Carlos Gonzales stepped out of the white Toyota, "What happen?" He asked one of the coyotes who was crawling up the bank.

"We got a call that air support was coming."

Carlos walked to the back of the truck, striking the side of the truck, "This was a good plan!" he yelled.

Another man drenched from the river walked up. "Senor, I will want all my money back," he said, wiping the water from his face.

"I'll get you across," Carlos said without looking at him.

"You had your chance," the man shot back.

Carlos glared at him with his beady eyes, "Don't test me!"

"This is no test. I want my $25,000!" the man demanded.

With the thunder from the blades of the helicopter who was still hovering over the river scanning everyone with their light, Carlos pulled his black-handled Smith and Wesson from his pants and aimed at the man. Without saying anything, he squeezed the trigger, dropping the man in the Mexican dirt. Everyone froze on the bank.

"Make sure everyone knows there are no refunds!" he told the first man and stepped back into the truck. "Get Erika on the phone," he told the driver.

Chapter 30

The office was buzzing with agents coming and going, and Lawson had just finished his report from the night before when his phone buzzed with a text from Lia. Reading her text that she hoped her grandmother didn't scare him off, he smiled and leaned back in his chair. Sweeny looked over his coffee cup that was sitting on his desk. "Do you smile when I text you?"

"Every time," Lawson replied while sending a text back to Lia.

Cap, who was unnoticed by the boys, stood over them with his coffee mug pulled up to his face. "If I didn't know better, I'd think you two were dating."

"Maybe if he started brushing his teeth in the morning," Lawson said still looking at his phone.

Sweeny covered his mouth with his hand and checked his breath, "Hey! I don't have bad breath. Do I?" He stood and got in Cap's face, trying to get him to check his breath.

Pushing Sweeny away, Cap said, shaking his head, "You two come to my office."

Sweeny followed Lawson into the conference room, still muttering "I don't have bad breath." He wouldn't let it go. Lawson just smiled, knowing that Sweeny was conscious about his breath.

"Pull the door closed," Cap said in his raspy voice. "We have a tip that some of these coyotes have been congregating at an apartment here in Presidio after they have led a group across." Cap slid the paper work across the table to Lawson.

Sweeny looked over his shoulder and recognized a familiar address. "Hey! Dale and I followed a Toyota to this apartment last week."

"And?" Lawson asked.

"Nothing out of the ordinary."

"Nothing here is ordinary," replied Cap. "Did Dale ever find his radio?" he added.

"No, sir," Lawson answered.

"You boys check this place out." Cap shuffled his files back together.

Lawson thought back to last night when the helicopter pilot said a white Toyota had emerged on the opposite side of the river, then back to Sweeny following the truck here on US soil. *Surely it's not the same truck. They wouldn't be that stupid? Or that smart?* he thought.

Dale was sitting with his feet propped up on his desk, proofreading Lawson's report, something that Lawson had asked early on, knowing that Dale was good at writing reports. "Probie, come go with us to check out that apartment you and Sweeny went to last week," Lawson said.

A raspy voice came from behind them, "Take Valentine. She's bored sitting around here." Cap looked at Valentine, who sat up, hearing her name.

"Come on, girl," Lawson waved her to lead them out.

Parking on the side of the apartment building opposite from the apartment they wanted to observe, the three agents stepped out, followed by Valentine. She had become a regular sight with the agents and was welcomed in most places Cap went.

"There's really no good place to get to watch the apartment," Sweeny commented.

"You want me and Valentine to set up on the roof?" Dale asked.

Lawson and Sweeny turned and gave him a puzzled look. "The roof?" Sweeny asked. "And just how is she going to get on the roof?"

Dale pointed to a small building on the roof with a door on the front of it. "The stairwell goes to the roof."

Lawson smiled at Sweeny, insinuating they didn't give Dale enough credit. "Good idea, stay low."

Dale and Valentine disappeared around the corner and jogged to the inside stairwell, meeting an elderly lady who walked out of her apartment and smiled as if it wasn't out of the ordinary to have an agent and a canine in their building. Dale pulled on the stairwell door, and finding it locked, he pulled out his Kershaw knife that was clipped to his front pants pocket and popped open the door quicker than using a key. Carefully opening the door that led to the roof, they slipped out and sneaked to the side to get a better view.

After a few minutes, Dale pulled out the new radio Cap had loaned him until they could find his. "I'm in place. I have a good view of the apartment," Dale said.

"Switch over to our channel," Sweeny answered him.

After Dale switched over to their private channel, the curtains in the apartment folded back with someone looking outside. "Someone is looking outside," Dale reported back to Lawson and Sweeny.

Shortly after, a figure came through the apartment doorway wearing sunglasses, ball cap, and a jacket and walked swiftly to the parking lot. "One just left," Dale said in the radio.

"Follow them?" Sweeny looked at Lawson.

"Are there others in the apartment?" Lawson asked Dale.

Watching the apartment, Dale noticed the curtains folded back again with someone still looking outside. "Someone is looking out now."

"No, let's see if there are others," Lawson said to Sweeny.

The figure who had left the apartment walked on through the parking lot and out onto the street. Looking back several times and not seeing anyone, Erika shed her glasses, jacket, and ball cap, throwing them in a trash can. Pulling her purse tight to her body, she jogged across the street and headed to the pharmacy.

"Why are you out of breath?" Lia asked as Erika walked in the door.

"I walked here."

"From your house?"

"From a friend's."

"Who?" Lia asked.

"A friend. Have you talked with Lawson today?" she asked, knowing Lia would drop the questioning once she mentioned Lawson.

A smile formed on Lia's face. "We texted a little this morning."

"Texting isn't talking. Ask him to lunch—I'll watch the store."

"I don't know, I have so much to do." Lia said looking at her desk and the paperwork that had piled up.

"You'll always have too much to do."

"OK," she smiled and picked up her phone.

"You busy for lunch?" she texted Lawson.

"Nope."

"Well, do you want to go to lunch?" she returned the message.

"Sure. Do you want me to pick you up?"

"I'll come get you," she smiled at her phone.

"I'll come get you!" he sent back with a smiley face.

Lia put her phone on her desk and walked back out into the store. "OK, we're going."

"Good! Now we have to do something to bring in more business to this soda bar?" Erika answered.

Since when does she care about business? Lia thought.

The door to the roof stairwell opened slowly and without a sound. Dale was so fixated on the apartment that he didn't realize Valentine had walked away. The light sound of two sets of shoes quietly crept across the roof toward the agent with his eyes glued to a pair of binoculars. Dale felt the cold steel object against his back and froze, wondering if he had time to go for his gun. In a split second and with superhero speed, Dale rolled to his back and drew his service revolver, aiming at the two figures standing over him.

"Holy Crap! Don't shoot, Probie!" Sweeny threw up his hands.

Looking at Lawson and Sweeny through the sights on his service weapon, Dale exclaimed "Don't do that!" and replaced his weapon.

"That was impressive!" Lawson said, helping Dale to his feet. "Bet you want do that again." He looked at Sweeny.

"I bet I don't, either," Sweeny said, putting away his radio.

Chapter 31

Two SUVs pulled up to an old mechanic garage in the southern part of Ojinaga, and a young man wearing coveralls and wiping his hands with a greasy rag walked out to greet them. A man dressed in slacks and a white t-shirt stepped out, and the young man nodded and pointed to the small room above the garage.

The visitor looked back at the SUV and pointed to a wooden stairwell leading to an exterior door that opened into a small room. Six more Cartel members stepped out of the vehicles and made their way to the stairs. The young man went back to a 80s model truck with the hood open, pretending he hadn't seen anything.

As the door opened, the seven Cartel members were greeted with a *"Hola"* by Jose Emmanuel

"Como estas," One of the men replied. Three other men stood behind Jose with grave expressions and dressed alike.

"Come in, come in." Jose motioned for them to close the door behind them.

"You have some sort of deal for us?" one of the men asked. "Right to business. I can respect that. Yes, as you know I am

in the smuggling business, primarily with people."

"Get to the point!" the impatient visitor pressed.

"If I help you smuggle your drugs in with my people, what would I make?" Jose went straight to the point.

The men looked at each other, surprised someone would ask for a cut of their profits. Their speaker glanced back at him. "I'm sure we could work something out. What's in it for us?"

"I make the people I am smuggling in carry the drugs. If they get caught and arrested, we only lose the drugs and not our people," Jose replied.

"And how are we going to get our money from the buyers?"

"My coyotes will bring it back."

"And how can I trust that one of your coyotes will not run off with the money?"

Jose paced the room. With each step, the wooden floor creaked and moved, making his men uncomfortable with his peculiar demeanor. He stopped in front of one of his men. "Because my men know not to double cross me. They know they cannot run and cannot hide things from me." His voice grew with emotion.

His men became even more uncomfortable. "Did you think I wouldn't find out that you are stealing from me?" He poked the chest of one of his men.

The Cartel members looked at each other then back at Jose, who directed his speech to them. "You ask me how I can trust my men?" Without warning, he drew a small .38 caliber pistol from his waist and stuck it to the forehead of the man he was referring to. The words "Please no" were the only thing heard before Jose squeezed the trigger, spraying blood and bone and brain matter across the room and on the opposite wall.

Everyone in the room jumped, and five of the Cartel members drew their weapons. The limp body lay on the wooden floor with blood oozing through the cracks and falling to the garage floor below. "You can put away your weapons," Jose said, replacing his gun in the waist of his slacks. "No one steals from me. And if we do business, no one will steal from you."

"I'll have to ask what your cut will be from my boss. Give me a day?" the Cartel speaker asked, staring at the slain body.

"Take your time. You know how to find me," Jose replied.

The men scrambled out the door and down the stairwell. The young mechanic was standing in the parking lot shaking as blood dripped over the 80s model truck he was working on.

"Clean this up and let the others know I will never be double crossed!" Jose ordered his men.

Sweeny was sleeping on his couch with his arms stretched over his head when a football landed on his stomach. The impact startled him, causing him to sit straight up. "Good! You're up. Let's throw," Vicky said, standing in front of the couch with a pair of cleats that were a size too small on her feet.

"Don't you want to play house or with dolls?" Sweeny asked, rubbing his stomach, thankful the football hadn't landed two inches lower.

"Dad!" Vicky placed both hands on her side and gave him a dirty look. "I don't play with dolls!"

There was no winning when he talked to Vicky about playing with the girl things most eight-year-olds played with. Sweeny downed a glass of water that was sitting on the counter top and followed her out to the front yard with the most grass of their property. Vicky stepped back and heaved a ball that was too big for her toward Sweeny with all her might.

"Good throw. You've been working on it," he commented.

"Recess."

Tossing the ball back, she tried her best to draw it in with her arms, causing it to hit her face. Sweeny didn't say anything. She looked down at the laces and placed her small hand on them, drew back and threw again.

"What do you think of Erika?" Sweeny asked, throwing it back.

"Erika? Why?" She ran after the ball she dropped.

"Oh, I don't know. I was thinking about asking her to eat supper sometime."

Vicky held the ball and looked at her dad, "She's OK. I really like Lia."

"Well, Lawson is talking to Lia," he chuckled.

"If he doesn't ask her out, then you should."

"It doesn't work that way," he answered.

"Why?"

Sweeny thought *I don't know* for a moment, then answered, "It just doesn't."

Sweeny had thought about asking Erika out since he and Cap spoke, but wasn't sure if the timing was right with Lawson and Lia starting something. "Well, what do you think?" he asked Vicky again.

"I guess it's OK. You gonna double date with Lawson and Lia?" She lit up.

"We'll see." He heard his phone ringing inside. "Hang on, I'll be right back." He jogged up the steps and darted inside to catch his phone before Sandra hung up. They visited about their plans for Sandra picking up Vicky at school and what night they were coming over for supper. Hanging up, he thought he heard a vehicle pull up outside and Vicky talking to someone. Looking out the window, he didn't see Vicky, nor did he hear her. He ran to the front door.

In the front yard, Lawson was catching a pass from Vicky. "You stealing my quarterback?" Sweeny asked.

"She's getting good," Lawson smiled at Vicky and in return received a big smile back.

"Uncle Lawson, guess what?" Vicky said with an excited tone.

"What?" Lawson asked.

Before Sweeny could stop her exciting news, she blurted out, "Dad's gonna ask out Erika!" she said, throwing the ball.

The football bounced off Lawson right leg as he turned to Sweeny with a big grin, "Really?"

"Well, I just said 'what if,'" Sweeny tried to play it off.

"He's taking her to supper," Vicky said with a higher pitched voice and a big smile.

"I'll let you two work this out while I start supper. You staying?" Sweeny asked Lawson.

"Sure. This might be an interesting night," he smiled.

"I told him y'all should double date," Vicky said.

"What do you know about double dating?" Lawson asked.

"I know things. So... where is Lia?"

"For such a rough and tough kid, you sure worry a lot about me and your daddy's dating."

"You didn't answer the question," Vicky persisted.

Lawson pulled his phone out of his back pocket. "There she is now," he pointed to the text Lia had just sent thanking him for lunch.

Vicky snatched the phone out of his hands and started texting her back. Lawson didn't see the harm of her talking with Lia and walked in to question Sweeny. After a few minutes of teasing Sweeny, a thought hit Lawson: *What if she's texting Lia about Sweeny asking Erika out.* "Vicky!"

Chapter 32

Lawson lay in bed not knowing whether to laugh or be worried as he read the text conversation between Lia and Vicky early that evening. *Since when does an eight year old know how to text? And what in the world are they teaching that she would know about dating?* he thought. His phone rang, *small world!* It was Lia.

"Hey," he answered.

"Tell me Sweeny didn't put Vicky up to texting me," Lia replied.

"No, that she did alone. Please don't say anything—it was just a simple question that she took too far."

"Is he interested in Erika?" she asked.

"I think it's more him wanting someone to visit with," Lawson played it off.

"Ok. I've known Erika for a long time and love her to death. But she's not really someone Sweeny would want to date. She's been pretty mysterious in the last six months and hanging around people I don't know."

"I don't think he's interested, just small talk gone wrong. What are you doing?"

"Boxing up a few things here at the store."

He rolled over and looked at the digital clock on his bedside table, "Its 11:00 p.m., and you're still at the pharmacy?"

"It never ends. I'm running some deliveries in the morning, then Erika is supposed to watch the store for the afternoon so I can catch up on some cleaning at my house. What about you?"

"I have to go out to the stables in the morning, and I'm off during the afternoon," he replied.

"My uncle had horses; that's something I miss."

"Well, I'm sure I can pull some strings if you want to go riding tomorrow afternoon."

"Really?" She didn't mean to sound so eager.

"Yea, call me when you're done running deliveries, and I'll come get you."

"Ok, deal."

"Call you in the morning." He hung up.

Lia quickly picked up a few items and threw the boxes in the back and locked up. She hadn't ridden horses since her middle school days and had missed it greatly, so the thought of riding excited her. The back tires on her jeep spun out, leaving her parking lot as she shot home to clean so she would have tomorrow afternoon clear.

It was just before noon when Lawson called Lia. She had been done with her deliveries for over an hour and was impatiently waiting for his call. When the phone rang, she gave it three rings before answering it. "Hello," she said in a chipper tone.

"You ready?"

"Yep."

Within 10 minutes, he pulled into the pharmacy to find her standing outside wearing a white top, boots, and a pair of jeans that defined every curve in her legs. *Wow!* He opened the passenger door for her. "So when was the last time you rode?" he asked.

"Honestly, it's been a while. I hope I don't embarrass myself."

"Nah, you'll be fine." He aimed toward the stables.

Two horses, one bay and the other sorrel, were saddled and tied to a walker as they pulled in the gate. An agent was sitting on a bale of hay whittling a piece of wood, waiting for Lawson to return. "I got Sam and Sorrel saddled for you. Sam is probably the easiest to ride. When you get back, just tie 'em up and I'll take care of them," the man instructed them, disappearing into the barn.

"Sam or Sorrel?" he asked Lia.

"Sam!" she replied.

Once on the horses, they rode out an aluminum gate and headed toward the mountains in the distance. The air was warm, but they felt some relief from an occasional breeze from the south. Leaving slack in the reins, Lia let Sam lead the way as if he had made the trail a million times. Sorrel and Lawson were close behind as he admired Lia's long dark hair swaying back and forward with every step Sam made.

Trotting up beside her, Lawson said, "Well Mrs. Gonzales, you didn't seem to forget much on riding."

His narcotic smile caught her off guard. "Yea, it feels good to be out here. I've been so engrossed with the pharmacy, I haven't taken time off."

"I say we forget our day jobs and savor the day," he replied

Giggling, she responded with "You're not going to go all *Carpe diem* on me, are you?"

"I might," he grinned.

They continued to ride toward a ravine and headed north on a dried river bed. The agent at the barn had told Lawson about a small lake two hours from the barn. His instructions were to follow the river bed. The sky was filled with soft white clouds that quickly changed shapes standing out against a deep blue background. "This is the perfect day," she said, and Lawson agreed without saying anything.

They came up on a clear half-acre pond lined with green grass, the water seeming to take on the color of the sky. Lawson was surprised to find the oasis and even more surprised that more people didn't know about it. He stepped down off of Sorrel and walked him up to the water for a drink, and Lia followed suit with Sam. "So, do you bring all your girlfriends here?" She elbowed him.

"No, this is my first time here. I normally take them to the creek where you found us," he smiled.

"Oh, so you take your girlfriends skinny dipping," she continued to pick.

"They just can't keep their clothes on with me around," he laughed.

"Well, Mr. Caine, it's gonna take more than your smooth talking to get me in that water," she teased him and walked to the other side of Sam.

Letting Sorrel's reins go, he followed her around Sam and snatched her off her feet, cradling her with one arm under her knees and the other under her back. She screamed and dropped the reins of Sam; the two horses paid them no attention and took advantage of the green grass.

"My smooth talking might not get you in that water, but there are other ways," he taunted her, dangling her off the water.

"You wouldn't dare!" she said, squinting her eyes at him. The thought crossed his mind, but he wasn't sure how she would take it if he *did* drop her in the water.

Setting her down on her feet, he replied, "Today might be your lucky day."

With his back to the half-acre lake, she said, "But not yours," and placing her hands on his chest, pushed him with all her might backward into the water. What she didn't expect was his firm grasp on her wrist at the last moment pulling her in with him. After the initial shock, the water was warm and inviting.

"Oh, my gosh!" she exclaimed, breaking the surface. Lawson was just laughing. She turned and walked back to the bank with soaked clothes, and Lawson stopped laughing for fear she was mad. As she began shedding her boots, shirt, and jeans, though, Lawson felt a strong lump in his throat. He climbed on the bank and stripped down to his boxer briefs, and before he could lay his clothes in the sunshine along with hers, Lia was back in the water splashing him.

He turned and jumped back in the water, pulling her arm to the center of the pond and threating to dunk her underwater. They laughed and wrestled in the chest-deep water until he finally gave in, "OK, OK, I give," he laughed.

Lia sank down to neck level, covering her bra and cleavage. "You always give up this easy?" she taunted.

"I know when I've been beat," he grinned cautiously, pulling himself closer to her.

Feeling her heart skip a beat, Lia closed the gap between the two and wrapped her arms around Lawson's neck, resting them on his shoulders. Trying to swallow the lump in her throat, she closed her eyes as Lawson slowly approached her lips and let the moment happen. As their kiss became wetter with the clear deep blue water from the pond, she heard rustling on the bank.

Opening her eyes in time, she saw Sam bite the butt of Sorrel, causing him to trot off. Pulling back from one of the best kisses she had ever had, she told Lawson, "Your horse is running away."

Lawson spun around in the water to see Sorrel trotting over the dirt ridge, "Crap! Sorrel!" he yelled, not really expecting anything. "Hang on, I'll be right back," he said, wading out of the water and jogging over the ridge. Lia laughed at the sight of Lawson running after his horse in only his boxer briefs.

She stretched out and floated on her back with a peaceful grin. Lawson appeared without his horse. "OK, I need to borrow Sam," he said, taking the reins.

"I'll rent him to you," she joked, but he was in the saddle and breaking into a lope before he heard her. Then the funny sight of Lawson riding over the ridge on a horse in his boxer briefs made her laugh. *You just can't make this up*, she thought.

A few minutes later, Lawson and the two horses walked over the ridge. Lia waded out of the water and with the fear of one of the horses running off, they sat on the bank while their clothes dried out, holding onto the reins of both horses.

With damp clothes and carrying their boots, they came riding out of the ridge as the sky turned into waves of fire, the clouds breaking into a bright red in the setting sun. They rode close to each other, *the perfect ending to any day*, she thought.

Chapter 33

Sweeny leaned over the table and grabbed the syrup. "I don't mind handing it to you," Lawson replied.

"I asked you twice. What's wrong with you this morning? You seem to be in another world."

Not realizing he had zoned out, Lawson said, "Sorry, I've got a few things on my mind."

Lawson hadn't come down from his high from yesterday's trail ride with Lia; in fact he hadn't slept all that great, either. He had texted Lia early this morning wishing her a good morning, but hadn't heard back yet. Not worried, he took another sip of his coffee.

"Lia's world?" Sweeny asked.

"What?" Lawson asked, zoned out again.

Sweeny set down his fork, "OK, what in the world happened yesterday?"

Lawson smiled. "You didn't!?!" Sweeny said in a loud voice. "Shhh. No, nothing happened." He looked around at

everyone staring at them.

"Something happened."

"We went riding out of the stables and just had a nice evening."

The waitress returned to the table and refilled their coffee and waters. Dale had wanted to meet them for breakfast, but Cap had different plans, and the two of them ventured out to chase a possible lead of a small group seen in the Big Bend National Park. As they stuffed themselves with chocolate chip waffles and maple syrup, they never noticed Erika enter the restaurant.

"So everyone is out working and you two are enjoying breakfast," she picked on them.

"Someone has to hold down the fort," Sweeny replied with a mouth full of waffles.

"Fort or restaurant?" She pulled up a chair and ordered a cup of coffee.

"Where's Lia?" Lawson asked.

"At work. What did you do to her?"

Lawson looked up surprised, "Do? What's the matter?" he asked, concerned.

"I'm not complaining; she's been floating ever since she came in this morning. Even after she found out I left early yesterday, she still wasn't upset. Thanks." She held up her cup saluting him.

"Well, this one isn't worth shooting today," Sweeny pointed at Lawson.

Lawson went back to eating. "Did you guys ever catch any of the guys that had the delivery trucks prepared for them to cross the river?" She took a sip from her mug.

Lawson looked at Sweeny with a funny look. "No, we never did," he replied, thinking Sweeny had told her.

"Crazy that they had trucks waiting on them" she added.

"You'd be surprised at what we find," Lawson continued to

eat.

"How did you know about that?" Sweeny asked, relieving any thoughts he told her.

She quickly crawfished her story. "Oh, a friend said something. So what did you two do yesterday?" she hurried on, trying to change the subject.

"We just went horseback riding. Who is your friend?" Lawson asked.

Sweeny's radio, which was facing him on the table, came alive with Cap's raspy voice calling them. Sweeny collected the radio and walked outside to avoid disturbing the other tables of people. Before the door shut, Erika excused herself to the bathroom, leaving Lawson sitting alone with an unanswered question. Minutes later, Sweeny walked back in. "Cap needs us. He thinks they have a possible visual on Jose."

"Really!" Lawson jumped up and waved at the waitress, dropping a twenty on the table. He waited for a split second on Erika to come out, but Sweeny called for him from the door. *Strange,* he thought about Erika.

"Switch over to our channel," Cap replied before they could get out of the parking lot. Their truck tires smoked as Sweeny fishtailed, coming out onto the highway running with sirens and lights. The excitement of finally catching Jose was driving their adrenaline and racing heart rates.

"Go ahead, Cap." Lawson spoke into the mic on their channel.

"You boys go by and get a plain vehicle. I want to tail this possibility."

They looked at each other with the disappointment of not running hot to the scene where Cap and Dale waited. "10-

4. I'll get my truck," Lawson said. Empty water bottles and trash shifted in the cab as Sweeny made a strong U-turn in the middle of the street.

They wasted no time parking and running to Lawson's truck to catch up with Cap and Dale. They pulled their M4's and gear bags, throwing them into the back seat of Lawson's truck. "Cap, we're on our way," Sweeny replied.

"They are in a tan Buick heading west on Hwy 170. You can probably intercept them at the high school."

"10-4." Lawson raced to the parking lot of the high school. Lawson felt his pocket vibrate with a text, and already excited, he frantically pulled his phone out to see a text from Lia. "Sorry I haven't replied yet. Erika left me hanging and I had a ton of things to catch up on here. How is your morning?" the message read.

He tossed the phone to Sweeny, saying, "Answer this text. "Do I look like your assistant?"

Lawson started to answer and drive at the same time. "Give it to me!" Sweeny snatched the phone from his hand.

"Tell her—"

"I know what to say," Sweeny cut him off.

A half dozen turns later, Lawson pulled into the parking lot and positioned his truck so they could see the Buick coming down the highway, "Cap, we are at the high school."

"We've been made here. They are speeding your way. I've called in to the state police. We might as well take them down now."

Hunched over the steering wheel and staring down the highway, Lawson looked back at Sweeny, who was still texting Lia. "What are you saying?"

With a big smile, Sweeny replied, "Just what she needs to hear."

Lawson reached for the phone and Sweeny snatched it away, laughing and texting at the same time, "Honey, I loved watching your butt bounce on the saddle yesterday and wished I was the saddle—"

"Damn it, Sweeny!" Lawson left his seat, wrestling Sweeny for the phone before he sent the message. As the commotion was taking place inside Lawson's truck, they never saw the Buick turn off the highway five blocks before the school and bypass the high school and the state police that were coming from the opposite direction on Hwy 170.

"Here!" Sweeny finally gave in.

Lawson checked the text, which simply read, "Busy, I'll call you in a few."

"Ass!" Lawson said sitting back down in his seat just in time to see the state police pass them. Pulling out behind them, they saw Cap's truck come into view, and as the police pulled over to speak to Cap, Lawson and Sweeny pulled in behind them.

"Boys, you had to have seen them!" Cap yelled over the officers.

Sweeny and Lawson looked at each other, knowing the answer and with their expression, Cap knew they had missed them. "Well, Damn!" Cap pulled his cowboy hat off and slapped his truck with it.

"How would they know we were waiting for them? And that Cap called the State boys?" Sweeny asked Lawson.

"I don't know—it's as if they know where we are before we get there."

Then, simultaneously, they replied, "Dale's radio!"

Chapter 34

The doorbell sounded as Lawson walked in the pharmacy, and Erika poked her head around the corner from the store room. "Someone here to see you," she yelled at Lia.

"You don't have to yell in front of—" She realized it was Lawson as she walked out of her office. The warm smile that formed across her face gave Lawson the reassurance of yesterday's horseback ride. She motioned him over to the empty soda bar. "Can I get you something?" she asked.

Taking a chance and seeing that Erika had returned to the store room, he leaned over the counter and gave Lia a small peck on the lips. She looked toward the store room and not seeing Erika, grabbed Lawson by the shirt and pulled him back to her and gave him a long and passionate kiss. "Wow," he whispered.

"That's what I thought too," she replied.

"Do you treat all your customers like that?" he asked, smiling.

"Just the ones she likes!" Erika yelled from the back room.

"Stop being noisy," Lia yelled back.

Erika appeared from the door. "You two need to get a room," she added, throwing a roll of waded tape at Lia. "So, did you catch who you were after this morning?" she added, looking at Lawson.

"Not yet," Lawson answered, wondering how she knew. It was the second time in one day she had asked about cases that she shouldn't know anything about—and now it was the first time to give Lawson a suspicious attitude about her.

"Where is Sweeny?" Erika asked.

"He went to pick up Vicky." Lawson turned to Lia, adding, "Tonight is her dance recital. I know she'd want you to come."

"Are you asking?" Lia cocked her head and asked.

"Maybe?" He said, slow and dramatic.

She smiled, "I'd love to go."

"Don't worry about me standing here," Erika said.

"Do you want to go?"

"No, but thanks for asking." She walked back to the store room.

Lia signaled him to sit on one of the stools as she fixed him a chocolate shake. Everything on the bar and around it was still new from the lack of business she had, even with the promotion she had been doing. It was a bigger worry than she let on, but right then Lawson Caine was sitting across from her, and that was all the business she was thinking about, even if she was treating him to the shake.

"What time is Vicky's recital?"

"7 p.m. I can stop by and pick you up," he said, thinking it would be the first time he saw her house.

"That would be fine," she replied.

Finishing his shake, Lawson said, "I better head home—I've got a few things to do before tonight. See you at 7?"

"Yep." She took his hand and with a marker wrote her address.

Throwing a yellow cotton blouse in a pile of other clothes that she didn't think would work, Lia stood in front of her closet, scanning the other shirts hanging. *Nothing looks good!* She grabbed another shirt and stood in front of her mirror. *Nope!* She threw it with the others. Slipping out of the jeans she had on, she tried a pair of shorts with a long-sleeved, button down demi shirt. *Better!* She raced to the bathroom to fix her hair and makeup.

A knock on the front door echoed through the small two-bedroom house that was across Presidio from Lawson's house. Lia jogged to the door and pulled it open, "Come in, and give me a minute." She ran back to the bathroom, leaving Lawson standing in the doorway. He walked in, looking at the living room and kitchen, being as nosey as she was when she visited his house. A brown leather couch backed up to one wall of her living room sat across from a flat-screen TV mounted to the wall.

"Sorry if I'm too early," he yelled toward the bathroom.

"You're good," she yelled back, focusing on her eyes with a

mascara brush.

He made his way into the kitchen that was partially decorated with a few southwest pictures and a yellow Mexican ceramic plate. A picture of Lia and her grandmother sat on a small china cabinet, but Lawson picked up the picture beside it that was Lia and a slightly older man. "Who is this in the picture with you?" he yelled.

"That is Roberto. My older brother," she answered, looking around the corner.

"You don't talk much about your family," he said.

She smiled not knowing how to answer him. "You'd like Roberto. He is different than the others."

"Meaning he wouldn't disagree about you and me."

"You ready?" She appeared from the bathroom, not hearing his question.

"Yep." He replaced the picture and led Lia out to his truck parked in front of her house.

A few minutes later, they pulled into a parking space at the high school where Vicky's recital was being held. Cap and Sandra parked beside them.

Sandra jumped out with a big smile on her face and quickly made her way to Lia. "I'm so happy you're here," she said, hugging her tight.

Lia was happy with the greeting. "Thank you, me too."

They walked in through a set of double doors to an auditorium packed out with parents, grandparents, and what seemed like everyone else in Presidio. Sweeny was standing in the third row, waving as though he had been waiting for them all afternoon. "What's with all the hurry?" Lawson asked him. "It's one thing to hold a parking spot at a rodeo, but you try to hold seats at an elementary dance recital. These moms are brutal," Sweeny said, relieved he didn't have to hold them any longer.

"We need to work on getting these two to church," Sandra said to Lia, pointing at Lawson and Sweeny.

"It's starting." Sweeny pointed to the stage curtains opening, hoping she'd drop the church conversation.

"I'm not going to stop trying," Sandra gave Sweeny a look.

Two sets of girls came out dancing across the stage, and when the third set of girls came out, Vicky was in the middle. Her hair was pulled back and almost unrecognizable with the amount of makeup she was wearing. Lawson leaned past Lia to look at Sweeny. "How in the world did you get her to wear makeup?" he asked.

"Like pulling teeth," he replied with a "proud dad" expression.

"She's courageous!" Lia replied, just as Vicky made eye contact with her. The expression change on Vicky's face was as if light was just created. A big smile filled her face, and she lost her place in the opening dance routine, but she didn't care— Lia was there!

During the recital, Sweeny turned his head to Lia. "She hasn't danced this well ever. She really likes you."

"Oh, I'm sure she's dancing for you." Lia didn't know how to answer.

After the girls' final bow, the curtains closed. "I'm heading back. Lia, join me," Sandra said, pushing her way out of the aisle.

"We'll wait here," Lawson replied.

Sandra and Lia disappeared back stage, leaving the boys with Cap. "What did you think, Cap?" Lawson asked.

"It was good," he replied, thinking about his pack of cigarettes in his truck. "So you boys think these coyotes have Dale's radio?" he asked, changing the subject.

"Starting to make sense. They seem to know where we are since Dale lost his radio," Lawson replied. "Something else: Erika has mentioned two busts gone bad that nobody knows about."

"She was there when Dale lost his radio," Sweeny said.

Cap nodded, "Hmm."

Sandra and Lia returned with Vicky glued to Lia's side. "You did great, kiddo," Sweeny praised her, getting back a big hug in return.

"Can Lia go eat with us?" Vicky asked.

"I don't see why not," Lawson said.

The five of them headed out to Cap's favorite restaurant.

Chapter 35

With the truck idling and the parking lights on, Lawson and Lia listened to the sweet melodies of country music while parked out front of Lia's house. He wondered if she would ask him in, but wasn't sure what his answer would be. She was tucked back in his passenger seat on her side, facing him with her legs folded back and resting on the seat. He was talking about his friends in Paris, Texas, but she didn't hear a word; she just watched his lips moving, thinking tonight was perfect.

"Vicky sure does like you," he said, pulling her out of her trance.

"She is a sweet girl. Sweeny is doing a great job as a dad."

"He worries about it. He thinks she's around too many guys and not enough girls. That's why he made her join dance."

"Well, Lawson Caine, thank you for the date. It was fun," she said, sitting up.

He took advantage of her sitting up and gently reached around her head, pulling her face closer to his. Taking a deep breath and fighting against her racing heart, she closed her eyes in time to feel his lips against hers. The cab of the truck was dimly lit with the instruments and radio creating the moment. Lawson reached under the center console and lifted it, creating another seat for Lia to scoot closer without unlocking lips.

As things became more heated, she turned her body and straddled Lawson with the steering wheel in her back. She barely fit and started thinking maybe that wasn't such a sexy move after all. With the unexpected move, Lawson hadn't had time to move his arm and with it caught between them he tried to move it, causing her to move back enough that her back lay on the horn, with a car passing them honking, back thinking they were honking at them. Lia's eyes widened before they started to laugh together, and when she did, she honked the horn again, and this time the neighbor's front porch light came on.

"I think you've made your point," Lawson laughed.

"Yeah, we should call it a night," she said waving her shirt to cool herself down.

Lawson opened his door and helped her out first before climbing out behind her. They walked to the door holding hands, and being a chivalrous guy he stopped shy of entering the door. "Thanks for a great evening," he said.

Standing up on the threshold of the door, she kissed him one last time, whispering "Thank *you*." She slowly closed the door, watching him walk back to his truck. *Dang, he has a fine— Keep focus, Lia!* she thought to herself. *Should I have asked him in?* She smiled, pulling the collar of her shirt back, allowing cool air to cross her cleavage. She felt her phone buzz in her pocket, and pulling it out, she saw that she had missed several calls from her father and a text that read, "I know you were out with that agent! I don't approve of this! Call me ASAP!" *Well, crap!*

Early the following morning, Sweeny pulled up to Cap's house and carefully slid Vicky out of the cab, carrying her to the front door. She was still asleep and in her nightgown. Sandra opened the door and stepped aside so Sweeny, who was dressed in uniform, could carry Vicky to their spare bedroom and tuck her in the bed. Cap was waiting in the kitchen, also dressed in uniform. "Thanks, I didn't want Dale to be the only one there this morning. The state boys believe this is going to be a big bust."

"Part of the job," Sweeny shook his head.

"Get some sleep, momma and you take care of them." Cap kissed Sandra on the lips and patted Valentine on the head.

She and Valentine walked them to the door, saying "Please be careful." She closed the door.

Cap pulled out of the driveway and headed toward Hwy 170. Taking the mic off the clip, "Unit 121 to 167," he grumbled over the radio.

"167," Dale replied.

"Switch over," Cap implied to their channel.

"Go ahead, Cap."

"What's your 20?" Cap asked.

"Had to run back to the office. The troopers are staged near Bakers road. I'll be right back."

Cap replaced the mic. "Reports say they have almost 30 immigrants moving north, each carrying a large amount of drugs."

"So, Jose has them carrying drugs now," Sweeny replied. The headquarters in Presidio had received reports from informants that Jose had struck a deal with the Cartel family and had shot one of his own men. Tonight's bust would be the first with illegals carrying drugs.

Their patrol truck crawled in to Bakers Road with a half-dozen state police cars and officers staging for the bust. Cap stepped out and lit a cigarette; it was just after 2 a.m. and the first time in a long time they had been called out in the middle of the night.

"Good morning," one of the state troopers said in an energetic voice.

"Boy, he is too chipper this early," Sweeny said under his voice so only Cap could hear.

"Morning," Cap replied in his raspy voice.

"We are waiting here until we hear from one of our boys that—" he started to say before he was interrupted.

"Sergeant! The vans are coming this way!" a young trooper said, running up.

The state trooper studied the young officer for a second, then yelled to the group, "Everyone move to the second staging area! Move!" he yelled out.

Within seconds, every vehicle disappeared to a secondary staging area a mile west of Baker's Road and set up again—all but Dale. Since Dale had spoken to Cap on their own channel, he had forgotten to switch back over and missed the call that everyone was moving. He was speeding back to the staging area that he had left, Bakers Road.

Two Chevy vans pulled over to the side of Bakers Road and waited for the group of immigrants to meet them there. The coyotes had planned to load the drugs in both vans and leave the group to fend for themselves in an area that had nothing to support people crossing the border. Just as the coyotes were near the vans, they spotted a set of headlights speeding their way, and as the lights pulled onto Bakers Road, they ordered the people to run back to the river with the drugs. The headlights belonged to Dale's patrol truck.

"Where in the world is everyone?" he said to himself.

Two sets of headlights blinded him as the vans charged toward his truck, and holding his arm over his eyes he heard the sound of breaking glass.

"What in the hell was that?" he exclaimed, and just as he realized what the sound was, two more bullets entered his front windshield, missing him by inches. He ducked down and grabbed his mic, yelling "I'm taking fire!"

The state sergeant looked at Cap, "Is that your boy?"

"167! What's your 20?" Cap replied in his radio.

"Bakers Road!" The sound of gunshots could be heard through the radio. Sweeny ran toward Cap's truck before anyone said anything.

"Damn it, Cap! Your boy screwed this up!" the sergeant said.

Cap ignored the comment and ran after Sweeny, who was already sitting behind the wheel. Cap didn't argue and jumped in the passenger seat, shouting "Hit it!" Rocks sprayed the police cars as Sweeny jetted toward Bakers Road.

Nearing the road, Cap and Sweeny could see the cloud of dust surrounding Dale's truck and the red taillights of the two vans speeding south on Hwy 170. Sweeny slid to a stop, and a sudden fear of losing a team member overwhelmed him. "Dale!" he yelled, jumping out of the truck. Dale's windshield was littered with shattered glass, and the side doors were almost unrecognizable with bullet holes. Sweeny opened the driver's door to find the cab empty. He shined his light in the cab then around the truck.

"No blood," Cap said in a calm voice, looking through the blown-out passenger side window.

Three police cars slid to a stop behind Cap, with the others chasing the two vans. A shadow appeared from the field next to the road, "I had to bail," Dale said.

Sweeny felt his blood pressure go down. "Probie, you scared the hell out of me."

"Good thing you bailed out. No-one could have lived through this," Cap said, looking at his truck.

"What in the hell do you think you are doing!" The sergeant yelled, walking up. "We've worked for weeks getting intel and you screw it up in one night!" His voice rang out over the area.

"I didn't know that everyone had—" Dale started.

"And you are going to answer for this!" The trooper interrupted him and stuck a finger in his chest.

In reaction, Sweeny shoved the trooper, whose feet got tangled, dumping him into the ditch, and without words two other troopers jumped on Sweeny in defense of their sergeant. Dale, who wasn't going to let Sweeny fight two alone, grabbed one of the troopers by the back collar and dragged him to the ground, but the sergeant, who had regained his footing, tackled him to the ground and drove his fist into Dale's jaw. Sweeny was on his back with the other troopers holding him down as he struggled to get up and help Dale.

A loud explosion froze the officers in place. Cap racked another shell into his shotgun. "Another punch thrown is going to answer to me!" he barked.

"This isn't the old west! You're not going to pull out a gun and expect to get away with it," the sergeant bellowed back.

"It might not be the old west, but it's the old me!" Cap squinted his eyes.

Everyone got up and dusted themselves off. "You'll hear from my superiors," the sergeant replied.

"Do you think I give a shit?" Cap said with the shotgun resting on his shoulders.

The sergeant ordered his men back to their cars and to help with the apprehension of the two vans. The three set of taillights and flashing blue lights disappeared before anyone said anything.

"I'm sorry, Cap," Dale replied, wiping the blood from his mouth.

"Don't worry about it. Let's get this truck back to headquarters," Cap said.

"We might need to leave it for the incident report," Sweeny replied.

"Screw the report."

Sweeny and Dale didn't argue and followed Cap back to headquarters.

Chapter 36

The following morning, Cap called a meeting with the team members at their favorite diner over breakfast.

The guys were sitting around the table drinking coffee and scarfing down eggs and bacon, waiting on Cap to give them a lecture on getting along with other agencies. The conversation started with Vicky and her dance recital, then led to Dale's truck being shot up. "Last night was an honest mistake. You boys stay in communication at all times when we're out on a call," Cap said over his steaming cup of coffee.

"And don't punch the sergeant," Terry laughed, looking at Sweeny.

"I didn't punch him. He fell over his own feet," Sweeny defended himself.

"OK," Cap silenced the table. "We have to go to Marfa today."

Everyone stopped eating and looked at Cap. "For what?" Lawson asked.

"You boys get in a fight with the state boys and you don't think the chief has something to say?" Cap answered. "Don't worry—I told him everything, so he's more upset with me."

"But let me guess," Sweeny replied, sitting up straight and pulling his mug to his face, "Do you think I give a shit!" He mimicked Cap in a raspy voice. Everyone laughed.

Cap smiled, "Something like that."

"Howdy, boys," a voice spoke up behind Dale and Lawson. Lia stood behind them with a small wave.

Lawson pulled a chair beside him for her. "Good morning," he said.

"Sounds like you boys had an interesting night. You OK?" she asked Dale.

"I'm fine," he sheepishly answered, eating a piece of bacon. "How'd you hear about last night?" Sweeny asked.

"Front page of the paper," she said.

Cap looked up from his plate, then surveyed the room for a paper. After finding one on the edge of the diner bar, he sat back down and read the article with his reading glasses on the edge of his nose. "What's it say about me?" Sweeny joked.

"Well, hell," Cap replied in a low voice. Everyone looked at him ready for the story. "One of the state boys totaled his car in the chase last night."

"Was it Sergeant Serious?" Sweeny joked.

"No, but whoever wrote this article didn't spare us any fault. Finish up and lets go," Cap ordered.

"Where are you going?" Lia leaned over and whispered.

"Marfa. Chief wants to see us. Can you come over tonight for supper?"

"I have to go see my family, but I could come over later?" she answered, not wanting to tell him that it was really her dad that wanted to see her.

They worked on finishing their breakfast while telling Lia about last night's fiasco with the state police. She laughed with Sweeny's exaggeration of the story and how he wrapped it up with his creative boxing match. "Say, where is your sidekick?" Sweeny asked, insinuating Erika.

"I can't keep up with her these days."

"Well, we're gonna be at our swimming hole tomorrow if you girls want to stop by," Sweeny said.

"What makes you think I want to see you swimming in the buff?" she laughed.

"It's every girl's dream." He stretched his arms out.

"Y'all finish up," Cap interrupted, dropping a five on the table and standing to retrieve his hat from the back of his chair. "A word," he said to Sweeny, nodding to the door.

"What did I do?" Sweeny grinned and followed Cap outside as he pulled out a smoke.

Looking back in to make sure the boys had stayed and that Lia was still seated with Lawson, Cap asked Sweeny, "You think that girl is part of this missing radio?"

"Lia? Nah, she doesn't seem like she'd be the type. Erika, on the other hand, is a little shady."

"Get close to Erika—I have my suspicions about her."

"We'll do that," he answered Cap.

"Just you. I don't care for Lawson to know. He's not thinking clearly, being in love and all." Cap pulled in a puff of smoke and exhaled.

"Lawson? He's not going to let anything interfere with his judgement," Sweeny defended him.

"I'm not saying he's slacking. But he's defiantly love blind," Cap said as the door opened with the rest of the team coming out to join them. Lawson walked Lia to her jeep, gave her a small peck on the lips, and told her he'd call this afternoon. "Load up," Cap said as Lawson rejoined the group.

Later that day, they were sitting in a small conference room with the Chief Patrol Agent chewing them out about the fight with the state police. Everyone sat in the room quietly, not making a sound, not because they were intimidated by the chief, but because it was Cap's order. After the chief was done with his lecture, he asked Cap to join him in his office. The guys walked out and gathered in the lobby of the station.

"Heard you guys went rounds with the state boys last night," another agent asked, walking through the lobby.

"Something like that," Lawson answered since everyone was sulking over their lecture.

"Ah, I wouldn't let it bother you. Bunch of us are going to shoot pool and have a few beers after our shift. Y'all interested in a little tournament between your station and ours?" the agent asked.

The guys looked at each other. The tournament sounded OK, but the beer sounded better. "You're on," Terry answered before anyone else.

In the chief's office, Cap sat patiently in front of the chief and his desk. "Cap, the last thing we need is stories like this one." He pointed at the paper.

"You know that's just a bunch of crap!"

"Maybe so, but the public doesn't know that," the chief answered, with Cap agreeing.

"Alex Sweeny is pushing the limits with this agency, and if I hear of anything else with him involved, I will suspend him."

"Sweeny didn't do anything that I wouldn't have," Cap replied.

"That could be the problem. You're teaching the young agents the old school of doing things. This is a new era, and the tactics you were taught don't fit anymore."

"It's kept my boys alive." Cap stood, adding, "If you don't like the way I do things, then fire me. If not, I'm too busy to sit here and listen to your political BS. Why don't you grab a side arm and join us for a ride? This office is ruining you," Cap pointed at him.

"James," the chief's voice became softer, "you are one of the best in this organization. I knew that when you and I came through the academy together. But I'm getting heat from the highers to be more presentable to the public. The war on the border is a hot topic right now, and I'm just asking for you guys to do your job and lay low."

"That's all I've ever asked for," Cap answered and started out the door.

"James?" Chief called. Cap stopped and looked back. "You know I'm on your side."

"See you on the battlefield," Cap replied in a raspy voice.

Walking through the lobby heading for the door, Cap fumed, "I need a beer."

"Funny you should say that," Sweeny replied as the team followed him out.

***

Lia sat on the faded floral couch in the living room she had grown up in with her father standing over her pointing his finger at her. She sat silently listening to his lecture on why Mexicans shouldn't mix with Anglos, but when he made the comment that it was his decision, she lost it.

Rising to her feet, she snapped, "You are not the boss of me anymore, and I will date whoever I wish. This isn't the old days and predetermined love."

"Sit down and show me the respect I deserve," he ordered her.

"Show me some respect by understanding me," she flipped it back on him.

He paced out the door and came back in, "If you choose to see this American, then you are banned from this house."

With those words, Lia's mother walked in, "That is being too harsh. She is my daughter too."

Her father threw up his hands and stormed out the front door. Lia looked at her mother and said quietly, "Mom, I really like him."

With a stern look and following her father outside her mother replied, "You better love him if you're willing to bring this between your father and yourself."

Outside with her husband, "What is it about this guy?" she asked Lia's father. "I've never seen you this upset."

"I don't like him. I wish I could tell you, but it's something about him," he replied, staring off in the distance.

Chapter 37

The lights of Ojinaga flashed in the windshield of Lia's Jeep driving home. Several mom and pop bars were open with drunk men littering the streets. Lia continued to wipe the tears that had formed in her eyes leaving her home and drizzle down her cheek leaving mascara lines. The words from her father about respect felt like a knife grabbing deep into her heart, she had always worked hard at show her father the upmost respect but felt like a failure with this fight. Her phone buzzed with a text from Lawson. After reading it she put it back down on her seat and took a deep breath hoping it would help fight back the tears but had the opposite effect, she broke down crying.

Lawson sat in his living room with the only light coming from his TV. He watched the blank screen on his phone resting on the armrest of his chair hoping for a reply, nothing. *That's strange.* He thought. Then the thoughts of her father entered his mind, he knew with her going to see her family there was always a chance he would ask her about him. He became engrossed in a movie and after 30 minutes into the show he felt himself doze off. It was either the few beers he had or the trip that made him tired but it didn't matter only that he didn't hear his door shut and the footsteps that entered the living room.

A hand reached out and pulled on his shoulder, opening his eyes and startled he saw the figure standing in front of him. With tears still in her eyes Lia stood in front of him with her hands to her side and silent. Lawson knew the tears were from her father but with her in his house he felt like he knew her decision. He opened his arms inviting her to crawl in his lap, not expecting her to bury her head in his chest sobbing. He held her tight against his body letting her crying not saying a word.

The following morning Lia woke to the bright sun light shining through Lawson's bedroom window. His sheets and feather comforter felts warm to her body and as she stretched her arms and sat up a sense of peace came over her. She tip toed to the living room where Lawson was still asleep on the couch wrapped in a blanket. She sat on the edge of the couch, "Good morning." She whispered in his ear.

"Did you sleep ok?" He asked rolling over without his eyes open.

"I did. I would have slept on the couch."

"Nah, I sleep here sometimes." He lied trying to be a gentleman.

"I'll make us some coffee. What time do you have to be at work?" She asked walking into the kitchen.

Lawson waited for her to leave the room and made his escape to the bathroom. "I am taking the day off." He replied while peeing.

She laughed hearing him in the bathroom, "You know, I might just do the same if you want to hang out?"

"Ok." He said standing in the doorway with a toothbrush in his mouth.

She covered her mouth, "I bet my breath is bad?"

"I have an extra tooth brush."

"For all the girls you have over?" She grinned.

"It's a four pack." He gave her a smirk.

"I'm joking." She walked past him and shut the bathroom door leaving him holding his toothbrush.

Walking back out she was greeted with a cup of coffee, "Wanna go fishing?" He asked.

"You know how to wow a girl in the morning." She picked.

"It's just fishing." He answered.

After loading his fishing gear, going by Lia's house, and stopping by the diner for breakfast with the other team members, that were mad he took off the day, he and Lia were on their way to a farm north of town with a few good fishing ponds. The sun was on a vengeance with its heat but the steady south wind kept the day from being a sweltering loss.

Lawson stopped and visited with the farmer on their way in and returning to the truck a strong smell of suntan lotion hit him. Opening his truck he found Lia with a guilty look, "I'm sorry. I should have stepped out before putting it on." She said holding a bottle of 35spf.

"You're not going to burn." He said rolling his window down. Driving to the first pond, that had an aluminum boat pulled up on the bank, the farmers yellow lab followed them.

"Hello." Lia knelt down and petted the dog, "Are you going to help us fish today?"

Lawson loaded their poles, tackle box, and cooler in the boat but before he could push it farther in the water the lab climbed in. "Come on boy, get out." Lawson pulled on the dog.

"Can't he go?" She asked. He looked at the dog and thought that it probably wasn't a good idea but let him go anyway. Paddling out the yellow lab sat at the feet of Lia and panted happily with her scratching his head. Baiting one of the poles he handed it to Lia who casted it toward the center of the pond.

"So your father isn't happy with us dating?" He asked knowing the answer but felt like they needed to talk.

"No, he's pretty upset. I'm sorry."

"What do you think?"

"I'm here." She smiled.

"I don't want to come between you and your family."

She thought back to her sister's wedding and the comment that Roberto made about her dating whoever she wanted. "I'd like for you to meet Roberto."

"He's not going to punch my lights out for dating his sister?" He joked.

"Ha, no. Roberto is the sensible one of the family. Maybe the rebel. He was the first to leave home and be successful."

"What about the brother I met on the street?"

"Carlos? He's my brother, but he's bad news too."

"Would you say you're more like your mother?" he asked.

"Grandmother," she didn't hesitate.

"Grandmother?"

"I'm not all hippie and medicine woman like her. But I was the first to finish college and start a successful job—until I decided to open my own pharmacy," she laughed.

"Seems like you're doing pretty good at the store."

"I am on the medicine side... huh, maybe I am closer to my grandmother than I realize," she shook her head. "But I wish the soda bar would take off."

Before Lawson could ask another question, her pole doubled over with a fish on the other end. She screamed with excitement. "Reel it in!" Lawson exclaimed.

She reeled and got the fish close to the boat, only to have it make a run, pulling out more line. She reeled it in again, only to have it run again, and after the third time, the yellow lab stuck his head over the side of the boat. "Back up, boy," Lawson said.

"He just wants to see the fish. What is it?" she yelled, fighting the rod and reel.

"Catfish, and a big one."

The fourth time she got the fish near the boat, it surfaced, and that was all the yellow lab needed to be invited into the water. The boat rocked back and forth with the dog baling in the water. Lawson did his best to coach the dog back to the side and out of the way of Lia and her fish. He paddled beside the dog and grabbed him by the collar. Pulling him in, Lawson didn't anticipate that the weight of the dog might shift that side of the boat downward. Lawson went in head first.

Surfacing, he could hear Lia bellowing with laughter, still reeling the fish. Lawson felt the muddy bottom of the pond and hurled the dog back in the boat, which also pushed the boat, Lia, and a wet lab toward shore. He felt his pocket, thinking *my phone!* He quickly turned it off and looked back at the boat that was a good twenty yards away, with Lia still laughing and holding a nice-sized catfish.

Chapter 38

After a shower and a change into dry clothes, Lawson cleaned the only fish they had caught, her fish. Their trip ended after Lawson dried out and having a soaked phone, they went back to his place and put it in a bowl of rice to dry it out. With the two large catfish fillets, Lawson sliced serval limes, and placing them on his grill, he cooked the fish with a blackened spice. Lia opened two beers and walked out on his back deck, sitting in one of the chairs.

"Today didn't turn into a total bust. I still caught a fish," she grinned.

The house phone rang from inside. "Hang on, Mrs. Fisherman," he said, opening the door to answer the phone. Returning, he reported, "That was Sandra—the church is having a drive-in movie night for a fund raiser and wants us to come."

She sat her beer down. "Better not drink this, then. I forgot it was tonight."

"Cap wants me to bring my patrol truck. He thinks we need good PR since Dale's incident the other night."

"I don't think this town thinks any different of the Border Patrol. Y'all have been as fair and nice to people as any other agency," she said, trying to replace the cap on the beer bottle.

"I'm not even sure what they are playing tonight."

"*Cars*. It has some good high-speed scenes that y'all can take notes for your driving."

"Ha-ha. You're one to be talking," he pointed his spatula at her.

***

Jose Emmanuel stood over the slain body of one of his coyotes with smoke still rolling out of the barrel of his pistol. Four other coyotes stood wide eyed and shaken, praying that he wouldn't turn the barrel toward them. "We have a radio just for this reason!" he screamed at everyone in the room. "And now I have to explain to the Cartels that we have to try again to get their drugs across the border." He referred to the night the bust went bad.

"You keep shooting your coyotes, you're gonna have to smuggle people in yourself," Carlos replied, sitting calmly in a chair behind the four men.

"I don't need any advice from you," Jose said.

"No, we need to throw the border patrol off their game." Carlos stood and walked in front of one of the men. "Pull that squirrelly man to the side and tell him to give the wrong info to the Border Patrol. A huge crossing 50 miles north of here. 200 people."

Jose stood listening to Carlos and nodding his head in agreement. "To make sure we keep them there, take 50 people, but don't let them cross," Jose added.

"We cross in the same place that went bad the other night," Carlos said, then turned back to the man. "Find out if they have sensors in that area?"

Jose started pacing the floor, then stopped and faced another man. "I want you to smuggle a small group over tonight. Rape the women and start a new tree in that area. That will give them something to look for." He smiled and began to walk away, then stopped again. "No! Rape the women, then kill them. That will stir the nest." He walked out of the room.

***

Three border patrol trucks parked side by side with doors wide open for the kids to climb in sat in the front row of the drive-in movie. Lia wasn't able to get her door fully open before a little eight-year-old girl pulled herself into the seat holding an extra ice cream sandwich. "I saved this for you!" Vicky said excitedly.

Lia looked at the smooched bar and smiled, "Thank you sweetie, you read my mind."

"She's been watching the highway for Lawson's truck for 20 minutes," Sweeny said, relieved Lia came with Lawson.

Sandra hugged Lia. "Heard you caught the only fish today," she said, smiling.

Lia looked back at Lawson, surprised he would confess. "I did. But I couldn't have unless someone held back the dog."

"Ha-ha," Lawson pulled their folding chairs out of the truck. "Where's Dale?"

"He's patrolling," Cap said sitting in a chair eating an ice cream bar Vicky had given him.

"Is he gonna be OK alone?" Lawson was surprised Cap let him go out after his truck got shot up.

"He's got Valentine."

Lawson looked at Sandra. "And you're good with that?"

"I feel safer that she's watching after my boys," Sandra smiled.

"That and it was her idea," Cap answered.

Lia was having trouble opening the ice cream bar, and when Vicky wasn't looking, Sweeny traded the smashed bar for a new colder one. "Thanks," Lia grinned.

The sky darkened with the sun setting and a little south wind continued to keep the area cool. The screen came alive with the start of the movie, and the sound flowed out of the vehicles that were parked throughout the pasture. Vicky managed to crawl into Lia's lap and snuggle under a light blanket she had brought. Vicky explained every scene as if she were a Hollywood critic. "You don't need to tell her everything," Sweeny said.

"She's fine," Lia smiled.

"So you let her show you up today?" Sweeny turned to Lawson.

"What can I say?"

"How'd you cook it?"

"Same way I showed you last time, with limes and blacken seasoning," he said, seeing someone with popcorn. "Do you want a popcorn?" he asked Lia.

"Sure, and water!" Vicky answered.

"Yeah, that would be great," Lia laughed.

"Cap, Sandra?" Lawson asked.

Cap held up two fingers. "What about me?" Sweeny asked.

"Come on, you're going with me." They walked through the cars and trucks to a make-shift concession stand with the priest serving everyone.

"Well, good evening, gentlemen. Popcorn and a coke?"

"Popcorn and water," Lawson replied.

"Noticed you brought Ms. Gonzales to the movie. Something going on there?" the priest asked, being nosey.

"I don't know, Father, maybe."

"She is a great girl with a successful business. Does this mean I'll be seeing you in church?"

"Yes sir, possibly so."

"Takes a girl to get him there," Sweeny replied.

"I'll take it, however I can get you gentlemen there. And I know Ms. Gonzales has a friend that comes with her occasionally; perhaps you too can join us?" The Father looked at Sweeny.

"Father, I might not be the one you want in church," Sweeny grinned.

"I don't believe that. Mr. Sweeny, God's doors as well as mine are always open to you."

Sweeny's grin left his face, "Thank you." Lawson noticed the nice remark stuck a nerve. Walking back to their trucks, Sweeny commented, "He has never stopped asking us to church."

"No, he's persistent."

Sweeny turned to Lawson. "I need to start going with Vicky. Doesn't seem right that I'm playing basketball and she's with Sandra."

Walking up, they handed everyone their waters and popcorn and found Vicky had fallen asleep on Lia. Sweeny gently ran his fingers through Vicky's hair. "I guess we played too hard today. Do you want me to take her?"

"She's fine," Lia smiled.

Lawson and Lia softly talked back and forth during the movie while Cap concentrated on the screen, not having seen the movie. Sweeny, however, sat quiet in deep thought, glancing at Vicky sleeping on Lia. The thought of him robbing Vicky of a mother began to haunt him.

Chapter 39

As Lawson drove to church, he kept thinking of what he was going to tell Sweeny about not playing basketball. He kept playing the conversation in his head, knowing Sweeny would pick on him relentlessly. Lawson's surprise was not that Lia was waiting for him on the front steps of the church dressed in an off-white, sheer panel dress that complemented her figure, but that Sweeny was standing next to her in khakis and a short sleeved, button-down shirt.

"What are you doing?" Lawson asked Sweeny.

"Going through open doors," he replied just as the priest walked out. "Good morning," Sweeny greeted the priest and walked in.

"Doors?" Lia asked.

Lawson smiled. "Something a friend said last night." He winked at the Father walking in.

The priest looked to the sky with his hands cupped. "Thank you!"

"I better text Dale and Terry and let them know we aren't going to make it," Lawson said, pulling his phone out.

"Where is Vicky?" Lia asked Sweeny, but before he could answer she sprang in Lia's lap.

"Wow! You look pretty!" Vicky greeted her. "I'm glad someone noticed."

"You look pretty," Lawson looked over his phone at her. With a big smile across her face, Sandra sat beside them with Cap sliding in at the end. He saluted to Lawson and Sweeny with his index finger to his eyebrow.

"Please tell me you are coming to lunch," Sandra said to Lia.

Lia looked at Lawson, then back to Sandra. "Yes, ma'am." "Where is Erika?" Sandra asked.

Lia turned and checked the door. "I don't know—she said she would be here."

"Regardless, she is welcome to lunch too."

The service started with the pipe organ playing. The priest delivered his message about seeking a relationship with God before worrying about a bunch of rules. The sermon seemed to be spoken more simply and directly than normal, and Sandra knew he was speaking less "churchy" for the boys sitting in her pew. Lawson glanced several times at Lia and the slim dress she was wearing that defined her dark, sexy legs. *I can't think like this in church. Dang, she is good looking!* He didn't hear much of the sermon.

Sweeny, on the other hand, was drawn into the message and heard something he had never heard. "It would be pointless for a bunch of perfect people to come to church. The church, which is a group of people, not a building, is for people who struggle in life," the priest affirmed from behind the pulpit.

After the service, the priest was at the door shaking people's hands and being surprised at the comments that it was his best sermon. Sweeny and Vicky walked out holding hands. "It was good," Sweeny said.

"Which part?" the priest quizzed him.

"Your part." He shook his hand and followed Cap and Sandra to their truck. The priest pulled the doors closed and walked back up the aisle. Jumping in the air, he tried to click his heels together and fist pumped into the air.

The court next door was empty. "Wonder where Dale and Terry are?" Lawson asked.

"I wonder where Erika is, too."

"Dale said he went home after nobody showed up," Sweeny said, helping Vicky in his truck.

"I'll meet you at the Garrett's." Lia gave Lawson a small peck and head to her Jeep. On the way, she noticed the pharmacy lights on and people inside. "What in the world," she said out loud and pulled in. Opening the door, she found Erika behind the soda bar and three Mexican men sitting on the stools eating ice cream.

"Hey, I had some friends I wanted to show the soda bar. How was church?" Erika asked.

"Good," Lia replied, confused. "Can I speak with you for a minute?" She pointed outside.

Following her out, Erika said, "What's up? I'm sorry I stood you up for church—"

Lia stopped her. "Why are you here? We don't open on Sunday."

"We need the business. I'm sorry; I thought you'd be happy I'm trying to bring in business."

"I am. No, I'm sorry. This is just a side of you I'm not used to."

"Lia, we've been friends since childhood. When have you ever not known me?"

Lia hugged her. "Lock up when you leave."

Erika saluted her, "Aye, aye, captain." Lia left knowing that Erika was acting weird, but just couldn't put her finger on it.

Walking back in the store, Erika watched Lia pull away. "She's gone."

Lia's brother, Carlos, walked out from the back. "My sis would lose her cool if she knew I was here. Where were we?" he asked.

"You were saying we had an even greater resource on the inside of the Border Patrol agency than Erika," one of the men replied.

"Yes we do, thanks to Erika." Carlos kissed her on the cheek.

Lia lightly knocked on the Garrett's door, and Sandra opened the door, saying "Young lady, you know you don't have to knock here." She hugged her again.

"I wasn't sure. How can I help you?"

"Set out drinks; come and I'll show you."

They passed through the living room, where Cap had a football game on the TV and the boys sitting on the couch with their feet propped on the coffee table. Dale was sitting on the end of the couch. "You made it?" Lia smiled.

"Yep. I'm not talking to you," he said, staring at the TV.

"What did I do?"

"You ruined our basketball game."

"Come by the store and I'll give you a free root beer float."

"OK, sold!" He winked at her.

She continued into the kitchen and gathered glasses with ice in them and placed them on the table. Once everything was set, Sandra called everyone in the dining room, and standing by the table, Cap blessed the meal and they took their seats.

"Erika couldn't make it?" Sandra asked.

"No ma'am. She was at the store when I drove by with a few men she was treating ice cream to. Kinda weird for her. I'm a little worried about her," she said, retrieving a roll from the basket being passed around.

"I'm sure she's just finding a new place with you and—" She stopped her sentence.

Lia wasn't sure why. "New place?" she asked.

"I might be putting my foot in my mouth. Since you and Lawson have started dating."

Lia grinned at Lawson. "Yes ma'am, maybe so."

After the food was devoured, Cap kissed Sandra on the forehead and called Valentine to follow him back to the living room to catch up on the game, the boys following right behind him. Vicky stayed to help Lia clear the table. Sitting in his chair, Cap turned to Lawson, saying, "You and Dale grab us a beer from the frig."

Lawson looked at Dale. "Probie." The two disappeared into the kitchen.

"You getting close to Erika?" Cap quickly asked Sweeny. "I need to call my informant."

"The squirrelly man?"

"Yes, he seems to know more than anyone. I'll set it up." Lawson and Dale returned with the beer.

Chapter 40

With so much vacation time accrued and the willingness that Erika was giving at the pharmacy, Lia and Lawson decided to take another day off and go hiking. One area that Lawson hadn't spent much time was near Chinati Peak. Other agents had caught immigrants near the area, but it was far out in the middle of nowhere. The area had been off limit to the public for years, and with most of it private land, it was near impossible to get there. The land owner had told Lawson any time he wanted to hike, he was welcome.

The dome-shaped hump of the peak could be seen from miles and is highest point of Presidio County at over 7,700 feet above sea level. The peak is surrounded by other smaller jagged peaks and rugged canyons. One of the agents had shown Lawson a trail that wound through the cliffs and brush-filled drainages to reach the peak.

They had started out early in the morning to beat the heat, but it had quickly caught them before they were a quarter of the way of their 15-mile hike. Lawson had their only backpack, with Lia closely trailing him.

She stopped briefly on a ridge that over looked the desolate land. "Wow."

"It pretty up here," Lawson agreed, stopping to pull out a water bottle and handing it to her.

"Thanks—I hope I can make it up there." She looked up at the summit.

"If not, we'll go as far as we can. They say it's an awesome view."

"Onward." She pointed up the scarce trail.

They reached a point in the trail that was almost straight up, and Lawson helped pull Lia up to several flat ridges. They could see the top, and with no evidence that others had been there, he felt they could do it. Lawson pulled himself up to the finial peak and reached down, grabbing Lia's hand and hoisting her up to him. Both of them took a deep breath and turned in a 360, admiring the view from over 7,000 feet.

"This is probably the prettiest place I've ever been to. I can't believe this is here," she said with her hand over her eyes shading the sun.

Lawson set down his backpack and took out another bottle of water. "Yeah, I can't believe I haven't been here yet."

They sat on the dirt watching clouds passing over the dried land and throwing shadows on the mountains and valleys. Lawson felt Lia's hand work it way on his, and he turned his hand over and locked fingers. With a soft, warm smile from her, he leaned toward her, giving her a kiss. She scooted close and snuggled up beside him—a place that she felt safe.

After soaking up the endless view, they began their trek down, Lawson going first and helping Lia where he could. They reached a point that she was worried about and had expressed concern about going up. "It's OK," Lawson said. "Just put your foot here." He pointed at a small ledge. She placed her boot on the ledge, but without warning the rocks gave away and her foot came crashing down on Lawson's hand that was holding his balance.

It was if everything went into slow motion—Lia's foot stopped at Lawson's hand, but he lost his footing scrambling to regain his place. Lia fell to her stomach and grabbed Lawson's hand. He looked behind him at the drop to a sharp canyon many feet below. "Lawson!" Lia screamed. He struggled to hold her hand and the rocks at the same time, and he could feel the blood running down his leg from his knees as they brushed up against the side of the mountain. "Lawson! I can't hold—"

The last thing Lawson saw was Lia leaning over with her hair falling on both sides of her head, desperately reaching for him. Then... nothing.

***

Sweeny parked alongside the service station that sat across the corner from the yellow and pink building where Lawson and Sweeny had met their informant before. He looked both ways, then walked across the street and up the stairs that led to the room above the shop below. Opening the door, he found the informant sitting at a table pushed up against the glass windows.

"*Hola*," Sweeny said before walking in.

The man remained sitting and waved him in, and Sweeny thought it was a little strange even for this man. He scanned the room, seeing that an empty chair sitting across the table from the man was pushed back. "What can you tell me?" Sweeny asked.

"Please sit," his informant pointed to the chair.

"I'm good," he said, sliding away from view of the window. "Senor, everything is fine. Please sit." The man offered the empty chair again. It wasn't that the man was acting strangely that made Sweeny nervous, but the wink the man gave him—

the signal that Sweeny had taught him if he was ever made.

The man stood and put his arm around Sweeny, trying to push him to the chair, but Sweeny felt something sliding into his back pocket. "I'm good standing," he replied, needing a distraction so he could buy time to get out. Pulling his phone from his front pocket, he said "Hello?" He faked an incoming call, then said, "It's in my truck." He spoke loudly into the phone. Covering the phone, he looked at the informant. "I've got to run to my truck, but then we'll sit and have our talk."

"*Ce*," the man replied.

Sweeny quickly made his way to his truck, cautiously looking over his shoulder. He knew by the actions of his informant he was being watched, if not targeted. Cranking the truck, he had it in drive before he shut his door and sped off. Turning onto the highway that led back to the check point to cross the border, he noticed a blue truck swing past a slow car and speed toward him. Not taking any chances, Sweeny floored his truck and made it to the check point before the blue truck could get close. He watched it turn around.

"Sweeny, how are you?" A border agent asked at the checkpoint.

"Good," he said, still watching the blue truck drive off in his rearview mirror.

After crossing, he pulled over and reached for the piece of paper that the man had stuffed in his back pocket. The note told him that Jose Emmanuel's men had come to him and asked him to give Sweeny false information about a crossing north of Presidio. The real crossing would be at the same place the two vans were caught. It also read that they had a radio from one of the agents and that a girl named Erika was working for Jose. Sweeny set the note down and thought for a moment, then picked it up and read on. What he read next was the most chilling part of the note. There is also someone else helping Jose, but the informant didn't know who it was—they were being very quiet about this person, mostly because it was a Border Patrol Agent.

Sweeny dialed Cap's number on his cell phone. "Cap? We need to meet."

***

"Lawson!" Lia screamed. She leaned over the edge as far as she could, but couldn't see him. She screamed his name repeatedly, but heard nothing back. Panic mode set in. She slid down the trail on her stomach to a ledge that stuck out farther than the others, her knees and elbows bleeding from the jagged rocks.

"Lawson! Please answer me!" She lay on her stomach and stretched out over the edge. From there, she could see Lawson's limp body below on a large rock. She made her way down farther and reached him just as he was gaining consciousness. Kneeling beside him, her instincts kicked in, and she began to examine him. "Where are you hurt?"

"My head," he moaned.

"Can you move your legs?" she asked.

He sat up blinking his eyes, trying to regain his vision, "Yeah, I don't think anything is broke."

She took out a bottle of water from the pack he was lying on and had him drink. "Let's get you down." She helped him to his feet.

"I'm OK," he said as he became more aware.

They sat for a time letting him get his wits, then headed down. The six-mile hike out felt like 100 miles with Lawson's head pounding and both of their legs and arms chewed up by the rocks. Reaching his truck, she opened the passenger door for him. "What are you doing tomorrow?" he smiled, climbing in.

"Sleeping in," she said to herself, walking around to the driver's door.

Chapter 41

"What the hell happen to you?" Sweeny said, seeing Lawson limp in the office.

"I took a fall on Chinati Peak yesterday," he answered, pouring a cup of coffee. Lawson and Lia had cut their hiking date short yesterday after they made it down the mountain. They spent the remainder of their day watching TV from his couch.

"You went without me?" Sweeny asked, throwing a pen at him.

"That's a pretty view from up there," Dale piped up.

"You've been?" Lawson asked, surprised since the landowner was protective of his place and only allowed people he knew there.

"Yep," Dale answered, not giving any information.

Lawson struggled to sit in his chair with his uniform pants rubbing against his skinned-up knees; Lia had told him to bandage them, but he insisted on letting them air out. He felt like he had been run over by a truck and with his head still pounding, he was gorging himself on Advils. Today he was looking forward to staying in the office and catching up on paper work from the last few days he had been off, but that suddenly changed when Cap walked in.

"Heard you say you were up on Chinati Peak yesterday?" Cap asked, holding his mug.

"Yes, sir."

"Good, you can show us how to get there. Just got a report of some immigrants seen in the area this morning."

"You got to be kidding?" Lawson asked, not because it was a coincidence, but he wasn't interested in seeing the area for a while.

"Load up. Sweeny, ride with me." Cap slipped on his cowboy hat and refilled his cup.

On the drive to the mountain range, Dale rode in Lawson's truck with Terry trailing them in his new SUV that the other team members gave him grief over.

"Why in the world would coyotes lead anyone to that part of the world? There's nothing there and nothing for miles," Lawson said out loud.

"There's water and shelter. Plus the farmer is never around," Dale answered him.

"And how do you know this?"

"Don't say anything, but a few weeks ago I snuck out there and climbed the peak. I've been looking at it ever since I got here," Dale replied.

Lawson cut his eyes at him. "You know better than that." "I know."

"It's quite a view," Lawson said, turning right onto the highway heading north.

Sweeny waved the smoke lingering in front of his face, rolling down his window. "You know those things are going to kill you," he said to Cap.

"Hmm!" was the only answer he received.

"Do you think this is part of the diversion your informant was talking about?" Cap asked. Sweeny had filled him in on everything that had gone down in Mexico with his informant.

"Not this far out. Plus this diversion he was suggesting would take place on the river and no one would cross."

After a 45-minute drive, the three border patrol trucks pulled up to a very familiar parking area. Lawson had been there less than 12 hours earlier. With the dust settling, Dale unloaded the ATV from the back of Lawson's truck and parked it beside Sweeny's ATV. The peak of Chinati towered out of the barren land, casting a shadow toward the Rio Grande. A rusted, beat- up old truck parked feet from the agents. Lawson knew the truck that belonged to the land owner.

"Gentlemen," an elderly man greeted them.

"Good morning," Cap shook his hand.

"It could be," the old man answered. He had seen a small group of immigrants walking late yesterday evening, with two small girls.

"Why do you think anyone would be out here in the middle of nowhere?" Lawson asked the man.

"The only thing I can think is that they are meeting someone out here for a ride. These valleys are tough and a rugged terrain, no place for young people. That's why I called." He walked back to his truck, adding, "You can leave those here and follow me in your truck." He pointed to the ATVs.

They followed the old pickup down a winding dirt road that stopped at a knobbly ravine with dried underbrush and a small trail leading down. Dale looked down the lopsided, rocky path and then back at Lawson. "We're not going down there?" he asked.

"What's the matter, Probie? You worried?" Sweeny laughed.

"Part of the job," Lawson patted him on the shoulder. "Grab your packs and extra water—we're going on foot from here."

Cap gave Valentine some water by pouring it in the palm of his hand, "Let's go," his raspy voice ground out.

Within their first half mile they picked up on footprints and trash left behind. The Advil was beginning to wear off, and Lawson could not only feel his head pounding again, but wished he had listened to Lia about wrapping his knees. He rolled his pants leg above his knee, giving it relief from rubbing against the fabric.

"Dang, Bub," Sweeny said, looking at his scrapes. "Carpet burns are hell, aren't they?" he laughed.

"Shut-up," Lawson rolled his eyes.

Valentine, who was on point, froze before walking around the next bend in the trail. Cap signaled for everyone to stop and drew his SIG Sauer from his holster. Sweeny stepped in front of Cap with his pistol pointed up and slowly rounded the bend. As each agent came around the turn, they remained silent at the sight that was waiting them. A small tree proudly decorated with women's underwear stood in the next turn of the path.

Sweeny was the first to holster his weapon. "Son of a Bitch! Another rape tree."

"By the looks of it there is no age," Terry said, pointing at a small pair of panties that would fit a child. "This is sick!"

"This is what those volunteers showed you guys, wasn't it?" Lawson said.

"Yep."

"Take it down and bury it." Cap ordered.

Sweeny snatched a bra off the tree and caught the glimpse of something out of the corner of his eyes; at first he thought he was seeing things. After a few blinks, he pointed around a large rock nestled beside the trail. "Cap."

Cap walked up to Sweeny's pointing hand to find two young girls and an old woman lying in a pool of blood. "Call for air support and the sheriff's department," he said before examining any farther.

"Why?" Dale asked.

Lawson snapped his finger and gave him a dirty look. "Don't question!"

Sweeny knelt down beside the young girls. "They can't be 14 years old."

"By the looks of it, they were killed execution style." Cap pointed out the rope that tied their hands behind them.

Sweeny cocked his head. "Why? Why kill them here in the middle of nowhere? And execution style. That doesn't make any sense." His blood began to boil.

Cap stood up and looked around at their surroundings. They were close to a narrow canyon and an enormous cliff. "Dale, stay here. Sweeny, you come with me. Lawson, you and Terry scout west of here."

Lawson swung his M4 off his back and into his hands, and Terry followed suit. It wasn't long before they found themselves in a narrow valley with sage brush blocking their way. Lawson spotted a set of prints in the dirt. "Let's check out what's past this brush."

"It's probably a dead end. Maybe we should check out another area?" Terry suggested.

Lawson pointed at the footprints for Terry and squeezed past the brush. Within 20 feet, they came to a cavern washed out by rainfall. Lawson shined his light in the dark entrance, and beyond the opening were supplies, water, ammo, whisky, and cans of food. "Looks like we found something they didn't want us to." He pulled out his radio. "Cap? You and Sweeny make your way back to us."

Chapter 42

The team stood in front of the entrance to the washed- out cavern discussing whether they should take the items or stake it out. "I still say we stake it out,"
Sweeny argued.

Lawson ducked back into the cavern and examined the items once again, coming out into the light. "Don't you think this is a little strange?" he asked the team.

"What do you mean?" Cap asked.

"Everything is neatly organized in the cave. No trash. And why would coyotes execute people so close to a hide-out?"

Cap shined his light back into the cave. "Unopened whiskey? Hmm!" He tugged at his mustache in thought, then surveyed the area again. "We're being watched," he said in a quiet voice.

"How do you know?" Terry asked.

"This whole thing is a set-up or diversion." He looked at Sweeny. "I want everyone to walk back to the tree. Sweeny, slip off the trail before we reach the tree and scout the area. From here on, we make channel 32 our private channel." He started back up the trail.

Reaching the tree, they found Dale sitting in the shade and the tree freed of its horrific decorations, now buried in the scorched earth. He stood and walked to the team as they covered the bodies with emergency blankets from their backpacks. In the distance, a flash of light caught Lawson's attention, and he made his way behind Cap. "Someone is watching," he said.

On the next ridge, over 1,200 yards away, sat three Mexican coyotes perched on a large rock watching the team through a rifle scope attached to a Remington 30-06. "I think Jose's plan is working. The patrol agents are staying at the bodies," one of the men reported.

"Where is the other one?" another man asked.

"There's four. That's all of them," the first coyote answered. "No! There was five," the other man argued.

The man with the rifle turned and gave him a deadly stare. "Don't argue with me. There's four."

Within 200 feet, Sweeny squatted behind a boulder with his M4 resting beside him. "Cap?" he whispered in the radio.

"Go ahead," Cap's raspy voice replied. "I got three men within 200 feet."

"Hold your ground for a moment," Cap answered and looked at Lawson.

Sweeny looked over the rock in time to see the men arguing over the radio they had in their position—Dale's radio. "I saw the old man talking in the radio, but nothing came over ours!" one of the men said.

"You don't have the volume up!" another snapped at him.

Sweeny took advantage of them arguing and slithered on his belly closer to the men, bracing himself between a large sage brush and another large rock. He rolled over to his back and pulled his .40 cal H&K service weapon out, setting it beside him for quick grab. He carefully looked over the rock at the men who had their backs to him, a perfect place for Sweeny. *I have the perfect advantage to take them now,* he thought. *Come on, Cap, what are you waiting for?* He looked down at his radio, then leaned up on the rock and drew down on them with his M4. Taking the safety off, he started to tell them to freeze, but another cold barrel buried into the back of his neck. "Set the rifle down slowly, Senor," a voice said from behind him.

"Sounds like Sweeny has the advantage," Lawson said to Cap.

"As long as he doesn't do something stupid," Cap replied and put the mic to his mouth. "Sweeny?" he called into the radio. No answer. "Sweeny?" he said with a louder voice, but still there was no response. Cap turned and looked up at the ridge, thinking Sweeny couldn't answer because he was too close to the men.

Lawson saw movement on the ridge and pulled his M4 to his cheek, looking through his 4.5X14 Leupold scope. "What are you doing? You're going to give us away!" Terry snapped.

"Too late! They have Sweeny at gun point!" Lawson replied, taking off down the trail toward the ridge. He heard Terry's footsteps behind him, and looking back, wondered where Dale was. Valentine passed him as if she knew exactly where to go. Lawson's radio mic, which was clipped to his shoulder, came alive with orders, and by the sound of Cap's voice, the Sheriff's Department was on scene.

After barking an order to launch the helicopter, Cap called to Lawson. Knowing that Lawson was running and didn't have time to answer, he told him that the men were making their way south, which worked to Lawson and Terry's favor.

They jumped a small crevice and ran up a flatter incline to the ridge that Sweeny was on. Gun shots echoed through the mountain range, and Lawson and Terry stopped and looked at each other.

After three more shots rang out, Lawson set off again running up the trail, and Valentine zoned in on the shots and disappeared ahead over the trail. Four more shots sounded through the valleys as Lawson reached the ridge. He pulled his M4 to his cheek and advanced toward a large boulder with Terry to his side pointing his sidearm in front of him. Taking cover behind the boulder and out of breath, they could hear the shouts of one of the men. Lawson peeked around the rock to see a lifeless body lying face down in the dirt and Sweeny crouching in a small crevice with his H&K.

"I don't know how he does it," Lawson looked at
Terry. "What?"

"Sweeny has managed to kill one of them and is barricaded behind a rock," Lawson replied in relief that Sweeny was OK. He ducked around the rock again and whistled.

Sweeny looked directly at Lawson and gave him a big smile and thumbs up. "What do you want to eat for supper?" he yelled at Lawson.

"What did he say?" Terry asked.

"Don't ask," Lawson rolled his
eyes.

Terry looked around the rock at Sweeny. "Hey Terry! You coming to eat with us tonight?" Sweeny asked with a grin on his face.

"What are you having?" Terry replied.

Lawson pulled Terry back by the back of his shirt. "Will you two stop horsing around!" Four more shots ricocheted off the rock Lawson and Terry knelt behind, and Lawson gave Terry a dirty look.

"We could have grilled chicken!" They heard Sweeny yell from his post.

Terry raised his head so he could hear him. "BBQ?"

"Damn it, Terry, you're just egging him on," Lawson pulled Terry back down.

"Honey or hot!" Sweeny yelled back.

Lawson looked back around at Sweeny's position to find only his hat sitting on the rock and Sweeny gone. Lawson stretched out and looked to his left, but no Sweeny. Then he heard the conversation start again, "We should put bacon in with the baked beans," Sweeny said, kneeling beside Terry.

"And potato salad," Terry replied.

"Are you freaking kidding me?" Lawson was pissed.

Both Terry and Sweeny started laughing. "Relax. I just saw Cap sneaking up from the backside of those two men. Give him a few seconds to get in position," Sweeny said. Three shots rang out from a .308 rifle. "There's Cap now." Sweeny scurried around the boulder with his M4 pointed in front at the two men that had their hands up with Cap drawn down on them. "Cap! You would give John Wayne a run for his money," Sweeny replied, then demanded the two men lie on the ground face down.

"There's only one Duke," Cap said walking up with his weapon aimed at the back of the head of one of the men.

"Will y'all please get serious?" Lawson said, pulling his handcuffs out.

"What's his problem?" Cap asked out loud.

"He's upset because Sweeny and I were talking about supper tonight," Terry answered, cuffing the other man.

"What are y'all having?" Cap asked.

Lawson looked up at Cap. "Really?"

Chapter 43

Sweeny and Lawson were finishing up their report when Cap walked in and asked for Sweeny to join him in his office. Lawson didn't question Cap taking his report partner since Sweeny was in a threatening situation the day before. Many times Cap would talk with the members that were in hard positions and advise them to speak to the agency psychologist, which many times they would turn down.

"Shut the door," Cap told Sweeny.

"What's up?"

"You OK from yesterday?" Cap sat behind his desk.

"I'm fine. Why did you really call me in here?"

"One of the coyotes we arrested yesterday has been ratting out everyone this morning. We know that Erika works for Jose and that she had Dale's radio. We also learned there is another mole that is somehow involved with the agency."

"Lia?" Sweeny asked, sitting up.

"That is my first guess."

"Makes sense. Lawson is going to freak out," Sweeny replied.

"Lawson doesn't need to know any of this. I want you to get close to Erika and soon. Jose has a big payroll, and if you could somehow get on that, we could take down the whole operation."

"You're asking for something that could take a long time to get in."

"I think he is desperate since he has joined up with the Cartels. Just let me know everything. Only the chief and I know about this."

A knock came from the door. "Come in!" Cap yelled.

Lawson opened the door and handed a copy of the report to

Cap, asking "You OK?" as he looked at Sweeny.

"Yeah, I explained to Cap that I was gay and you and I have been secretively dating for over a year," Sweeny said, grabbing Lawson's butt.

Lawson slapped his hand and rolled his eyes. "You need anything else, Cap?"

"No, we're good. Take your boyfriend." Cap pointed at Sweeny.

Lawson and Sweeny left Cap's office to see Dale and Terry drive off, heading back to the Chinati area to finish with the investigation of the cavern and the rape tree. Lawson refilled his coffee. "You and I are heading to Big Bend today."

"I'm with you… sweetie," Sweeny grinned.

***

"Lia! Phone!" Erika yelled from the office.

Lia finished bagging a couple of bottles of medicine and handed it to an elderly lady with a "Thank you, Mrs. Richards." She turned and walked into the office. "You don't have to yell," she said to Erika, picking up the phone. "Hello."

"Lia," her father replied on the other end.

"Good morning."

"Your mother is telling me that I am too hard on you about seeing this border agent. We are having a family meal tomorrow, and we want you there." Lia heard a commotion in the background. "I mean, I would like you to bring your friend so that I can meet him."

Lia couldn't believe what she was hearing. The first thought that crossed her mind was that Roberto talked her father into allowing her to bring Lawson home, but she didn't care. "Really?"

"I'm not saying I'm OK with this... just that I am willing to meet him."

"Papa, you will like Lawson. He is very nice and a gentleman—"

Her father interrupted her. "I'm sure he is. 7 o'clock."

"Yes sir. Thank you," she said.

"OK. See you tomorrow. *Hola.*"

Lia hung the phone up with a huge grin. "What was that about?" Erika asked.

"Papa wants to meet Lawson."

"Wow, the old man is coming around. And speaking of the infamous border patrol agent," Erika pointed at the door as Lawson and Sweeny walked in.

"Come here," Lia waved Lawson back to the office.

"OK?" Lawson looked at Erika with a puzzled expression. Lia shut the door and told him her good news. Lawson was a little hesitant about the invitation since her father was adamant about them not seeing each other, but didn't express it with Lia so happy. She wrapped her arms over his shoulders to give him a welcome hug, but their hug quickly turned into a passionate kiss.

Keeping his arms around her, he leaned back. "I've got to go to Big Bend today, but would you like to have supper tonight?" he asked.

"Of course. But instead of cooking, let's just go get something."

"Sounds good." He leaned in for another kiss.

They walked out to find Sweeny and Erika sitting across from one another at the soda bar. "This is really good," Sweeny said, holding up a spoon of ice cream from a tall glass.

"Yes it is, if I can keep Erika from giving away all of it." Erika held up a five-dollar bill, showing that Sweeny had paid.

Lawson turned back to Lia and gave her a kiss, saying "I'll call you later today."

Sweeny dropped his spoon in the glass. "See ya," he said to Erika and followed Lawson out.

They were no more than a mile away from the pharmacy when Lawson received a text from Lia. "Sweeny asked out Erika!"

"You asked Erika out?" he said, holding his phone.

Sweeny shrugged his shoulders. "Yea, I figured it wouldn't hurt anything."

Another text came across Lawson's screen. "Double date tonight!" she added with a smiley face.

"We're double dating tonight?" Lawson asked Sweeny.

"Sounds good to me."

As the day progressed, their conversation changed back and forth from Sweeny and Erika to why the cavern was set up. Sweeny was biting at his lip to tell Lawson about his informant and what he had learned about the major smuggling happening soon, but Cap had asked him to keep it under wraps. What bothered him the most was that he felt he was betraying

Across Borders

Lawson's trust by setting up Erika with the possibility that Lia was involved. It was a long and painful day for Sweeny; he had never kept a secret from his best friend.

That night, Sweeny insisted that they take separate vehicles. Lawson was confused as to why, but didn't press the issue. Lawson and Lia were sitting at the table when Erika and Sweeny walked in. "Look at the cute couple," Lia commented.

Tugging his shirt, Sweeny replied, "We can't help it."

"You two are meant for each other," Lia added.

Erika gave her a smirk. "We are just eating." Sweeny pulled out her chair for her, then sat.

After a night of eating and laughing at their stories, Sweeny excused Erika and himself. Walking out, "Where are we going?" Erika asked with a seductive grin.

It was tempting to Sweeny, but he was focused on one thing. Getting in, he asked, "I don't know—where do you want to go?"

"What does your place look like?" she asked.

Earlier in the evening he had dropped off Vicky with Sandra, and though his house was unoccupied, inviting Erika to the place his daughter slept was out of the question. "What about the stables? Nice view of the stars."

"That sounds nice," she batted her eyes.

They pulled around to the back of the horse barn, and Sweeny turned his headlights off, allowing their surroundings to be lit up with stars from above. He let the tailgate down, and both of them sat with their legs dangling over the end watching the moon rising over the mountains. A light breeze blew around the barn, and with the insects singing, their night came alive. Erika wasted no time pushing Sweeny down on his back and climbing on top of him, forcing their kiss.

Taken by surprise with Erika's forced aggression, Sweeny wondered what it would hurt if he just let happen whatever Erika was planning, but the thought of his daughter came to mind. *Dang it!* He pushed her back. "Hang on a second," he said, grasping for air.

Erika sat up. "What's wrong?"

"Nothing, I was planning—"

She interrupted him, "Planning? I'll stop you there," she said and climbed off.

Sweeny looked at her, puzzled. "I was saying that I was planning to watch the stars and visit for a while."

"I didn't come out here to visit. Are we going to do this or not?" She started to unbutton his shirt.

He sat up and changed the tone of their conversation, "OK, the truth. I asked you out because I am looking to make some extra money on the side."

"I'm not paying you for sex."

"Ha-ha, I know you're in with some of the coyotes and I think I can help—"

She interrupted him again. "I'm not in with anyone," she replied, offended.

"Erika! I saw you take Dale's radio, and I have seen you with others that are known coyotes. I'm not interested in turning you in—I'm interested in making money," Sweeny convincingly argued.

She gave him a baffled look. "I only took Dale's radio for a joke. Someone took it from me."

"Erika, I'm not stupid."

She stepped down from the tailgate and paced the ground, saying "How do I know I can trust you?"

"Because I would have reported and/or turned you in last week," he became more convincing.

"And if I was involved, how would you make money?"

"By making sure no one is around the areas the coyotes plan to smuggle people across. But only legit coyotes, not these guys that are leaving people to die," Sweeny said. *Come on! Buy this!* he thought.

Erika walked to the cab of the truck and dug through her purse, Sweeny followed her to the passenger side. "How do I know I can trust you?" she asked from inside the cab.

"You can trust me on this," he lied.

Just as Sweeny was taken off guard with her aggressive move on him in the back of the truck, he was even more surprised when she wheeled around and stuck a .38 cal revolver in his face, "And if you do anything to—"

The whole area came alive, not with the stars and insects, but with the half-dozen agents popping out of the shadows with their M4's pointed at Erika. "Drop the pistol!" one of them yelled.

Sweeny shook his head. "Why in the hell did you come out!" he growled.

One of the agents took her by the arm and forced her to the side of the truck. "Maybe so you wouldn't get shot," the agent replied.

"She wasn't going to shoot!" He kicked the dirt, angrily insisting "Damn it! I had this!"

"Sweeny. You're what I thought you were, a fraud!" Erika exclaimed with her face buried in the side of his truck.

"Maybe so, but you and every coyote are going down. Rape and kill young girls? They will pay with their lives!" Sweeny replied.

"Pray they don't get to your little girl," she hissed with an agent cuffing her.

"Sweetie, anyone that comes near my family will lose more than their life."

The agent spun Erika around to walk her to an SUV, and with a demonic glare, she tossed back over her shoulder, "You better build a fort. We're coming after everyone, especially that little girl of yours. There's a nice tree that needs decorating."

One of the agents pushed her face into the side of the SUV.

"Get that bitch out of here," Sweeny replied with chills of fear running up his spine.

Chapter 44

The following day, not a word about Erika being arrested was breathed by anyone involved, under Cap's orders. Lawson texted Lia three times during the morning before getting a reply at noon: "Not happy right now. Erika stood me up at work. I have no clue where she is. Pick me up at 6 to go to my family's house."

"What's that about?" Sweeny sat on Lawson's desk.

"Oh, she's pissed. Erika didn't show up this morning. You sure you don't know where she is? You haven't said much about what you guys did after you left."

"Like I said, we drank a few beers and watched the moon rising. Nothing big." Sweeny clinched his teeth; he hated lying to his best friend. He was more worried about Lawson finding out that Lia was involved with the coyotes.

Dale walked in, announcing "Terry and I are heading back up north."

"Be careful," Sweeny replied sitting back down at his desk.

Dale looked at him with a puzzled expression. "Ok...." He didn't recall Sweeny ever saying to be careful. "Cap," Dale said, slapping the door-jam of Cap's office walking out.

"Hang on to that radio," Cap replied.

Dale laughed, "Yes sir." He waved at Sweeny and Lawson and walked out of the office. The wind had picked up and dust was swirling in the parking lot as Dale picked up his pace and jumped in the truck with Terry. Sweeny watched from the window as Terry's truck disappeared.

"What was that about?" Lawson
asked. "I can't say 'be careful'?"

"It's just not you," Lawson said, shuffling papers. "I'll be back," he added heading to the administrative assistance office.

Sweeny stuck his head in Cap's office. "We're going to have to tell him by tomorrow."

Cap nodded his head. "Tomorrow."

Lawson stayed close to the office during the afternoon, helping with unfinished reports and talking with the sheriff's department about the three bodies found the other day and the stash of phony supplies. Sweeny was sitting at his desk just before 5 o'clock checking his email, and reading something that didn't resonate well with him, he made a bee line to Cap's office, pulling the door shut. "The Sheriff's office doesn't think we have enough on Erika to keep her! What the hell?" Sweeny fumed.

"I was on the phone with them earlier. She has lawyered up, and what I am being told is that they only have her on the radio thing—which she is sticking to her story about it being a joke."

"She confessed to me at the stables!"

"Whether she did or not, it looks like she is slipping through the cracks," Cap replied.

"Cap, she threatened my family. She directly threatened Vicky. You and I both know that she is very well connected and could easily come after us," Sweeny's voice shook.

Cap sat up with the tone of Sweeny's voice. "You can bet your ass nothing is going to happen to Vicky or yourself. We'll make sure of that. They are holding her another 24 hours, and unless we come up with more evidence, she is going to walk. Head home—you've had a stressful day."

Sweeny snatched his keys off his desk and headed to his truck, thoughts of moving Vicky to his parents' place in Houston crossing his mind, but the thought of running wasn't. He sped to Cap's house to pick up Vicky, then headed to their favorite restaurant.

Lawson, freshly showered and dressed, walked out to his truck twirling his keys on his index finger. Nervousness wasn't even close to describing his emotions as he cranked his truck and headed to Lia's house. Before he could put his F250 in park, Lia was skipping down the steps, dressed in shorts and a casual t-shirt with a pullover. She made it to the passenger door before he had time to step out and open the door.

"You ready?" she asked in an excited voice.

"I guess," he answered.

"What's wrong?" she asked, definitely sensing something off-key.

"Just nervous."

"Don't be—my mother is excited you're coming, and Roberto is looking forward to meeting you."

"And your father?"

"You wouldn't be going if he wasn't interested in meeting with you." She leaned over and kissed him. "Everything will be fine."

"Why would you let her bring this border agent here?" Carlos asked his father.

"If Lia is dating this man, then maybe I should meet him. Why are you so afraid of him being here?" Lia's father looked at Carlos over his glasses.

"Afraid! I'm not scared. Just stupid to invite him here. I'm going to get a drink!" Carlos stormed out of the room.

Lia's mother stepped aside, allowing Carlos to enter the kitchen. "Thank you," she said, looking at Lia's father.

"Don't thank me yet. I only said I would meet him." He went back to reading a book he was holding.

As Lawson turned into Lia's family's house, a red heeler puppy ran out to meet them. Lawson took a deep breath and opened his door, and Lia picked up the puppy and grabbed Lawson's hand. "Come on," she grinned.

The front door opened to a woman wearing a floral apron and a big smile. "Amalia," Lia's mother called her.

"Mama, this is Lawson Caine. Lawson, meet my mother."

"It's nice to finally meet you," he said as she shook Lawson's hand.

Lia's father appeared behind her mother, "And this is my father. Papa, this is Lawson."

Her father reached around her mother and shook Lawson's hand. "Please come in," he said.

As they walked into the small mortar and stone home, two smaller children ran into the living room and each hugged one of Lia's legs. "This is my little sister and brother," Lia said, trying to shake free of their death grip.

They continued into the kitchen, where Roberto was walking in the back door. He smiled, giving Lawson a sense of easiness. "This must be the famous Border Patrol agent I keep hearing about," Roberto grinned and shook Lawson's hand.

"*Famoso*? Ha!" Carlos said from the kitchen table with a glass of tequila sitting in front of him. Lawson recognized him immediately from meeting him a few weeks back with Lia, and he wondered if Carlos was still packing the black-handled pistol.

"It's nice to meet all of you," Lawson said, casually looking down at Carlos, who didn't look up.

"Please, let's go to the back and eat. Everything is ready." Lia's mother ushered everyone outside.

In the back of the house, two of the picnic tables were pushed together and covered with a red-and-white-checkered table cloth. Smoke was still pouring from the grill sitting on a small brick patio only feet from the table. Everyone filed out of the house and gathered around the two tables. Lia and Lawson sat on one end close to her father and Roberto while her mother walked around the table making sure everyone had their plates with piles of food. Carlos stumbled out of the back door and took a seat at the opposite end of the table.

"How long have you been with the Border Patrol?" Roberto asked, starting a conversation.

Before he could answer, Lia's father piped up. "We don't need to bombard Mr. Caine with questions."

"Papa, how else do you start a conversation?" Roberto spoke to his father. It was clear to Lawson that Roberto was not as intimidated by him as the rest of the family.

"It's OK. A few years now," Lawson answered.

"Mr. Gonzales, Lia tells me you are a plumber," Lawson said to her father.

Carlos coughed loudly, choking on a piece of meat, then started laughing, *"Fontanero?"* He referred to plumber in Spanish while laughing. Lawson wasn't sure what was funny about the question.

"Carlos!" Lia's father snapped at him. "Yes, I am," he answered, looking back at Lawson.

Lia stepped in with a question to redirect their awkward conversation. "Roberto, how long are you staying this time before journeying out to another world trip?"

"Yes, Roberto, how long till another trip?" her father repeated the question.

Chapter 45

Lawson was relieved that Lia's father was accepting him sitting at their table, but could easily tell he was keeping his distance with his conversation. Roberto kept the table laughing at his last adventure in the Caribbean and picking on Lia about childhood stories. Everything was going great until Carlos, who had had more drinks during their meal, stood up and asked a blunt question: "What are your intentions with my sister?" he sputtered out.

"Carlos! Sit down—you're drunk, and nobody wants to hear from a drunk," Lia snapped at him.

"I don't, sis. You bring home this gringo and we're all supposed to OK with it?" he answered, stumbling back.

"Go sober up," Roberto stepped in.

"I want the *culero* to answer!" Carlos laughed and taunted Lawson.

Lawson wasn't sure why Lia's father was silent during Carlos's outburst, but he looked at Carlos. "We are friends," he answered, staring down Carlos.

"Are you banging her?" he laughed.

"Papa!" Lia begged her father to step in, but it was clear he was keeping quiet. "Mama!" she turned to her mother.

"Carlos, go inside," her mother insisted.

Lawson turned to her father, who was steadily staring him down. It was clear that his welcome was over. Lawson nodded and turned to Lia's mother. "Thank you for having me, but I believe I better leave."

Lia didn't argue with Lawson wanting to leave and stood with him, but Roberto stepped in, saying "Carlos, go inside or I'll—"

"You'll what?" Carlos started laughing. It was at that moment that Lawson realized that Lia's father was scared of Carlos.

Lia and Lawson walked through the house to head to his truck when Lia stopped and looked back. "I'll meet you at the truck," she said, walking back toward the back yard.

"Are you sure?" Lawson asked, but she answered his question by walking through the back door. Lawson wound his way through the small house and out the front door, where he was greeted by Carlos.

"You come back here, and I'll kill you! Understand?" Carlos pulled his black-handled pistol from his waist, but before he could bring it down pointed at Lawson, Lawson blocked it with his left hand and sent his right fist crashing Carlos' jaw, lifting him off his feet. The pistol hit the ground before the limp body of Carlos, and Lawson tossed it into the bushes that lined the front of the house.

Lia's little brother, who had followed Carlos, saw the punch and ran to the backyard, shouting, "Papa, Papa, Lia's boyfriend knocked out Carlos!" The chair that her father was sitting in fell to the ground as he rushed through the house to find Lawson still standing over his son. Before Lia and Roberto could round the house, her father threw a punch toward Lawson, who sidestepped it and pushed him away, causing him to fall. All Lia saw was her father and brother on the ground with Lawson standing over them, fist drawn.

"Lawson!" she screamed.

"Get in the truck, Lia!" he demanded, knowing the area was getting more and more hostile. She began to say something, but he repeated his order. "Get in the truck!"

Lia started to cry and looked at her mother, who was making her way to the front. She mouthed the words to Lia, "Go." Lia saw Carlos coming to and knew that if she stayed things could get even worse, so she climbed into the truck, looking back at her family. Her father was being helped up by Roberto; her mother was standing in the door holding her younger sister, and her drunk brother was picking himself up—not the family dinner she had ever imagined.

"Why!" She screamed at Lawson with his truck speeding out of their street.

"Why? He pulled a gun on me!" Lawson answered, confused about why he was being yelled at.

"My dad?"

"Your brother! Your dad just fell." Their weight shifted as he rounded a corner.

"Stop!" Lia yelled at him.

He gave her a puzzled look. "What are you doing?" he asked, still driving.

"Pull over! Now!" she screamed again. Lawson pulled into an abandoned store parking lot. She opened the door before the truck came to a halt and stepped out, slamming the door and walking away from his truck.

He threw the F250 in park and stepped out. "Where are you going?" he called out, but she didn't reply. "Lia!" he called again, but she was totally tuning him out, and he could only watch her walk off down the busiest street of Ojinaga. The sun had set, and the city was beginning to darken with nightfall, a few street lights flickering as they turned on. She waved down a car with an older couple in the front seat, and as Lawson watched, she slid into the back seat and disappeared around the corner.

What the hell? Screw this, I don't need it! He climbed back into his truck and slammed the door. His tires peeled out on the loose rocks as he aimed toward the border, fuming. The scene at Lia's family's house played over and over in his head: *What could I have done differently?* The thing that stuck out was that her father never stepped in, giving him the biggest clue that he wasn't welcome.

He slammed on his brakes, pulling over to the side of the street, *No! I'm not going to let this happen.* He spun the truck around and raced to the place he knew Lia was going—her grandmother's.

Stopping at a stop sign, he could hear his phone buzzing with a text message. He searched the seat and console, but figured it was on the floor. He unbuckled his seat belt and reached for the phone that had slid against the passenger door. It was a message from Dale: "Call me." *Not now, Dale.* He continued his race to Lia's grandmother's house.

In the distance, he could see the car with the older couple coming out of the dirt road that led to her grandmother's house, *Dang, they got here fast.* He turned down the now dusty road, thinking *I hope this turns out better.* He parked in front of the clay shack with the porch he had repaired last time he was here. The blue heeler met him on the front porch, and he bent down and petted him. The door opened and Lia's grandmother stepped out wearing her unusual attire. She was carrying something in her left hand. "Lawson," she greeted him.

"Abuela." Lawson returned the greeting. "Can I see her?"

"She is upset. Why don't you let her cry out whatever has her upset?"

"I don't think she understands—"Lia's grandmother interrupted him, "Her family?" She smiled and nodded her head. "Amalia has had a tough time growing up with a troubled family." She grabbed Lawson's hand and led him out from under the porch and toward his truck, where she turned his hand over and peered into it before letting go. "You are still heading toward death! You must take action now."

"Why do you think I'm heading to death, and how would I take action?"

She handed him a small hand-woven dream catcher with red and white feathers dangling from leather ties. "Place this above your headboard for a few nights and bring it back to me."

Lawson stared at the dream catcher. "I want to talk to her." "I am sorry."

With respect to her grandmother, he opened the door to his truck. "I hope she knows how I feel about her."

"Me too," Lia's grandmother replied.

Lawson drove out, and turning onto the blacktop, he dialed Dale's number. After a few rings, Dale answered. "Hey, Dale, what's up?"

"Sweeny isn't answering his phone. I'm still at the office and an attorney keeps calling demanding the report of Erika's arrest. What do I do?" Dale said.

"Erika? What report?"

"It's news to me too. Evidently Sweeny arrested her on smuggling charges. What do I say to this attorney?"

"Nothing! I'm on my way in now!" Lawson hung up, confused, and dialed Sweeny's number.

Chapter 46

With Sweeny not answering Lawson's phone call, Lawson sent a text, "What is going on with Erika? Why is she arrested? Call me!" The message sent, Lawson lay in bed awake during most of the night, continuing to replay the day with Lia's family. He picked up his phone to send her a text, only to set it back down for the 10th time without sending it. *What would I say, what could I say?* It did look like he fought both her brother and father.

While he was contemplating whether to call in sick, his phone finally rang with Sweeny's return call. "Why haven't you called?" he asked.

"Sorry, I'll explain everything today. You need to head in, we just got word that Jose and the Cartel are moving a historic amount of drugs today." Sweeny didn't give Lawson any time to answer and hung up.

"Well, crap!" Lawson rolled out of bed. He quickly jumped into a cold shower to wake himself up, even though it was a sleepless night. He finally shot Lia a short text, asking "Can we meet today?" He snagged his gear bag and walked out looking at his phone, but finding no reply. Driving to the office, he noticed that the pharmacy was closed, and an elderly lady was standing at the door with her hand shielding her eyes looking in the door.

Pulling into the crowded lot behind the office, he parked and walked in. The office was unusually packed with agents and deputies, and when Cap noticed him, he waved Lawson to his office. "Glad you could join us," he commented, with Sweeny, Dale, and Terry already sitting.

"Glad I was kept in the loop!" Lawson answered, staring at Sweeny.

Cap caught his attention. "We'll have time to explain that, but right now we need to focus on the facts of what is going down. We know that Jose has planned a diversion north of here while he leads a massive exodus in the Big Bend Park. Our plan is to send decoy agents to the diversion and stage a large number of deputies and agents close to the Big Bend area."

"How do we know this?" Lawson was getting the feeling he had been kept out of more than just Erika's involvement.

"We have inside information," Cap replied.

Lawson thought for a moment, then connected things together. "I don't know the extent of Erika's involvement. Is Lia in jeopardy?"

Cap took a deep breath and looked at Lawson. "We don't know if Lia is involved or not." He looked at the other agents. "Y'all give us a minute," he said to the others.

They started to walk out. "Not you," Lawson pointed at Sweeny. "Why are you two keeping vital information from me?"

Sweeny closed the door. "Because we weren't sure if you would be thinking clearly."

"What?" Lawson's voice could be heard in the other office.

"Listen, Compadre," Cap interrupted. "We have a crucial mission ahead of us today. I need everyone on top of their game today. It was my decision and my order that you were not told about Erika. Here is another order: No conversations with Lia on this matter." Cap pointed his finger at Lawson.

"I don't think you'll have to worry about that," Lawson sat in a chair.

Cap realized something else was going on. "Maybe you should stay in the command post today."

Lawson looked up at him. "I'm good," he said convincingly.

"You and Sweeny have point on this," Cap changed his tone.

Sweeny and Lawson walked out to an empty office with the agents and deputies already outside pairing up and heading to their places. Cap pulled his door shut and looked at the empty and dark office. "You've taken care of us to this point. Help these young men make good decisions both at their jobs and at home." He pulled out a St. James medallion hanging from a gold chain under his shirt. "We're all on a journey, guide our steps." He looked up at the ceiling, saying a quiet "Amen," and walked out.

As Lawson and Sweeny rode out to their staging area, the truck was quiet. Sweeny didn't know what to say and started, "I'm sorry. It killed me to keep you out of this."

"I'm not really that upset about Erika," Lawson replied, looking at Sweeny, "but do you think that Lia is involved?"

"I don't know." Sweeny didn't want to answer. "I know that Erika is part of Jose's smuggling ring. She's locked up right now, but the department is letting her go unless we get hard evidence to hold her." Lawson remained silent. "She's dangerous, Lawson, you should have seen her eyes when this went down. She didn't hesitate to let me know that both Vicky and I would die."

"Vicky? She said that?"

"In an unmannered, barbaric way. No emotions, just ice cold brutality in her eyes." The thought of it sent chills up his spine.

Their radio interrupted them with Dale's voice. "We are in place on the north side."

"Dale's OK being part of the decoy?" Lawson asked.

"Not really, but he'll get over it." They pulled up to the mobile command center located a few miles from the border in Big Bend. Teams of agents and deputies filed in, leaving one giant dust cloud hovering over the area. The cloud suddenly rose with air support landing in a designated area. "I don't think I've ever seen a larger operation," Sweeny said stepping out of the truck.

As everyone was patiently waiting for Jose to make his move south of the border, Erika and her attorney sat across from an officer. "I believe your 24 hours is up, and unless you have anything on my client, we will be leaving." The officer sat quiet and frustrated about releasing someone they knew was dangerous and heavily connected to Jose Emmanuel. Sweeny sat in the mobile command center, unaware that the threat to his family was walking out of the county jail texting on her phone.

The radio came alive in the center with Dale's voice. "We have movement across the Rio, four trucks and 20-25 people."

"Keep us informed," Lawson answered and turned to the other agents in the command center. "Let our eyes on the border know."

After 20 minutes, Dale's voice came back. "They are still just sitting on the banks and walk around the rafts they have. Anything on your end?"

"Nothing!" Lawson replied and looked at Sweeny. "I'm getting nervous now. You sure your informant was correct?"

"Yes," Sweeny answered, unaware that his informant's body was swinging by his neck in the upstairs room of the building they had met in.

Across town, Sandra walked into her living room, where Vicky and Valentine were watching TV. "Sweetie, are you hungry?"

"Sure," Vicky answered. Sandra walked back to the kitchen to fix a grill cheese. Vicky, glued on the TV, never hearing the clanking noise outside. Valentine lifted her head and stared at the door. She stood as the door knob slowly turned.

Chapter 47

Cap walked into the command center. "It's been over an hour. I am starting to think we've been snowed."

Lawson called Dale, asking, "What's happening there?"

"The same," Dale answered.

"Have you called your informant?" he asked Sweeny.

"Several times, still no answer."

"And our eyes in the sky haven't seen any movement?" Cap asked.

"No sir," Lawson answered.

"Let's wrap this up. Leave a few agents in the area. We need to let these guys get back to their jobs." Cap walked out pulling a cigarette from his shirt pocket, but before lighting it, he turned back in. "You two go over and find out what is happening. I don't need to report to the chief with nothing." He lit his cigarette and pulled out his cell phone.

The team did not yet know that word had come to Jose about the sting operation, and with the Cartel's agreement he shifted his mass movement 30 miles farther south and easily moved 300 people and over two tons of drugs into the US. That word was a phone call he had received earlier that morning.

Cap paced the ground waiting for Sandra to pick up the phone, but after the sixth ring it went to voice mail. "Hmm!" He took another drag off his cigarette.

Lawson and Sweeny walked out of the command center Sweeny saying "Tell Sandra that I am heading out with Lawson. I'll get Vicky this evening."

"I will. If I can get her to answer the phone and—" Cap stopped and answered Sandra's call. "I've called several times," Cap he said fretfully.

"I'm sorry," Sandra told him. "The neighbor walked in, and Valentine almost attacked her. If she hadn't screamed, I'm not sure what Val would have done."

"Well, I left her to protect y'all. She's just doing what she is trained to do," Cap replied and walked back to the command center talking to Sandra.

The two boys quickly headed home passing the pharmacy, "Why isn't the pharmacy open?" Sweeny asked.

"I haven't had time to tell you. We had a falling out over her family yesterday."

"Didn't go well?" Sweeny asked.

"I'd say not. Her father definitely doesn't approve me. Her brother pulled a gun on me, and her father came at me, tripped, and fell to the ground. It looked like I knocked both of them out."

"Did you?"

"Just her brother. He is bad news."

"Pulling a gun? I'd have knocked him out too. Dude, you don't need to be around that. What did Lia say?" Sweeny asked.

"Nothing. She went to her grandmother's. Crazy!"

Lawson parked his patrol truck in his drive, and after changing clothes, the two of them headed across the border. They stopped briefly at the check point and after being waved through, headed to the bright yellow building where Sweeny had met his informant many times. Sweeny laid his work cell phone on the seat and pulled out the phone he used to communicate with informants.

"He's still not answering. Let's just head to the building and see if there is any sign of him." Sweeny pointed down a busy street. Pulling to the side of the street across from the bright yellow building, they surveyed the streets and the windows for any signs of the squirrelly man. Sweeny looked back down at his phone. "I'll be right back," he told Lawson.

Lawson followed him across the street, saying "You're not going alone."

They made their way to the side of the building and preceded up the stairs to an unlocked door. As they slowly opened the door, the smell almost knocked them down. Sweeny looked at Lawson. "Only one thing makes that kind of smell. Death." He swung the door open to reveal the man hanging from the exposed trusses. "Damn!"

Sweeny started to enter the room, but Lawson latched onto his arm. "No, we don't need to be here." He studied the streets for anyone paying them attention and quickly led Sweeny back to his truck. As Lawson was pressing the unlock button on the remote, a voice yelled from behind them. They turned to find an older man jogging across the street, waving them to stop. Lawson signaled Sweeny to step behind the truck, and Sweeny knew it meant to pull his Glock 23 from his waist.

"Agent Caine! It is me. You helped save my family not long time ago," the man said, excited to see Lawson.

Lawson had to think back, but realized it was the man they had caught crossing a few weeks back, the same time Sweeny had kicked in the face of one of the coyotes. "Yes, I remember you."

The old man shook his hand. "You saved me, anything I can do. You tell me."

From the other side of the truck, Sweeny interjected, "You can tell us where to find Jose Emmanuel."

The man looked at Sweeny, then back at Lawson with a concerned look they had seen many times, a look of fear. "If you know, I will protect you," Lawson replied.

With a change of expression, he pointed south on the street. "Go to the end, turn corner. Brown building, upstairs." He turned and quickly walked away.

Sweeny looked at Lawson. "You kidding me? Let's go!" He jumped in the truck.

"We don't need to blow this," Lawson argued. "We should call the Mexican police."

"Let's make sure he is there. I don't want to look like a dumbass."

Thinking about it for only a moment, Lawson agreed and drove to the end of the street. Things started to look familiar. "I've been here," he said, looking at the buildings.

"When?" Sweeny asked.

Then Lawson recognized a store front down from the brown building. "Lia brought me here to buy some items for her store."

They stepped out of the truck and looked around the street, a young boy sitting with his back against the building watching them. It was obvious they were out of place, two white young men driving a nice truck in the heart of Ojinaga.

Sweeny pulled a twenty out of his pocket and flashed it in front of the boy. "Jose Emmanuel?"

The boy laughed and rubbed his index finger and thumb together. "Dang!" Sweeny said, pulling out two more twenties. The boy never said a word and pointed at a single door that opened to a set of stairs. Sweeny slowly opened the door and looked back at Lawson. "You ready?"

"I've got a bad feeling about this," Lawson said, following Sweeny up the creaking steps. Reaching the top, they found another door with light coming from under it and voices inside. Sweeny put his ear to the door.

Sweeny shrugged his shoulders about what to do, and Lawson agreed he didn't know either. The door from below opened with two men walking in, so Sweeny and Lawson were stuck. The two men walking up the steps froze, staring at the two undercover agents, and Sweeny did the only thing he knew to do. He opened the door and walked into a small room with Lawson and three other men.

The older man turned and faced them, surprised to have American visitors. Lawson's expression was even more surprised. "Mr. Gonzales?" Lawson asked.

Sweeny shot Lawson a puzzled look. "Mr. Caine?" The older man paused for a brief moment. "Have you come to apologize?"

Lawson looked at Sweeny, explaining "This is Lia's father."

The two men entered the room behind Lawson and Sweeny and walked around them, staring at them confused why they were there. "I was actually looking for someone else."

"And who might that be since you are not here to apologize?" Lia's father asked in a serene tone.

Lawson couldn't believe that out of all the buildings in Ojinaga, he would accidently interrupt Lia's father. "I am sorry. Carlos pulled a gun on me, and I just reacted. I never intended to be disruptive or dishonor you and your family. I was only—"

Mr. Gonzales interrupted him, "I found the gun in the bushes after you left. Yes, my son was out of line. I should have invited him to leave earlier in the day."

Lawson drew back. This was a different tone from Lia's father than the day before. "I am sorry for interrupting your meeting," Lawson said, looking around the room.

"It is our plumbers' union meeting. Or that is what you would call it in the states. Why don't you come by the house later, and you and I will clear up this misunderstanding."

Lawson looked at Sweeny, then back to Mr. Gonzales. "Yes sir, I will. Again, I am sorry." He pulled on Sweeny to follow him.

Walking down the stairs, "What are the chances we would be led on a wild goose chase and end up at Lia's father's plumbing meeting?" Sweeny said.

"I don't know. He was much more understanding than he was yesterday."

Sweeny snatched the young boy up. "I want my money back. I asked you about Jose Emmanuel. That was Jose Gonzales up there." He pointed to the second story.

"*Ce!*" The young boy replied, "Jose Emmanuel Gonzales!" He pulled his arm free. "Everyone knows that."

Lawson's complexation turned pale white as he stared at Sweeny, then back up at the building. "Lia's father is Jose Emmanuel?"

Together they raced back up the stairs with pistols drawn, Sweeny lowered his left shoulder and exploded into the room. Shots rang out as two men standing in another doorway leading to a back stairwell began firing at Sweeny and Lawson. Lawson switched sides on the door he was kneeling in front of and fired five shots back, causing the two men to leap outside to avoid being hit. Their door shut, giving Sweeny and Lawson an opportunity to run to the wall on both sides of the door. Peeking out the window, Lawson could see Jose and three other men quickly running to a dark-colored Buick.

"You OK?" Sweeny asked.

"I don't know," Lawson replied, lowering his pistol and walking around the room.

Chapter 48

Sitting in Cap's office, Lawson was finishing his bottle of water. "Cap, we had him. I can't believe I was so naive. A plumbers' meeting!?!" Lawson said, frustrated.

"If you ever stumble upon a wasp nest and they don't get upset, there's no need to stir it up. You boys are lucky they didn't cut your throats. We now know who he is. It's just a matter of time," Cap said in his raspy voice.

"And the Mexican Police?" Sweeny asked.

"Well paid. They aren't cooperating with anyone. He's a free man as long as he stays on that side of the border."

"And Erika?"

"Same. But if she shows her face here, we have enough to hang her." Cap took out his leather pouch of tobacco and rolled a cigarette for later.

"You haven't heard anything from Lia?" Sweeny asked Lawson.

"Nothing."

"She's clean. Her business too. All indications show that she has nothing to with her father's corruption and criminal business."

"I told y'all she wasn't involved," Lawson defended her.

"We still have a mole connected to Jose. I'm going to tell you that the state boys still believe Lia is feeding information to her father. Keep your ear to the ground," Cap pointed to Lawson.

"We have a mole?" Lawson asked, confused.

"Fill him in on everything. I have to make a call," Cap said, picking up the receiver to his desk phone.

Lawson and Sweeny walked out of the office, "Yes! Fill me in on everything. A mole? Wouldn't that be Erika?" Lawson asked Sweeny.

"We're being tight-lipped about it, but through the note I was given and through information from the state police, we might have an agent that is feeding Jose information. My bet it is one of the state boys and not an agent. They are the ones that are the most worried about it," Sweeny answered.

Terry and Dale walked in, followed by Sandra and Vicky. "Look who we found outside," Dale said, smiling at Vicky.

She leaped into her father's arms and gave a big welcoming wave to Lawson. "Are you seeing Lia today?" she asked.

"Maybe so." Lawson didn't want to answer the real question.

"I just saw her at the pharmacy," Dale piped up from his desk.

Sweeny looked at Lawson with Vicky still in his arms, "Go! I'll cover for you here."

Lawson nodded his head. "Thanks." Grabbing his radio, he headed to the door.

As the door closed, he could hear Vicky asking her dad why she couldn't go, and Lawson smiled at the thought. She was infatuated with Lia, and because of Lia showing enthusiasm at the dance, Vicky had decided to stay with it a few more months. As Lawson pulled out of the office lot and headed toward the pharmacy, he wasn't sure what to expect. *Have Erika and Lia already talked? Has her father contacted her?* A million thoughts careened though his head, but the biggest thought was *Is there any hope for us?*

He pulled into the parking lot and drove past the windows, peeking inside to see who was in the store with her. An elderly couple stood at the counter with only one car in the parking lot, so believing it was safe, he parked and walked to the door. Saying a quick prayer for this conversation to go well, he entered. Lia was handing the couple a bag of medicine and thanking them for their patients while she was closed for personal reasons. Lawson smiled at the couple as they passed him heading out.

"Can we talk?" he asked.

She was finishing with the computer and the couple's order. "There isn't much to talk about."

Lawson looked around the store and leaned over to glance in the office. "I haven't seen her either or heard anything," she said, not looking at him.

"What?" he asked.

"Erika—I haven't heard from her. It's not like her to just up and vanish. But here lately, I don't know what to expect."

"Well, that's what I came to talk to you about," Lawson cautiously replied.

She put down a notebook. "You came to talk to me about Erika?" she snapped.

"And your dad."

"I should have listened to him from the start," she replied, walking to the soda bar.

Lawson followed her and sat on one of the stools. "Erika was arrested two days ago," he began.

"For what?" Her expression changed.

"For aiding in the smuggling of illegal aliens." Lia remained motionless and just stared at him. "She was let go by the state for lack of enough evidence to hold her."

"So, she is innocent?"

"No, we've known that she was helping with the smuggling. We had to take her in with little evidence, but after yesterday we have enough to lock her away for life," Lawson replied.

"Life?" she replied, shocked. "Where is she?" she asked. "We don't know."

"What? How long have y'all known?" She sat up.

"I'm not sure how long Cap and Sweeny have known. They kept me in the dark until recently," he answered.

"So what about me? Am I a suspect too?"

"No. But I—"

She interrupted him, "This isn't where you tell me that you were using me to get to her, like in the movies?"

"No."

"This is a lot to process." She walked to the counter and picked up her phone then walked back.

"Lia," Lawson took a deep breath. "We have uncovered the smuggling lord. The man that is behind the deaths of hundreds of men and women... and children. The man that Erika works for."

Lia's eyes widened. "Erika? Who?"

"Jose Emmanuel." Lawson answered. Lia again stood in one place, staring at him as if waiting for the entire answer. "Jose Emmanuel Gonzales. Your father."

"What are you doing?" Lia asked.

"What do you mean?"

"Why are you attacking my family? First my brother and now my father... for the second time."

Lawson was shocked and stuttered trying to answer. "I'm not attacking your family. Again, your brother pulled a gun on me."

"Get out," she said, looking down. Before Lawson had time to react, she picked up the notebook and threw it at him. "Get out!" her voice grew intense. He stood up with the notebook falling to the tile floor, and reaching down for it, he felt something hit his back and fall to the floor. "Get out!" Lia screamed, her voice trembling.

"Lia, I don't—"

Tears began rolling down her face. "Lawson, leave!" her voice shook. He walked to the door and looked back at Lia, who was now crying. He opened the door and walked to his truck. The sign swung in the window as Lia flipped it to the Closed position. She watched him slowly pull out onto the highway and then fell to her knees in the middle of her dark and empty store. Tears flooded the floor in front of her.

Lawson called Sweeny. "Hey. You still at the office?"

"No, Vicky and I are heading to the house. How did it go with Lia?"

"Not good. She didn't know anything about Erika, and when I mentioned her dad, she went off," Lawson replied.

Sweeny could hear Lawson take a deep breath through the phone. "Lawson, I don't know."

"About?" Lawson asked.

"Is she being honest? Maybe she isn't directly involved with her father, but how could she not know?"

"What are you saying?" Lawson was getting upset.

"Watch your back, Lawson. I don't trust her." Sweeny looked at his phone, saying out loud, "You don't have to hang up on me."

Chapter 49

With tears still in her eyes, Lia drove across the border toward her house, the thought of her father being a smuggling lord making her sick to her stomach.

Still, the fear of it being true became more real. The days and nights that he was gone during her childhood, the fact she never saw him actually working, the fact that they were never without money, and the many times sketchy men were at her house all added up to something she had denied her whole life.

Her little brother and sister met her as she put her Jeep in park and followed her to the door. Their normal hanging off her legs didn't happen this time with their sense that something was wrong, and walking in, she found her father sitting in the leather recliner he was accustomed to. She gently pushed her siblings into the kitchen with her mother. Before she could question her father, Carlos walked in with Erika. The two girls stood silently staring at each other.

"I was hoping this day wouldn't come," her father said, sitting up.

"I'll talk with you in a moment." Lia held out a hand toward her father. She turned back to Erika. "How could you?"

"How could I?" Erika repeated.

"I trusted you." Lia fought to hold the tears back.

"I never betrayed you! I've always been on your side," Erika defended herself.

"I trusted you to be a better person than this...." The words wouldn't come to her.

Carlos stepped in to say something, but Lia stopped him with the same hand she held toward her father. "All of you! You're disgusting! You are the very people I prayed to protect my family from, and now—"

She struggled to talk. Her mother walked to the kitchen doorway cleaning a plate, "And you knew about this?" Her mother remain silent.

Her father stood. "Have I never not taken care of you and your brothers and sisters? Have you ever had to struggle the way so many people here have?"

"At the cost of lives?" she snapped.

"Not everyone is worth saving," he replied. It was in a demeanor that she had never seen from her father. His tone and body language changed, changed to evil.

"We give people the chance at a better life in the states." Carlos started to say.

"Your life is worthless to me, so I'd be careful with your words right now!" Lia growled at Carlos. He quickly cowered down. "You've raped and killed innocent children!"

"Well, I never taught this. Some of our men like to make names for themselves, and making a name is good business."

"You should all know that the border patrol knows who you are. You will never be able to cross the border again." Her body shook with emotions she had never experienced before. "I can't be here," she said and walked out.

Erika followed her and grabbed her arm before she reached her Jeep, "Lia, think about this before you react. Your father has protected you your whole life and this is how you're going to repay him? This might not be the ideal life, but it's a good one, and the money is as good as it gets."

Lia locked eyes with her. "I don't know you any more. *Listen* to yourself. You sound like the demon my father is."

Carlos walked up. "Sis, you have no idea. This is the life you were meant for!" She glared at him with daggers from her brown eyes. "You can give me all the dirty looks you want, but hear me," Carlos threatened. "If you come between this family and this business, the rape and killings those kids got will be nothing compared what will come to you!" he snarled.

She pulled free from Erika and climbed into her Jeep. The thought of leaving her home for the last time didn't have the sadness she expected. Instead, an overwhelming sense of being free came over her. She headed to the one place she knew she could get answers.

Watching Lia drive off, Carlos said to Erika, "She is going to cause trouble."

"Let her cool off, and then I'll talk with her." "The border patrol men need to go," he said. "I agree."

"Any ideas?" Carlos asked.

"Taking Sweeny's little girl is a great start," she responded to him with a smile.

He nodded his head, "Then do it!"

Lia's grandmother stood on her front porch hanging a hide from a young coyote that had killed her chickens. She watched the dust blow in a slow breeze as Lia's Jeep drove down the dirt road and came to a rest in front of her shack. The blue heeler sat beside her grandmother waiting for Lia to open her door, and through the windshield her grandmother could tell that she was still upset.

Closing her door, she walked up to her grandmother and without saying anything, rested her head on the shoulder of the weather-beaten old woman. "I hoped this day would never come," she replied to Lia.

Lia looked up. "You knew?"

"Unfortunately. Never agreed, but I knew," she answered. It hit Lia that she was the only one of her family who visited her grandmother, and her grandmother never came to their house. She always thought it was her eccentric nature, but now it was adding up.

"Why?" Lia asked.

"That is a question many ask. Why do bad things happen? Come inside." She put her arm around Lia and guided her inside.

***

A light knock sounded from Cap's door, and holding the remote to his TV, he hollered at Sandra, "Someone's at the door."

Sandra walked into the living room. "By all means, don't kill yourself answering the door."

"It's probably that crazy neighbor," he replied.

She held her index finger to her lips, insinuating that Cap was talking too loud if it was the neighbor. He could hear her welcoming someone inside, and by her tone it was the neighbor. Sandra walked back in the living room, saying "Someone is here to see you," and she smiled as Lawson followed her in the room. Cap nodded his head, clearly seeing Lawson was upset.

He retracted the footrest to his recliner and stood up, "Sweetie, do you have some sweet tea made up?"

"Yes, I'll bring y'all a glass," she replied from the kitchen.

Cap nodded toward the back porch and walked out with Lawson. They sat in two rocking chairs that Cap and Sandra would sit in during the cooler times of the year. Sandra walked out with two tall glasses of sweet tea, and handing them their drinks, she turned on a fan that Cap had set up in the corner of the porch, then walked back in.

"Love is a complicated thing the good Lord made," Cap started.

"I don't understand. Out of all people I fall for a smuggling lord's daughter."

"Hmm!" Cap made his normal noise when he was thinking. "I'll have to say... it's a first for me."

"Cap... what do I do?" Lawson took a swig from the tea to hide his shaking voice.

"Well... we are all made different. Just because her father is an evil man doesn't make her damaged goods. It's funny how our hearts see clearer than our eyes."

"What do you mean?" Lawson looked at him.

"People see what they want with their eyes, but the good Lord looks at our heart. It's what's in our hearts that He knows what we really want. So... what our heart sees is what we really want." He pulled out a cigarette from his shirt pocket. "The old saying *follow your heart,* well... there's a lot of truth in that." He took a long drag. "This world has eyes, but lacks much heart."

A single tear rolled down Lawson's cheek, and afraid that Cap might see him crying, Lawson let it fall to the ground. *Heart?*

Chapter 50

ollow your heart! Sounds like a movie line, Lawson thought as he crossed the border. *Another sleepless night,* he yawned around his cup of coffee. It was early, but the sun was well on its way to bring another hot fall day. The checkpoint was busy with trucks carrying cargo to both countries for supplies. Mornings were normally busy for the checkpoints. Lawson figured that by meeting in the morning, there would be less stress and hopefully less tension. Besides, it wasn't every day a border patrol agent visited a smuggling Lord's home. *If Cap and the other team members knew I was heading to Jose, they would have a fit.*

Lawson knew that Jose was safe on the Mexican side of the border, and perhaps if he would meet with Lawson, he would release Lia from his grasp. Lawson had no idea that Lia had already made her mind up that she was done with her family. He parked his truck in the drive and said a little prayer that this would not blow up in face and that Carlos wasn't there. He checked his Glock before concealing it in the small of his back. "Here goes nothing," he muttered.

Lia's mother grew wide-eyed when she opened the door and found Lawson standing on the front porch. "Senor Caine?" she said loud enough for anyone in the house to hear.

The door widened with Jose standing beside her. "You came here for war?" he asked, just as surprised as his wife.

"No, I came here for peace," Lawson replied, holding both hands up.

"You are either up to something or crazy," Jose replied.

"Neither—I'm here to talk about Lia. Nothing else," he said. Jose and his wife stepped aside and waved him in. Walking into the small house with its aroma of fresh coffee, a strong feeling came over him. *What in the hell am I doing here?*

"Coffee?" Lia's mother asked.

"Yes, please," Lawson replied as Jose pulled out a chair for him at the kitchen table.

"So, Senor Caine. What is it that you want to talk about?" Jose sat back in his chair.

It was becoming more and more of reality that he had made a bad, if not stupid choice by coming to their house. "There is bad blood between us and we don't see eye to eye, but I love your daughter. I promise I am the right man for her and I'll always take care of her."

"So what do you want?" Jose cut him off and got to the point.

"Leave us in peace."

Jose rubbed his chin with his right hand. No one had ever approached him with such audacity, and the thought of it intrigued him. "You are a brave man. I like that," he told Lawson. "You're in the wrong business."

The words stunned Lawson. *Did he just offer me a job?*
"Wrong business?"

"Who knows you're here?"

"No one."

"Come work for me. You will make a fortune." He paused for a moment. "And you will have my blessings and peace with my daughter," he added, knowing that if he could bring Lawson into the family, Lia would come back.

"I don't believe I could work for you," Lawson stuttered.

"All I ask is for information, nothing else." He squinted his eyes. "Think about it."

Lawson kept quiet, thinking back on what Cap told him: "If you walk into a wasps' nest and they are not upset, don't shake the nest." He now found himself in a wasps' nest, but the wasps were not upset. If he turned Jose down, he might be able to walk out. "Can I think about this?" Lawson looked at him. Jose smiled with the thought of two agents working for him,

"Yes, one day." He raised his cup to his wife to refill.

Seeing a good time to exit, Lawson stood. "I have to get back before anyone knows I'm gone. Lia is still with her grandmother?" he asked her mother.

"*Ce,*" she answered.

He turned to Jose. "I'll tell the other agents at the check point I went to see Lia. No one needs to know I was here."

"I agree," Jose responded, walking Lawson to the front door. "You and Lia can have a good life. You both will be safe," he smiled at Lawson. Chills ran up Lawson's spine as Jose patted him on the shoulder.

The sound of another vehicle came from the drive, and Carlos emerged from a white Toyota truck with a profound expression. "To what do we owe this visit?" he asked with a sinister tone.

"Senor Caine is thinking about helping," Jose replied.

"No agent is just willing to help," Carlos said.

"Well, he is, and with his help, the whole family will be in." Jose paused, "All but Roberto."

"Roberto is a lost cause. And you, gringo, I don't believe for a minute you're here to help." Carlos stepped back and reached for his pistol.

"Put it away," Jose snapped at his son.

"Did you check him for a gun?" Carlos replied.

"Of course not, he's a law. He'd be stupid not to carry a gun," Jose said, stepping between Lawson and Carlos. "This is my decision, not yours. Now I said go!" He pointed to the white Toyota.

"I'm leaving," Lawson held his hands up and made his way to his truck. Jose and Carlos argued behind him in their native language, and Lawson picked up his pace, wanting to be out of their yard. Lawson heard Jose yell "No!" at Carlos just before the passenger-side window of his truck exploded, shattering glass over the driveway. Out of reaction Lawson spun, ducked lower, and pulled his Glock 23 from the small of his back.

"No!" Jose yelled at both men, who were in a standoff. "I didn't come here for this!" Lawson yelled.

"But you came here. And no gringo who's banging my sister is going to be part of this organization!" Carlos snared back.

"This organization's decisions will be made by me!" Jose snapped.

Carlos slightly tilted his head with an ominous grin. "Receiving my father's forgiveness for killing you is easy." Lawson eyed the trigger finger of Carlos and could see the fingernail turning white from pressure on the trigger. A deafening explosion rattled Lawson's head, and the impact of the sound blurred his vision. The smoke quickly vanished from the barrel of his Glock before Carlos' body fell to the ground.

Jose stood in shock as his wife stormed outside screaming and kneeling beside the lifeless body of her son. Lawson walked backward, not lowering his gun; he knew he had little time to get back to the border before Jose ordered the end of his life.

With his wife screaming, Jose couldn't decide whether to go after Lawson or help with Carlos. "You just dug your grave!" Jose said in a calm, eerie tone.

Lawson climbed in his truck still aiming at Jose, who was standing in the same place, not taking his eyes off Lawson. He put his truck in drive and peeled out, jetting to the border crossing. Not stopping for red lights or stop signs, Lawson floored his truck. Crossing into the US, he pulled over at the checkpoint and with shaking hands took a deep breath.

"Lawson, you OK?" An agent approached him. "What happen to your window?"

Lawson didn't answer him and pulled out his cell phone. "Cap?"

"Lawson?" Cap replied on the other end. "I've screwed up... bad."

"I'm at the office."

Chapter 51

"The Federales are going to have a field day with this," Cap paced his office. "Did you know about this?" He pointed at Sweeny.

"No, he didn't," Lawson answered.

"Damn it, Lawson! Have you learned anything from this station?" Cap stopped pacing and put both hands on his desk, leaning toward the two boys. "When we act alone or go rogue, we put this entire division at risk, both physical and political."

"Since when do you care about politics?" Sweeny asked.

Cap shot a look at Sweeny, then back at Lawson. "I have no choice. You're suspended until farther notice."

"Suspended? He ought to be decorated for killing a key member of the smuggling ring." Sweeny spoke up.

"I don't need anything else from you! You are treading on thin ice to be next." Sweeny started to say something. "No!" Cap shut him up, "I need you, so don't say anything else." He looked at Lawson. "Badge and gun." He held out his hand.

Lawson didn't say anything; he knew he had done something stupid and put his team in danger. There was no doubt that Jose had alerted all his men, and in fear that they would retaliate Cap put the entire border division on high alert. After handing over his badge and gun, he walked out of Cap's office to face his team. Dale and Terry stood in front of their desks awaiting the outcome of his meeting. "I'm sorry, guys." Lawson put his head down and walked toward the door.

"Don't worry, Lawson, we'll nail this son-of-a-bitch," Dale replied.

"Be smart Dale. These guys don't care about anything. If they get a chance at you, they'll take it." Lawson looked Dale in the eyes. He was proud of the agent that Dale had become and was thankful he was with the team.

Terry started to say something when his phone rang, "Hang on," he said, answering it and heading outside.

Lawson shook his head. "Always on that phone."

With the rest of the team walking out, Terry covered his free ear to hear better, and walked farther toward the gate. Sweeny put his arm around Lawson. "Just think of all the beer and fishing you get to do for the next few days."

"Is that supposed to make me feel better?" Lawson asked.

"It would make me feel better," Sweeny replied.

Terry walked back up to the team. "Sorry," he apologized for being on the phone.

Lawson looked toward the building, seeing Cap standing in front of his window watching the team. "Y'all keep me up to date on what's going on." He opened his truck door and climbed in. "I might have to drink a beer or two while fishing," He smiled at Sweeny, then pulled out. Passing the closed pharmacy, he thought there was no way Lia would ever have anything to do with him now. After all, who would want to date the person who killed your brother?

***

Lia stood paralyzed in the small kitchen of her grandmother's house; she had just received a phone call from her mother. The news that her brother, Carlos, was dead wasn't as surprising as who killed him. She felt the room tighten in and the air become hard to breath. Her grandmother grabbed her arm and sat her at the old wooden table. "Who?" her grandmother asked, knowing with Lia's expression someone had died.

"Carlos," she whispered.

Her grandmother shook her head with the news and wet a towel for Lia. "Here, place it on your forehead," she said, handing over the towel.

"It was Lawson," she said in a faint voice.

"Lawson?"

Lia looked at her grandmother with dry eyes. "Lawson killed Carlos."

"That is not the death I saw," the old woman said under her breath. She lifted Lia's face by raising her chin and looked deep into her brown eyes. "Child, this is not over. I see the same death in your eyes."

"What are you talking about?"

"Lawson is walking into death," she replied.

"Lawson is going to die?" Lia's voice escalated.

"Death doesn't take favorites." Her grandmother took a deep breath, "You must go find him. The only way I will know who Death is after is by the dream catcher I gave him."

"Abuela, you know I don't believe—"

"If you love him, you must find him." The words scared Lia. She kissed her grandmother and headed toward the States.

Chapter 52

"And you are sure?" Jose stood talking on the phone in a room filled with his men. "Going fishing? Where?" He smiled at one of his men, "Thank you. You don't really care for your agent friend, do you?" he asked the person on the other end of the phone. "Yes, you will be paid very well for this." Jose hung up the phone.

"What did our Border Patrol friend tell you?" asked one of the men.

"Looks like Senor Caine is going fishing in a remote area. Remember, I kill him. Understood?" Jose raised his voice.

"*Ce*," several of the men answered.

"Let's go." They walked out of the room and down the narrow stairwell to several vehicles. Jose climbed in the passenger side of a grey Honda Accord, "Let's get across the border before everyone else," he said, pulling out a fake ID. Minutes later, a young border patrol agent took the driver's ID and Jose's fake ID, looking in the window. "What brings you to the US?" the agent asked.

"Visiting my daughter," Jose replied.

"OK." The agent handed their ID's back. "Be safe out there," he added, and waved them through.

As the Honda Accord disappeared into the town of Presidio, another agent approached the young agent. "Here is a picture of Jose Emmanuel, and he also goes by the last name of Gonzales. The Chief thinks he is crossing over today," he mentioned.

The young agent's face turned pale. "He just passed through in a Honda Accord."

"You sure?" the agent asked.

"I'm very sure." Looking at the picture, "I looked directly at him."

The agent picked up the phone, "Cap, we didn't get the picture in time. Jose Emmanuel just passed through in a grey Honda Accord."

"We're on it." Cap hung up the phone at yelled for his team. He picked up the phone again, saying, "Put out an APB on a grey Honda Accord... pull 'em all over." He hung up the phone as Terry, Dale, and Sweeny walked in his office.

Cap grabbed his cowboy hat. "He's in Presidio. Honda Accord," he told them, walking to the door.

"Cap, do you really think Jose would cross the border at a checkpoint?" Terry asked.

"I think he's smarter than you give him credit for. Where's Lawson?"

"Probably at home," Sweeny said.

Cap pointed at their truck, "Get over there ASAP! And get him on the phone."

Cap ran to his truck as Sweeny and Dale loaded up in Sweeny's. Terry was the last one to leave the yard with his cell phone stuck to his ear. Cap was the first to kick on his lights and siren. "Do you think Jose would go to Lawson's house?" Dale asked Sweeny, hanging on to the truck handle.

"If someone just killed your son, you wouldn't wait around for revenge," Sweeny said.

With the sirens in the distance Lawson walked into his kitchen to fix a cooler of water and snacks. He was taking Sweeny's advice and hitting a small lake to fish and clear his head. He picked up a blue soft-side cooler, set it on the table, and opened the refrigerator for bottle of water. Closing the door, he jumped back, terrified and shocked at who was standing in his kitchen. "I won't do a lot of talking, but go to your grave and hell knowing that you cannot beat a Lord!" Jose raised the black handle of Carlos' pistol and aimed at Lawson's head.

"Know that when you get to hell, I want be there," Lawson responded, pulling his Glock from behind him and firing at Jose a faction of a second after Jose pulled the trigger.

Jose's shot grazed Lawson's shoulder, tearing his shirt but missing skin, and Lawson's wild shot struck one of Jose's men between the eyes. Blood sprayed the cabinets and counter top, and Lawson dove down the hall as Jose capped off three more shots, missing Lawson each time. "Why am I missing!?!" Jose screamed.

Lawson fired four shots through the hallway wall, backing Jose and his men out the kitchen door to the front porch. One of the men ran down the porch and opened the front door, then backed up beside the door. He never saw the shot coming that penetrated his chest and dropped him dead. Cap stormed the front of the house, blowing holes in the man standing beside Jose.

After the man fell to his death, Cap stepped on the porch face to face, pistol to pistol with Jose Emmanuel. "What makes you think you can pull the trigger before I do?" Jose taunted him.

Cap pulled his trigger. "Because I don't talk!"

Carlos' pistol bounced off the wooden porch as Jose grasped his right shoulder. Dale and Sweeny both put the barrels of their M4s to the side of his head. "Please move," Sweeny said. Terry grabbed Jose's hands and spun him around for cuffing, their eyes locking for a brief moment. Jose gasped for air as his wounded shoulder came to life with a hellish burn.

"Lawson!" Cap ran in the kitchen, stepping over the dead body of Jose's man.

Lawson slowly walked around the corner. "Am I glad to see you."

Cap holstered his gun and wrapped his arms around Lawson with his eyes beginning to water. "Damn, son, I didn't think we'd get here in time."

"He missed," Lawson replied with his head buried in Cap's chest.

Cap pulled him back and faced him. "Missed?"

"He was standing within three feet of me! He missed—I should be dead." Lawson's voice shook with shock setting in.

"Come on, compadre." Cap walked him out to a street flooded with Border Patrol trucks, sheriff's cars, and EMS vehicles.

Terry was standing guard over Jose as two EMS persons walked up the drive. Sweeny stopped Lawson. "You OK?" he asked, looking him over.

Lawson looked at his shirt ripped from Jose's shot. "Yeah, I'm OK."

As they walked off the porch, Cap followed, looking at the sky and mouthing the words, "Thank you!"

Chapter 53

Lia pulled off to the side of the street after reading the text from Erika; her father was now in US custody following a shootout at Lawson's house. *Why was Lawson the center to her family's tragedy?* Questions flew through her head to the point the air became thin again, and she struggled to catch her breath. She turned the air on high in her Jeep and put her mouth beside the vent, inhaling with deep breaths and letting them out through her nose. *Why did Lawson go to my family's house if he knew everything? Nothing makes sense.*

She dialed Roberto's number again, and again getting no answer she left a message: "Pick up, Roberto! Fine time to be on one of your trips. I need to speak to you ASAP. Call me!" Looking out at the mountains that seemed to stretch farther south than she realized, she said, "This is crazy" quietly to herself. Then she typed in a text to Lawson: "Where are you?" Moments later, she received her answer. "At Cap's house," Lawson replied. With the death of her brother, her best friend on the most wanted list, and now her father in jail, she might not be thinking clearly, but she wanted answers.

After letting Sandra know that Lia was on her way, Lawson sat on the front porch. His head had started pounding with everything that was happening. He heard her Jeep turn the corner, and by the sounds of the engine, she was heading his way and fast.

He expected her to explode out from the Jeep in hysteria, but to his surprise, she calmly walked up to the porch. "Lia, I never planned on any of this," he said.

She took a deep breath. "Just answer me one question. Did you use me to get to my father? Erika? My family?"

It came across his mind that no matter how he answered the question, it would never be believable, so he simply answered, "No."

"I want to believe you," she replied, trying to hide the shaking of her hands.

"I didn't know anything about Erika until recently, and I never expected your dad to turn out who he is. Especially for him to come after me today."

"What did you expect after killing Carlos? This is so crazy." She looked up, fighting back tears. "I've lost my entire family today." As the words came out of her mouth, she realized the magnitude of her loss for the first time.

The emotions overwhelming his thoughts, Lawson stood to his feet. "Please put yourself in my shoes—I don't know what to do."

"In your shoes?" The thought infuriated her. "What is going to happen to you with my brother's death?"

"I'll have to go in tomorrow and explain everything for reports, but I'm already suspended. Most likely I'll lose my job." He paused and looked at her, adding, "It was self-defense with Carlos."

"I'm sure it was—my brother was destined for the grave. I'm not sure why you were there," Lia went on.

"Right now I'm not sure either."

"I would like a better answer," she insisted.

He could see in her eyes that she hadn't gotten much sleep and had been crying. "I went for you," he said quietly.

"Me?"

"I guess I thought if I could make some kind of peace with your father that you and I could be together." The more he talked about it, the more it sounded crazy.

She sat in the place he had just stood up from. "Lawson, this is hard for me to say. I'm not one to express my feelings, but I found myself falling for you. There is something about you that pulled me in." She looked up at him. "Thank you for the time we spent, but I could never be with the man who killed my brother and arrested my dad, no matter how evil they are." She stood up, and walking past him, leaned in and kissed him on the cheek.

Lawson didn't turn around, but he agreed on two things. One was there was something that drew him to her, but the other was that he would always be the man who killed her brother and took down her father. Looking toward the house, he never saw Lia take the dream catcher that was sitting in his truck.

She turned with tears welling up and looked back at Lawson with one final thought: *I love you.*

***

Sitting at a table that was being entertained by Vicky, Lawson and Sweeny felt the safety of a man who was more than their supervisor—he had taken on the role of a father. Cap kissed Sandra and thanked her for a tremendous meal, and Sandra coached Vicky to help her in the kitchen while the three men made their plans for the following day. Valentine stuck to the heels of the eight-year-old girl as any good body guard would.

Cap had not asked, but demanded that the boys stay at his house. He knew with the actions that had taken place earlier that day, they would be a target, and he wasn't letting anything happen to his boys.

"I spoke to Dale. He said everything seemed to be quiet," Sweeny said, setting his napkin on his plate.

"Terry?" Cap asked, drinking his normal coffee after supper.

"MIA," Sweeny replied.

"That's not like Terry," Lawson responded.

"I'm sure he's preoccupied making sure his family is protected," Cap answered, not worried. "There's a good game on tonight," he added, making his way to the living room.

The boys followed him into the room as he got comfortable in his recliner and turned on an NFL game. With the voice of the commentator, Vicky quickly emerged from the kitchen and jumped in Lawson's lap. "It blows me away that you like football," Lawson commented. Vicky gave him a big smile and leaned back on him, getting comfortable herself.

"How did your conversation go with Lia?" Sweeny asked Lawson.

"About as good as you would expect with what happen today," Lawson answered.

"And?" Sweeny questioned.

"It's over."

Not understanding, Vicky whispered in Lawson's ear, "I like Lia." The words hurt, knowing she didn't understand. She added to her whisper, "And I like football because my daddy likes football."

Sandra walked in with slices of chocolate cake for everyone, and Vicky managed to slide out of Lawson's lap and squeeze into Cap's chair. Valentine lay beside the recliner.

Chapter 54

Lia finished packing the last of her deliveries to make that day. After a sleepless night, she wished that she could just close down the store, but people needed their medication. The back door quietly closed, and Erika walked in behind Lia, "Hey."

Lia jumped, startled. "Crap, Erika, you scared the fire out of me." She held her chest.

"I'm sorry, I guess with everything that's happened I'd be on pins and needles too."

"How did you get across the border?"

"One of your dad's men helped me across this morning. I got your text—what's up?" Erika asked.

"I've been thinking about this and my brother's offer to join with the family." Erika's eyes widened with her grinning. "But... I am only going to help because of the money. You know I am losing my butt here," Lia said.

"You have no idea the money that's involved. Your dad is going to be so happy," Erika replied.

"Hang on. Before we go any farther, I want it clear that I am not part of anything dealing with children."

"I understand. But you need to know that's part of the business. It bothered me at first, but once the money flooded in, I blocked it out," Erika answered.

The thought of it made Lia sick to her stomach. "What would I be doing?" she changed the question.

"Well… at first you'd be watching this side of the border. I can't be seen here now, so you would be doing what I did."

"Which is?"

"You have a great opportunity with the Border agents and finding out where they are so we can get people across. Are you and Lawson still on?"

"Not really."

"Can you be?"

"After what he did to my family, using him would be easy," she grinned.

Erika smiled, excited about Lia's decision. "I am so happy. I knew we would be working together," Erika answered.

"So if I am taking your job here, what are you doing?" Lia asked.

Still smiling, Erika replied, "After I recruited one of the agents to join, I've become a celebrity with all of your dad's men. I am handling the money and setting up families to cross."

"Recruited? Who?"

Erika raised an eyebrow. "I can't say. It was part of our deal. But if you could get Lawson…"

"He'd never help."

"Don't say never. We girls have a way of persuading men," she grinned.

Lia smiled back. "I could at least try."

Erika laughed, "That's my girl."

"OK, let's start," Lia said, standing.

"OK. I have a large family crossing tomorrow. We need to know where the agents will be mid-morning."

"Family? I can't help with children," Lia replied.

"The only way you'll get used to it is just dive in. Families are our business."

"I just don't want to see little girls get hurt. I know what my father's men do to them for examples."

Erika grinned. "It's the price of freedom."

Lia felt her stomach tighten up and her gag reflexes kick in, but fighting back against becoming sick, she replied, "I can't do this anymore." She pulled at her shirt.

"Do what?" Erika looked confused.

Cap and Sweeny stepped out of Lia's office. "Get your hands up!" Sweeny yelled.

Erika looked at Lia, "You bitch!"

"A bitch is a female dog. That defines you!" Sweeny snatched her hands and forced her over the counter, cuffing her wrists.

"You OK?" Cap gently laid a hand on Lia's shoulder. Five officers walked through the front door with Terry. Lia pulled a wire from the inside of her shirt. "I don't know." Tears filled her eyes as she spotted Lawson outside in street clothes standing beside Dale.

Terry pulled Cap aside and whispered in his ear, and Cap's complexion turned from a pale white to fiery red.

***

Lying on the floor in front of the TV, Vicky and Valentine watched a rerun of one of her favorite shows. With her head propped up and resting in her hands and her legs bent with feet in the air, Vicky heard a sound on the front porch. Valentine shot her head up and looked at the front door. The door knob slowly turned. "San! Someone's at the door," Vicky yelled, looking back at the TV.

"That crazy neighbor," Sandra said to herself, pulling a pizza out of the oven.

A deafening explosion filled the house, knocking pictures and plates from the walls and causing Sandra to drop the pan and fall back to the counter. In a daze, she tried to stand back up, but the room was spinning, and her ears were ringing. She forced her eyes wide open and rubbed her face. Then the thought hit her—Vicky.

She ran to the living room, and through the open front door, she could see two men running. Vicky screamed as the man had a death grip on her and forced her into a white Toyota truck. In shock, Sandra felt her pocket for her cell phone. Cap had asked her never to take it off her person, and pressing Cap's number, she saw Valentine lying in a pool of blood next to the place Vicky had been.

In a panic, she didn't see Vicky break free from the man and run to the side of the house, the men quickly chasing after her.

Cap heard the distinctive ring he had assigned Sandra on his phone, answering on the third ring, "Hey, can I call you back."

"They took her!" Sandra yelled, out of breath.

"Took who?" Cap's voice escalated for everyone to hear. The entire crowd of law enforcement officers around him stopped what they were doing and looked at him.

All she could say was, "White Toyota." And that was all she needed to say.

Cap ran to his truck, yelling at his men, "White Toyota. They have Vicky!"

With his body numb, Sweeny was the first to reach his truck and fishtailed leaving the parking lot aimed toward Cap's house.

Chapter 55

Sweeny shared his biggest fear with many fathers in the world, someone abducting their daughter. He had shown Vicky many times, while wrestling, that if someone ever grabbed her, to kick, punch, and scream as much and as loud as possible. The next thing was to bite and hard enough to draw blood, something Vicky had always followed up with "Yuk!"

Running toward the backyard, she wiped the blood from her chin, the blood that belonged to the first man that latched on to her. Sandra, in the commotion of talking with Cap, now caught a glimpse of Vicky's hair as she passed the bedroom window. She looked down at Valentine, praying that she would get up and help, but her body remained motionless. Sandra bolted to the backdoor, grabbing a kitchen knife and dropping the phone. Opening the door, she scooped the little girl inside and locked the door.

Both men made it to the back door and one threw a shoulder into the door. Crashing it open, the men trailed Sandra and Vicky back out the front door and toward the street. Sandra knew with Cap and the boys only a few blocks away, it wouldn't be long before they would be there.

Racing down Cap's street, Sweeny saw Sandra and Vicky running across the street toward the neighbors' house. "Thank you, God!" he prayed out loud, flooring the truck to cut off the two men. In one motion, Sweeny reached for his side arm with his left hand and slammed on the brakes, causing the tires to smoke against the pavement. With one shot and the truck still in motion, Sweeny sent the first bullet through the skull of the man that was the closest.

The other man dove behind a wooden privacy fence and fired multiple shots in the direction of Sweeny. He saw Cap and Lawson jetting toward him in their trucks, Vicky and Sandra storm inside the neighbor's house, but never saw the dark blue van pull in front of him. The sounds of AK47's echoed through the usually somewhat quiet streets of Presidio, Texas, pinning Sweeny behind his truck with only his service weapon.

"Sweeny!" Lawson yelled from his parked truck.

"One behind that fence," Sweeny pointed to the wooden structure.

"Sandra and Vicky?" Cap yelled back.

"Safe." He pointed to the neighbors' house.

A dark Latino man opened the van door and dumped a clip of Russian ammo into the front of Sweeny's truck, leaving it inoperable.

"Damn!" Sweeny covered his head with bullets ricocheting throughout the street.

With two fingers in his mouth, Cap whistled for his partner, but she didn't come. "You seen Valentine?" he yelled at Sweeny.

"No." Sweeny knew that was strange, for her not to be in on the action, nor had he seen her with the girls.

Three State Police cars skidded to a stop behind the van and the three officers unloaded their clips into the driver side. Looking around Sweeny's truck, Lawson could see the windshield of the van painted in blood. "Cap, we need to get that guy before he moves on us." He pointed to the fence. Lawson could hear another truck sliding to a stop and assumed it was Terry and Dale.

The man behind the fence made a break for it and ran toward Cap's backyard. Lawson fired several rounds wildly in the direction, but with the fence, trees, and other structures, the man made it to safety.

Sweeny looked under his truck at the van that had an unknown number of men inside. Then he locked eyes with the sergeant that he had punched. The sergeant pointed at himself, then Sweeny, held up the number one, then number two, then three. Sweeny and the sergeant stormed the van, blowing holes through the windows and doors, and Sweeny yanked open the door to find four of Jose Emmanuel's men dead.

Sweeny looked at the Sergeant. "Hope you're not still mad about the punch?"

The Sergeant laughed. "Only you, Sweeny."

Lawson, Cap, and Terry ran to the front of Cap's house and entered the front door one by one. Two of the State Policemen ran to cover the back, and a single shot rang out, then screaming from one of the troopers, "Hands up! *Manos Arriba!*" The Sergeant's radio came to life, announcing "We got him!"

Terry stepped out on the front porch of Cap's house. "Get EMS! We have an officer down!"

Sweeny ran to the porch, "Who?"

"It's Valentine!"

He entered the room to find Cap on his knees beside Valentine, holding her head. "It's OK, gal. You're going to make it," he spoke softly in her ear.

Lawson looked at Sweeny. "She's still breathing, but won't open her eyes."

"Come, girl, hang in there," Cap encouraged.

"Cap, the ambulance is pulling up," Terry said, walking back in.

"Here, use the rug to carry her, and let's move her to the ambulance," Cap ordered.

Lawson and Sweeny each grabbed a corner of the rug and started moving her, and once they got outside, she made a gasping sound. "Put her down." Cap's voice shook.

Sandra and Vicky made their way to the street, and once Sandra saw the boys and her husband on the front porch, she stopped Vicky. "We need to let them work," she explained, and walked her back to the neighbor's front yard.

Deputies from the sheriff's office gathered on the front yard to see if they could assist, and two EMT's ran up, pulling the stretcher with bags and oxygen strapped to it. Lawson and another deputy began removing the bags from the stretcher as the EMT's started working on Valentine.

Dale stepped on the porch. "Where in the hell have you been?" Sweeny asked.

Cap looked up, and before anyone could move drew, his sidearm and aimed it at Dale, ordering, "Don't move, you son-of-a-bitch!"

"Cap!" Sweeny yelled.

"Get cuffs on him! Now!" Cap ordered.

"What are you doing?" Sweeny yelled.

The deputies didn't question and drew their weapons, moving toward Dale. "He's the mole!" Terry said, pulling his cuff.

Lawson and Sweeny stood frozen behind Cap in shock. "Dale?" Lawson asked.

"She's not going to make it!" The EMT's hurried Valentine on the stretcher and rushed to the ambulance to get her to the hospital and get themselves out of the way.

Dale took a step back. "Don't act so surprised. It was only time before you figured it out. Lawson?" Dale said. "My last order is... you!" Dale reached for his sidearm and fired a single shot at Lawson.

Cap was the first to fire, sending two shots into Dale's chest, sending him back against the house. Terry quickly tackled Dale, knowing he was wearing a vest and Terry had only seconds to unarm him and get cuffs on before he came to his senses.

Lawson stood paralyzed—it was the third time in two days he had been fired upon within feet of a gun, and patting his chest, he couldn't believe Dale had missed too. He looked down to see if he could see blood, and looking back up, he caught Cap's pale look. "Cap?" he asked.

Cap stared behind him.

Everything played in slow motion as Lawson turned around and found Sweeny lying on the ground clutching his neck, blood pouring through his fingers, and the look he gave Lawson would become something that would haunt him forever. "Sweeny?" Lawson fell to his side.

Sweeny raised his free hand and locked hands with Lawson, not able to talk, but Lawson could read every word he wanted to say from the glare from his eyes. The scene around them broke out into mass pandemonium, but for Lawson, everything blacked out except him and Sweeny.

Lawson found himself reminiscing about the first time he met Alex Sweeny; the smile and glowing demeanor he displayed walking into the office set the tone for their relationship. Cap had asked Lawson to show Sweeny the ropes and introduce him to the others, and the vision of Alex riding shotgun with the window rolled down painted a picture of a brotherhood bond that would last longer than this earth. Out of all the incidents they had been in together, Alex had always made them more interesting with his witty approach.

Never had Lawson imagined he'd be the one walking Alex Sweeny to the grave. "Hang on, Sweeny! Do you hear me, hang on!" Lawson shook with terror.

Sweeny slightly turned his head toward Lawson and Cap, who was now kneeling beside him, and Lawson could feel the grip starting to loosen on his hand. "Sweeny, don't you dare go, you hang in there! Fight, damn it!" Tears started falling from Lawson's eyes onto Sweeny's uniform—and then, just as quickly as he had met Lawson, Alex Sweeny died.

"God, no! Please, someone, *do* something," Lawson begged, burying his face in the chest of his best friend.

Cap gently ran his left hand over Sweeny's eyes, closing them for the last time. The area broke into dead silence. The screams from a beautiful eight-year-old girl haunted the men.

Chapter 56

The following days were a blur, not only for Lawson, but for the entire team. The Chief sent another team to temporarily take over the Presidio station as the team mourned the life of their brother. To add to the loss, it was confirmed that the AK47's the men in the van had used were tracked back to a sting operation called *Fast and Furious* that had gone horribly wrong. Lawson hadn't returned to his house that was being repaired from the shootout only a few days ago.

Lawson had only traded a few simple texts with Lia, and as time was moving forward, he began thinking it was time for him to move on from Lia too. She had hired someone to help with deliveries for the pharmacy and moved to her grandmother's until she could figure what to do with her life. Dale Chanson was placed in maximum security and held for trial. Word from the state was that he would face a harsher sentence than any of Jose Emmanuel's men. He would certainly see execution.

Vicky hadn't spoken since the day she lost her father and was under the supervision of Sandra and a phycologist. Cap tried his best to get her to talk, but she would only grip a stuffed teddy bear that her father had won for her at the county fair. Valentine was clinging to life and not expected to make it, something they had kept quiet from Vicky.

"Which tie?" Cap asked Sandra. She pointed at his left hand, and he turned and wrapped it around his neck and began tying it.

Pulling it tight, he felt Sandra's arms wrap around his waist. "You're a tough man, James Garrett. Please don't hold it in," she said quietly.

He turned and hugged her tight. "He was a good man and I'll miss him," he said, then let go before she saw his eyes watering up.

Vicky was sitting on the couch wearing a dark blue dress, something Sandra thought she'd never wear, but she received no argument helping her in it. Sandra held her hand out for Vicky to join them as they walked through the living room, and she slid off the couch and followed them out to the truck. Lawson was sitting on the steps of the porch, "You ready?" Sandra asked him. He smiled and walked with Vicky.

Pulling up to the funeral home, Cap parked beside Terry's truck. The streets were lined with patrol trucks and cars from all departments, some from hundreds of miles away. The fire department had set their trucks at an angle for the procession to pass by after the service, and reporters and photographers stood in the shade of trees seeking a cooler place; they were kept back by the state police.

The sergeant from the state police came to Lawson to add his sympathies. "I don't know what to say, I'm sorry."

Lawson placed his hand on his shoulder and mouthed the words, "Thank you."

Terry and his wife walked up to the group. "How did you know?" Lawson asked.

"About Dale?"

"Yes."

"I had my suspicions, but the chief had asked me to keep quiet until they could get solid evidence to convict him. I'm sorry not to share it with you," Terry answered.

"It's OK," Lawson replied.

"Lia!" Vicky screamed. It was the first time in three days she had spoken. Lawson watched Vicky run to Lia and dive into her arms as Lia knelt on the parking lot. Trying to fight back more tears, Lia hugged Vicky tight, but with the little girl sobbing uncontrollably, she too lost it. Lawson walked up and place his hand on Lia's shoulder. She tried to stand, but with Vicky not letting go, she scooped the little girl up and held her.

"I'm sorry," Lia's voice shook as she battled to wipe away the tears flowing down her face.

"Me too," Lawson replied.

Lawson felt Cap's hand on his back. "Let's get these gals out of the heat," he said, shuffling everyone inside. Sweeny's parents met them at the door, and together the group made their way to the family section.

"Why don't you go with San?" Lia said to Vicky.

Sandra gave her a funny look, "You need to sit with us."

"I don't think I should. It's my family that caused this." Lia tried to pry Vicky loose.

"Not all of us draw the best family card. It's not your fault, and I know Sweeny would want you sitting with us," Cap replied, ushering her to the family seating.

The priest opened the service with prayer, then went into his message, and after a short sermon, added, "I would like to turn the eulogy over to James Garrett, who we all know as Cap. James." The priest held his hand toward the pulpit.

Cap stood and kissed Sandra, then pulled his suit coat straight and walked to the pulpit. Clearing his throat, he began. "I have served this country with a few departments, the first being the United State army. From there I joined the Texas Rangers and put in twenty years as a captain before moving to the Border Patrol. I say this to set the tone that I have served with many men during many difficult situations. From Nam to the borders of Mexico, we all had the same job, to protect this country. And it's with a heavy heart that I have lost many men and friends along the way. These men and women have given their lives so you and I can live free." He took a long pause.

"With the Border Patrol, many people think that our first job is to make sure illegals don't cross the borders. I'm here to tell you our first job is to protect you. The many illegals that cross daily are only wanting what you have, freedom and protection. When I first joined the Border Patrol, I thought that way, that someone was trying to cheat their way into the US. But that quickly changed when I found my first family crossing the border illegally. It was a father and mother and three small children. The man didn't need to say anything—I could see it in his eyes, he wanted what was best for his family. At that point, my heart broke and my mission changed." Cap took a sip of water.

"I made it a personal mission to help those who cried for help, no matter their nationality. A year later, that man and his family moved to the United States legally and found a better life. I visited him one day and he told me that it was because of the kindness he received from the Border Patrol that made him want to move here even more." Cap walked from behind the pulpit.

"Kindness. A trait that Alex Sweeny naturally had. Sweeny fought for those who cried for help and paid the ultimate price for you. The Bible says the greatest gift is for one to lay down his life for another. I believe King Solomon was the wisest person to have ever lived, and his first instruction was to be kind to each other. Something this country is quickly forgetting." Taking another long pause.

"I'm old and live by old-school rules. I think of these young men as my own sons." He pointed to his team. "Losing Alex Sweeny was more than losing a soldier and more than losing an agent—we lost a kind friend... and son. I hope and pray that you can learn from a young man and father what kindness can bring to this broken world." Cap began getting choked up.

"And together we can provide freedom and protection to all who seek it and to all who deserve it. May you rest in peace, Sweeny. And may you walk by the streams and brooks of heaven, hand in hand with the woman you loved."

Chapter 57

The following day, Lawson helped Lia carry a box to her car from the pharmacy. "You sure you want to close down?" he asked.

She had just sprung the news on him that next week would be her last week to be open. With everything that happened, she feared that people would stop doing business with the daughter of someone that was directly connected with the death of a beloved agent. "Yeah, I'm thinking about moving back to Mexico and possibly helping with a pharmacy." She took the box and set it in the back of her Jeep.

Lawson took a deep breath. "I can only wish that things would have turned out better."

She hugged him and then pulled away, knowing the longer she held him, the harder it was to leave. "Give Vicky another kiss from me." She climbed in her Jeep.

Lawson held her door, "I will."

She stopped and looked at him, "What are you going to do?" The Mexican Federales were still upset with Lawson killing Carlos and was demanding the US government take action.

"I don't know—I'll see what the agency is going to do."

She closed her door and rolled down the window. "Take care, Lawson." She gave a simple wave and drove out onto the pavement. Looking in her rearview mirror, she saw him give a wave and walk to his truck. Now that she was alone, she quit fighting back the tears and emotions, crying uncontrollably.

He made his way back to Cap's house, finding Sandra sitting on the front porch resting from planting flowers. "Did she leave?" Sandra asked.

"Yep," he replied.

"I was praying that things would work out with you two."

"Me too."

"Vicky wants to see Valentine, but I don't know; she's still unresponsive and will probably pass away. I used to know how to handle these things." Sandra fought back tears.

"Well, I was going to the cemetery. I can take her with me to put fresh flowers on his grave."

Sandra nodded and answered with a simple "OK."

Lawson knocked on the bedroom door where she was sleeping, "You want to go to your father's grave with some fresh flowers?"

"Sure." She slid down from the bed and followed him out.

"Where are you two going?" Cap asked, coming in the back door.

"Cemetery. You want to go?" Lawson
asked. "Not right now. You two go ahead."

Vicky pulled the seatbelt across her lap. "Did Lia leave?" she asked in a sober tone.

"Shedid, but I'msureyou'llgettoseehersoon," heresponded,

hoping he was right. They drove through the town of Presidio, where everything seemed back to normal and people were going on with their normal lives. Passing the school, they saw the flags out front flying at half-mast and a small group of high school kids waved, recognizing Lawson's truck. After stopping at the floral shop, they pulled into the cemetery.

Vicky hopped out and walked to her father's grave. Looking around, she said, "There's no vase."

"You can lay them on the ground for today. We'll bring a vase tomorrow."

"OK." she replied. "Lawson?"

"Yea." He looked down at her.

"What's gonna happen to Lia's dad?"

"How did you know Lia's dad was involved?" he asked. "Cap told me last night."

I wish he would have told me he told you, "He'll stay in jail for the rest of his life."

"So Lia won't be able to see him?" She looked confused.

"No, if Lia wants to see him she can. I don't know if she will."

She looked back down in thought and then back at Lawson. "If I forgive him, do you think Lia will go see him?" Lawson remained silent. "I don't want Lia not to have her dad too."

Lawson felt all the emotions welling up all over again. "How in the world are you so grown up?" He reached down and held her hand. "I think forgiveness is a good thing."

She repositioned the flowers and began humming the song "I Cross My Heart."

Lawson dropped Vicky back off at Cap's once they were done visiting Sweeny's grave, and headed to the place he was probably not allowed. After convincing the guard to let him, in he made his way to visiting area. A row of desks with half-inch thick Plexiglas divided the prisoners from the visitors. Lawson sat in a chair facing an empty chair with a dozen small holes cut in the Plexiglas allowing people to talk to the prisoners.

A guard walked Jose Emmanuel to the fixed chair and cuffed him to the desk, "Five minutes, Lawson." The guard said and took three steps back and observed their conversation.

Jose cocked his head. "Do you think being behind bars will keep me down?"

"That's not why I am here." Lawson stared him down. "Heard you lost your partner."

"I did."

"That bullet wasn't meant for him."

"I know."

Jose nodded his head with a half grin. "If you're going to ask if you can have my daughter's hand in marriage, you're wasting your time."

"She's gone." He wasn't sure if Jose already knew.

Jose held his hands up. "Well, Senior Caine, why did you come?"

"You took the life of a father."

With a smirk, Jose answered, "Some things happen. I lost a son and now my daughter." His voice grew angry.

"I took Vicky, Sweeny's little girl, to his graveside today. Out of everything she could have said or even talked about, she wanted to know about you and Lia. She was concerned that Lia would never see her father again. You want to know what she said?"

Lawson stood, fighting back emotions. "She wanted to know whether if she forgave you, would Lia get her father back! A little eight-year-old girl is willing to forgive the man that stole her father so that he could continue being a father. Me? My own self-desires were wishing and praying you to Hell, but I have to learn from a little girl that forgiveness is bigger than all of us! You're a son-of-a-bitch for taking my friend, but you go to your grave knowing that you and I are out-manned by an eight-year-old girl that forgave you!" Lawson slammed his fist on the Plexiglas.

Walking to the door, he looked back at Jose, who sat motionless and in a paralyzed state, overpowered by the gift of a little girl's forgiveness.

Chapter 58

After sweeping the inside of her grandmother's shack, Lia placed the broom next to a few small items belonging to her grandmother. One of the items was another dream catcher. "Abuela, I forgot I have the dream catcher that you gave to Lawson," she said, holding the other in her hand.

"He gave it to you?" her grandmother asked.

"No, I took it from his truck. I guess we don't need it anymore." She looked at her grandmother. "You were right, you know. We did have death in our future."

"Where is it?"

"Probably still in my car."

"Go get it," she insisted, pointing to the door.

Lia walked out and dug through her car, finding it under a bag. She returned to the shack, where her grandmother was now sitting at the old table. Lia handed the dream catcher to her. "Hopefully there is no more death in that," Lia replied.

Her grandmother looked at her. "Dear, this can't catch visions of death. That is something I just have. This is what it is called. It catches your dreams, the thing that you want the most." She walked over to the bed that Lia had been sleeping in and took down a dream catcher that Lia never noticed.

"When did you put that there?" Lia smiled at her grandmother.

"A while back." She held the small round dream catchers over the table and studied them. Waving them back and forth, she looked at Lia. "You are dreaming of him."

"A few times," Lia lied.

Her grandmother shook her head. "No child, you are dreaming of him every night. He is what you want. You cannot deny your dreams." She studied Lawson's. "He loves you very much."

"Just because he dreams about me doesn't mean he loves me."

"He dreams not only of you, but your children."

"Please stop." Lia stood, becoming upset.

"Denying it is only lying to yourself. You love him."

Lia wiped her eyes, admitting "I do love him."

***

After a long decision and avoiding any lawful repercussions, Lawson gave his resignation to the US Border Patrol— something that Cap was extremely upset about. After all, Lawson had taken out the second largest smuggling Lord of Mexico. Still, however he felt, Lawson made the decision, and after saying goodbye to everyone, he heading home to Paris, Texas.

It was a tougher decision to leave Vicky, but he knew that she would be well taken care of with Sandra and Cap until Sweeny's parents could decide what was best for her. Cap had told him that he was seriously thinking about retiring and moving somewhere where grass grew green and there were four seasons. He reminded Lawson that his ancestors came from Tennessee, a beautiful state, so he was considering there. Lawson made him promise that he would stop by Paris if that is where he ended up.

Terry fought the decision of whether to stay or move closer to his wife's family in Houston, but Cap explained that if he stayed, he'd have Cap's position, and that area needed a seasoned vet. Lawson hauled the last box into his parents' house, where he planned to stay until he could find his own place. His father had helped him get a job with the local sheriff's department, a place his father and uncles worked.

"Do you have everything you need?" his mother asked, poking her head in his room.

Looking around, he answered, "Yea, funny being back in my old room."

"It's nice to have you home," she smiled and closed the door.

He grabbed a box that he didn't recognize and opened it, realizing it was a box of items from his patrol truck. He started to close it, but noticed an unopened envelope. He pulled it out and set the box down. The wording on the envelope read *Open when I'm not around.* It was Sweeny's handwriting. Lawson tore it open and pulled out a handwritten letter.

Lawson,

I'm not one to get all mushy, so I'd rather not talk about this after you read it. Today, I met someone who looked just like Rachael. She is a waitress in a diner south of town. Everything about her was identical to Rachael, from the way her hair bounced back and forth when she walked to the dimples in her face. It was like seeing a ghost, but I couldn't keep my eyes off of her. It really screwed me up.

I feel like, No, I know that I am depriving Vicky from a mother. She really needs a woman in her life. You know how she walks around all tough and loves guy stuff, like football. She has been fighting me about dance and she wants to quit, which I hope changes soon. Anyway, she needs a mom to help her become a proper young lady I know she can be.

But I've also been thinking about what would happen if I died? Where would she go? I know Cap and Sandra are great, but they're getting old and really make good grandparents. My parents are OK, but she doesn't really know them. After losing Rachael, who was my best friend, I never thought I could have a friendship like that again.

You have become my best friend and I trust you with everything, including my little girl. I hope things work out between you and Lia because if anything were to happen to me I hope you guys would take Vicky as your own. She worships the ground Lia walks on and talks about her all the time. I know you're not a father yet but I started praying and one of the things I've been praying for is that I become a father like you're going to be.

Thanks for being my family,

Sweeny

P.S. You owe me beer!

Lawson walked back into the room with his mother and father. "Please don't be upset, but I think I made a mistake."

Chapter 59

Now, two years after Sweeny had past away Lawson found himself sitting in the cab of his truck looking over his gravel drive with his knuckles turning white from gripping the steering wheel. The warm breeze rocked the truck again as he stopped looking at his house and the unfinished railing that wrapped his front porch. The badge hanging from the rearview mirror threw sparkles of light in his eyes, and he looked down to study the picture of Sweeny and him after they caught a large stringer of fish.

"How did I get here?" he asked out loud.

"Fate!" a raspy voice replied from the passenger seat.

"I miss him, Cap!" Lawson looked back down at the picture stuck between the gauges.

"I do, too. But he would want you to move on. Face it, if the cards were turned and he was sitting here, you wouldn't want him mourning you." Cap took out a cigarette from his shirt pocket.

"I can't help but ask, if I had to do it all over again, what would I do different?" Lawson stopped Sweeny's badge from spinning on the rearview mirror.

"One thing for sure, I'd hung that little piss ant much earlier," Cap growled, referring to Dale.

Lawson looked at Cap and the starched white uniform shirt he was wearing. "I'll have to say, you good in that Ranger uniform."

Cap looked back at Lawson who sported the same Ranger uniform, "I can't believe you talked me into returning to the Texas Rangers."

"Well, at least 'Cap' matches your position now. I never thought the Rangers would be a fit for me. But I'm glad you came with me."

"Hmm!"

"I think Sweeny would have made a good Ranger."

"Yep, we just gonna sit here in your drive?" Cap pointed for him to pull up.

Lawson looked forward, but didn't remove his foot from the brake. Vicky came running around the corner of their house yelling that Lawson was home, with Valentine jumping in front of her as if she was tagging Vicky in their game. Vicky jumped on the running boards of the Ranger patrol truck as Lawson rolled down the window, and she piled through the window, sitting in Lawson's lap.

"You'll be ready to drive before long. Cap here is excited for you to drive him around when he gets too old to drive himself," Lawson laughed.

"Hmm! It'll beat riding with you all day."

Lawson let off the brake, easing forward. "Watch out, girl!" Vicky yelled at Valentine, who was following them up the drive. Lawson pulled Vicky into his arms and opened the door. "Did you have a good day?" she asked, excited he was home.

"I did. And you?"

"Yep. Notice anything different?" She smiled at him.

At first he didn't, then it hit him. "You're wearing make-up?"

"I figured I'd let her start with a little blush and lip gloss. We'll see from there," a voice replied from in front of the truck. Lia stood with her hair draped down her back and a warm smile on her face. In her arms was Lawson's 4-month baby boy.

"How's my little boy and beautiful bride?" He kissed her, taking Alex Jr. from her arms.

"We've had a great day. Been shopping, went to the grocery store, dropped off fresh flowers on Sweeny's grave, and made it back here in time to fix supper," Lia smiled.

"Supper? What are we having?" Cap asked.

"Ok, maybe I'm not fixing supper. Sandra's inside, Cap," she replied.

Lawson growled and acted like he was tackling Vicky. "Wait! Let me have him," Lia grabbed Alex from Lawson as he chased the squealing girl through the yard with Valentine playfully biting his ankle. "I can't catch you!" he said to Vicky.

She ran back up and dove in his arms. "I'll slow down next time so you can," she answered.

Lawson laughed, putting her down. "Sweetie, go ask San if she needs any help," Lia said to Vicky.

"Yes, ma'am." Vicky disappeared inside.

Lawson and Lia stopped shy of walking up the steps to their house. She turned and leaned into him. "I love you," she whispered, kissing him.

Lawson climbed the stairs and faced the west before entering the kitchen. The sky was exploding into a fiery red with the sunset, and he looked up at the sky and mouthed the words, "Thank you."

In *Waterproof*, Spencer LeJeune, the once-nerdy kid who grew into an attractive young man, puts it all on the line to find the Spanish Treasure Barge and to finally win over the heart of his childhood crush, Toni Benoit. After nearly twenty years apart, their reunited friendship quickly turns into a suspenseful treasure hunt, as they try to outwit a ruthless fifth-generation Spanish pirate. Will Spencer win Toni's heart and find the treasure before it costs him the lives of those he loves, and millions in silver and gold? Can Toni trust herself to fall in love—and can she tame the treasure-hunter's heart?

Waterproof is available in print and ebook editions at Amazon, Barnes and Noble, and other fine online retailers.

What do you get when you introduce a professional rodeo girl from a Georgia hay farm to an upper-crust composer from Manhattan? Mischief, music, and fireworks!

In *Field of Alicia*, Madi Coverton, a young widowed mother and professional barrel racer, never expected to meet concert pianist Michael Curry during her summer off from the rodeo circuit. What starts off as mutual interest and intrigue soon turn into wild adventures, building into an undeniable love that stirs the broken heart of the young widow. Will Michael follow his heart and leave the memories of his ex-fiancée behind? Can Madi learn to love again?

Fields of Alicia is available in print and ebook editions at Amazon, Barnes and Noble, and other fine online retailers.

About the Author

Lee DuCote has traveled researching cultures, people, and historical accounts to help create his stories. A native to Louisiana, he writes to give hope and encouragement to others, as well as to entertain and spark the imagination. Lee lives in the Ozark Mountains of Arkansas with his wife and family and is the author of *Fields of Alicia* and *Waterproof*. You can visit him and see more or follow him at the links below:

Connect with Lee DuCote

 www. leeducote. com

 @leeducote

 @leeducote

 www. facebook.com/ authorleeducote

www.ingramcontent.com/pod-product-compliance
Lightning Source LLC
Chambersburg PA
CBHW051334250626
47155CB00007B/2599